OTHER MYSTERIES BY
LAURA DiSILVERIO

The Book Club Mystery Series
Book 1: *The Readaholics and the Falcon Fiasco*

The Mall Cop Mystery Series
Book 1: *Die Buying*
Book 2: *All Sales Fatal*
Book 3: *Malled to Death*

The Swift Investigations Series
Book 1: *Swift Justice*
Book 2: *Swift Edge*
Book 3: *Swift Run*

OTHER MYSTERIES BY LAURA DiSILVERIO
WRITING AS ELLA BARRICK

The Ballroom Dance Mystery Series
Book 1: *Quickstep to Murder*
Book 2: *Dead Man Waltzing*
Book 3: *The Homicide Hustle*

WRITING AS LILA DARE

The Southern Beauty Shop Series
Book 1: *Tressed to Kill*
Book 2: *Polished Off*
Book 3: *Die Job*

continued . . .

The **Readaholics**
and the
Poirot Puzzle

A Book Club Mystery

Laura DiSilverio

AN OBSIDIAN BOOK

OBSIDIAN
Published by New American Library,
an imprint of Penguin Random House LLC
375 Hudson Street, New York, New York 10014

This book is an original publication of New American Library.

First Printing, December 2015

For more information about Penguin Random House, visit penguin.com.

ISBN 978-0-451-47084-3

Printed in the United States of America
10 9 8 7 6 5 4 3 2 1

Penguin
Random
House

Acknowledgments

At times, my gratitude for being able to write novels overwhelms me. I get up every morning and engage in work that excites and energizes me, that brings me fulfillment and a sense of having done something worthwhile. For that, I owe a lot of people thanks.

First and foremost, I thank my agent, Paige Wheeler, and my editors at Penguin Random House, especially Sandy Harding and Michelle Vega. Their insights and comments have made my books better, and their friendship has brightened my life.

Thank you also to the friends and fellow writers who have brainstormed with me, critiqued manuscripts or parts thereof, offered cover quotes, listened to me rant when stymied or frustrated by the writing process or the vagaries of publishing, and who lift me up with their generosity and brilliance. These include (but are not limited to) Amy Sagendorf, Linda Petrone, Hank Phillippi Ryan, Joan Hankins, Cindy Stauffer, Patrick Butler, Hans VonMilla, Glenn Miller, Jill Gaebler, Gretchen Gaebler, Catriona McPherson, Carolyn Hart, the sisters and misters of Sisters in Crime, my coconspirators in Mystery

Writers of America, Lin Poyer, Marie Layton, the amazing writers of Pikes Peak Writers, and many, many more.

I am grateful, as always, to the readers who have made Amy-Faye Johnson and the Readaholics part of their world, and who share their thoughts and friendship with me via Facebook and e-mail and at conventions or conferences. Writing would be totally unrewarding without you.

Finally, thank you to my husband, Tom, and the best daughters in the whole world, Lily and Ellen. You give me joy each and every day, and I am so grateful for your love, laughter, support, and presence in my life.

Chapter 1

Choosing a book for the Readaholics to read is a tough task, and the five of us who make up the book club take the responsibility seriously. Usually. There was the one time we wrote the titles of books ranging from *Gone Girl* to *The Moonstone* on slips of paper, taped them on my folks' garage door, and threw darts to pick a winner. Margaritas were involved. (Trust me, the garage door, unpainted since Fleetwood Mac hit the top ten, and liberally pocked with woodpecker holes to start with, was not greatly harmed by our selection process.) Only Lola managed to get a dart to stick. Did I mention the margaritas? Her dart picked Elizabeth George's *A Great Deliverance*. And there was the time, at least two years ago, when we decided (I don't remember why) that we had to find a title that started with Q and found ourselves reading an Inspector Rebus novel. But mostly, we take the task seriously.

Which is how I ended up having a conversation six weeks ago with Brooke Widefield, my best friend, whose turn it was to pick a book. We were sitting in my sun-room, almost uncomfortably warm with the sun streaming through the panes that I had Windexed to streak-free perfection only that morning. The celadon green tiles gleamed, and the plants (chosen with much help from Lola Paget, who owned a plant nursery) stretched greenly toward the sunlight. I'd had an event that went late the night before, Friday, and I was makeup-less with my copper-colored hair in a ponytail, wearing a faded University of Colorado T-shirt and shorts that had fit better five pounds ago. Brooke Widefield, of course, as always, looked exquisite, mink-dark hair curling over her shoulders like she had just finished filming a shampoo commercial and green eyes emphasized by taupe shadow and mascara. Her crisp red capris and denim jacket could have been featured in a magazine spread about how to look chic rather than sloppy running weekend errands. I was the "before" photo and Brooke the "after." I was used to it.

"It's hard to find murder mysteries without murders in them," Brooke observed facetiously. "But since Ivy, well, I'm not in the mood to read anything too realistic."

Ivy Donner, one of the Readaholics and our friend since high school, had been poisoned in May and we were all still reeling. I found myself agreeing with Brooke that we didn't need a police procedural or urban noir book for next month.

"There are lots of books without serial killers or gore," I said, taking a swig of my diet soda. "Tons of 'em. Really, when you think about it, books with brains caked on the walls and criminologists deducing the killer's identity from blood-spatter analysis are a relatively modern development. What about something more old-fashioned, something pre–*Girl with the Dragon Tattoo*?"

"Dick Francis," Brooke mused. "Except sometimes he kills off horses and I can't take that."

Brooke had a soft heart for animals and volunteered at the Heaven Animal Haven, the no-kill shelter here in Heaven, Colorado.

"Dorothy Sayers?"

She wrinkled her nose. "After reading that one about the bells, I'm not much of a Sayers fan. Bor-ing. I'm more in the mood for something along the line of Nancy Drew."

"I don't think the others will be too *keen* on that," I said. "Get it? Carolyn Keene?"

Brooke groaned and tossed a throw pillow at me.

"I guess that's why they call them *throw* pillows," I said, catching it.

"Stop with the puns already," she said, "or I'm leaving." She made as if to rise.

"Fine, fine." I held up my hands in surrender.

"What about Agatha Christie?" she said. "We haven't ever read one of her books."

I thought about it. "I guess you're right," I said slowly. "I guess I assumed everyone had already read a lot of Christie, since she is the queen of mysteries." I paused for a beat and decided to confess. "I've never read a Christie book, though. Don't toss me out of the Readaholics."

"I've read all the Miss Marples." She put down her diet soda, being careful to place a coaster under it, even on the glass table. "I've never tried any of the others, though."

And that's how we came to be reading *Murder on the Orient Express*, the book jouncing on the van's passenger seat as I headed for my brother Derek's pub. I'd finished it the night before and was looking forward to the Readaholics' discussion tomorrow. I tried to anticipate everyone's reactions, but the only one I was sure of was Maud's. Our resident conspiracy theorist would be wholeheartedly enthusiastic about the book because it contained a conspiracy. I smiled to myself as I parked the car in the gravel lot. I had found the whole conspiracy thing totally unbelievable. Twelve people working together to kill one man? Puh-leeze. Murder conspiracies didn't work, not in real life.

We've all heard the advice about doctors not performing surgery on their own family members. It's against the Hippocratic oath, I think, or maybe the American Medical Association bans it. The same should hold true for event organizers. If there were an event organizer governing body, I'd be happy to propose a bylaw that made it unethical to plan parties for family members, especially brothers. Under that rule, such an act would be punishable by having to retake high school sex ed, listening to an endless loop of John Denver's "Rocky Mountain High," or a cross-country road trip with said family. In a VW Beetle. With no air-conditioning. In August.

I looked at Derek and said in my reasonable voice, even though my day's supply of "reasonable" was about exhausted, "You can't invite more people. The fire marshal's max capacity is two hundred and twenty. We've already invited three hundred, not counting the people who will come because they read about the opening in the *Heaven Herald*, or heard about it from a friend. A fair chunk of the invitees won't be able to come, especially the ones from Denver, but you're asking for trouble by sending out more invitations this late."

We were sitting in my brother's ready-for-grand-opening brewpub, Elysium Brewing, on the outskirts of Heaven, Colorado. The building had originally been a factory—shoes, I think—and the designer had kept an industrial vibe with exposed pipes and the original brick walls. They contrasted nicely with the new fittings installed late last month. On a sultry August day, the narrow windows were open and brilliant sunshine lit up the booths with their orange leatherette upholstery and made the woodwork gleam. When I'd heard the pub's decorator was going with orange, I was skeptical, but against the dark wood and the bar's brass fittings, it looked really good, especially in the evening under the soft glow from the antique-looking pendant lights. A nook near the front windows held sofas and bookshelves that gave the pub a homey feel. I kept meaning to scope out the books, which I suspected the designer had bought by the yard. From where we sat in a corner booth near the kitchen, I could barely glimpse the patio where Derek envisioned selling a lot of brews on long summer evenings, and the wide staircase that led to an open area with eight pool tables and an auxiliary bar on the second floor, offices on the third floor, and a rooftop space that would eventually be a venue for private functions. At the moment, though, it was bare and pebbly and unattractive, off-limits to the public. A humongous stainless steel vat with tubing spiraling around it took up a large chunk of space. It sat in a glass enclosure so Colorado's craft beer enthusiasts could watch the brewing process in action. Whoop-de-do.

The janitor mopped his way past us, leaving an odor of lemon cleanser that temporarily overpowered the hoppy beer scent that pervaded the pub. Derek ran a hand through his short hair, which was a deeper auburn than my coppery locks. It stood on end. "People won't all come at the same time," he argued.

"I know, but trust me when I say that guests with an invitation in hand are going to expect to walk right in, not have to wait in line until the place empties out enough that there's room for them." I'd owned my event-organizing business, Eventful!, for four years now, and I'd learned a thing or two the hard way.

"But we've got to invite Gordon's doctor sister, Angie, and her husband, Eugene—he's an accountant—now that they're back in town. Their daughter—what a tragedy. And that guy who's running for state senator against Troy Widefield—not that I want him to beat Troy, but—"

A tattoo of stiletto heels on the stairs and raised voices interrupted us. "—what the judge has to say, Gordo," a woman's voice said. "You can't just not pay

Kolby's college tuition. The semester starts in a couple of weeks. He's—"

"He's twenty-four and a useless parasite," came Gordon Marsh's voice. "I paid for his first attempt at college, and I don't feel I owe him another go-round. I gave him a job here and that's more than he deserves. I'm damn sure he drinks or spills more beer than he sells."

"He's your *son!*" The speaker, a slim brunette, came into view. In tight jeans, a Western shirt that strained the pearl snaps across her chest, and carefully feathered hair, she looked a decade younger than the fifty-two or -three she had to be.

"Don't remind me," Gordon growled. He appeared on the stairs above her and followed her down, his heavier footsteps in contrast to the angry tapping of her heels. Derek's partner in Elysium Brewing, Gordon Marsh was in his early fifties with a full head of dark blond hair sprinkled with gray. His tanned face had its share of lines, and he carried a little extra weight around his middle, but he was still a handsome man. He reminded me of a younger, blonder James Brolin. He had a reputation as a player, though, with a philosophy of love 'em and leave 'em. Lots of 'em, if rumors were correct. I was sure he thought of himself as a "stud." He'd tried his pitch on me when he first went into business with Derek, but I was having none of it. Sure, I'd gone out once with a guy who turned out to be a murderer, but I had to draw the line somewhere.

I'd asked Derek why he'd partnered with Gordon, and he'd told me Gordon was an investment genius, head of his own venture capital firm, GTM Capital, with a knack for underwriting start-up bars and restaurants that went on to be hugely successful. He had a unique hands-on approach to his projects, where he or one of his senior staff "embedded" with the company they were underwriting until it was well and truly launched.

"I need him. Don't piss him off, sis," Derek had said, stopping short of suggesting I date the man to keep him happy. He knew how that was likely to go over.

"You'll be hearing from my lawyer," Susan Marsh said, eyes narrowed to slits. "You can't do this to Kolby."

"The hell I can't!" Without warning, Gordon swiped a beer mug from the bar and hurled it in Susan's direction. It missed her by a good three feet, hit a booth, and shattered on the floor.

Derek was on his feet immediately, making calming gestures as he approached his partner. "Whoa, big guy, no need for this." He stood between Gordon and Susan, which made me nervous, but Gordon didn't seem inclined to launch more missiles at his ex-wife.

Susan, eyes big, scuttled out of the bar, but not without stopping to snap a picture of the broken glass with her phone. For her lawyer's use, I imagined. I was so startled by Gordon's sudden fury that I stayed seated, not sure whether to call the cops or let Derek handle it. The two men talked for thirty seconds, and then Derek clapped his partner on the shoulder and returned to me while Gordon headed up the stairs to the roof, shaking a cigarette out of a packet as he went. Derek had complained to me before about Gordon disappearing to the roof for his smoke breaks.

"What was that all about?" I whispered.

Derek shook his head. "I don't know. Gordon's been edgy lately, losing it over the least little thing. When we first started putting this deal together, fifteen months or so ago, he was brusque, sometimes rude, but you could always see where he was coming from, you know? I mean, yeah, he was out for number one, looking to structure the partnership contract in his favor, but that's just business. When I didn't lie down and roll over, he respected it, I think. I mean, our contract's fair." He ran a hand through his hair again. "Lately, though, sis"—he gave me a serious look—"I don't know how much longer I can put up with it. If I could afford to buy him out, I'd do it tomorrow. He's rude to the employees—that's why Sam quit—and he busted a crate of hops the other day when the delivery truck was an hour late. If he behaves like that around customers . . ."

I could see worry in the deep line between his brows and the way his jaw worked. I reached over the table to punch his shoulder. "Hang in there. Maybe it's the grand opening that's got him on edge. Hopefully, he'll settle down once we're past Friday night."

"Yeah, maybe."

He didn't look hopeful and I got the feeling there was more he wasn't telling me. I didn't have time to draw it out of him, though, since I was on the verge of being late for a client meeting. "Hang in there," I repeated, sliding out of the booth as gracefully as I could in my tan pencil skirt. "I'll be back at five."

I'd agreed to take a few shifts behind the bar until Derek could find a replacement for Sam, the bartender who'd left in a huff after a run-in with Gordon the day before. I'd put myself through college bartending, among other jobs, and I wanted to help out because Derek had begged me to and because I, like my folks and sisters, had a fair chunk of change invested in Elysium Brewing. I'd even persuaded the Readaholics to put off our discussion of *Murder on the Orient Express* until tomorrow night so I could work at the pub this evening.

"Thanks, Amy-Faye. You're a lifesaver."

"I'll add that to my résumé." With a smile and another shoulder punch, I left him sitting in the booth and headed for the parking lot and my van.

The van might not be the BMW Z4 I was currently drooling over, but it was a lot more practical in the event-planning business. I wouldn't have been able to haul 101 stuffed Dalmatians to Lulu Vancura's sixth birthday party last night in a Bimmer. They were party favors for 101 of her closest friends who gathered to watch the movie in the theater the Vancuras rented—through me—for the occasion. The party had gone well and I was looking forward to planning many more of Lulu's birthday bashes. Ka-ching. I hadn't thought about it much before, but doing birthday parties created a lot more repeat business for an event planner than doing weddings. I mean, people had birthdays on an annual basis, whereas most folks spread their two or three weddings out over twenty years. The lucky ones, of course, only wed once.

The van bumped over the railroad tracks and past the sign welcoming visitors to Heaven, Colorado, population 10,096. EVERYBODY WANTS TO GO TO HEAVEN, it said in blue script underneath, quoting the Kenny Chesney song. Heaven wasn't always named Heaven. When I was growing up, it was Walter's Ford. Then, when I was a high school sophomore, the town council, in a bid to attract more tourists and destination wedding business, voted to rename the town. Developers piled on the bandwagon, dubbing housing areas Jubilee Heights and Cherubim Glen and the like. Many of the streets got new names that reflected the town's theme, as well. The town's main drag, where my office is located, was rechristened Paradise Boulevard. (It was formerly John Elway Avenue.) Funny that I would grow up to be an event organizer and benefit from the veritable tide of brides and grooms that washed into town, tickled by the idea of getting married in Heaven.

Eventful! was headquartered on the ground floor in the back of an old three-story building that also housed the Divine Herb, a tea shop (that probably sold more coffee than tea), and a yoga studio. The two-person law firm that had had offices on the second floor closed suddenly last month, and the building owners were trying to rerent the space. I parked on the street and walked around to the French doors that opened onto our reception area, where my part-time assistant, Al Frink, sat at his desk. I shared my new insight about weddings vs. birthdays with him. A student at Colorado Mesa, he had gelled back the sandy hair that typically flopped over his high forehead. He looked like a teenage escapee from the 1950s in his sweater vest and bow tie, even though he was twenty-two. The college had hooked him up with me for an internship one semester and we'd clicked, so he'd stayed on.

"Cynical much, boss?" he asked in response.

"Realistic," I countered.

"You should pitch divorce parties, then," he said. "Lots of booze, a ritual shredding of wedding photos— or better yet, a bonfire—and all the honoree's single pals helping put together a Match-dot-com or eHarmony video. Maybe we could offer a free month's subscription. I'll get with the Match-dot-com folks this afternoon and see what kind of deal we can get." He pretended to make a note.

"Ha-ha." Inside, I wondered if he wasn't onto something. I couldn't, offhand, think of a tasteful way to advertise the idea, however.

He grinned, and then told me my prospective client had canceled. I shrugged philosophically. You win some, you lose some. And even when you win some—land a client—you occasionally lose if they're obnoxious or refuse to pay. I asked Al for an update on the several events he was working, and he filled me in, adding his usual too-truthful observations about our clients.

"That Bethany D'Andrea is a harridan. One of my SAT vocab words. Have you ever noticed how she manages to be nasty by only saying what sounds like nice stuff?" He put on a treacly accent. " 'Oh, honey, you've been so strict with your diet. It's too bad that your green dress is looking tighter.' 'I just love mauve and teal! I'd've done my house in those colors, too, sweetie, if they weren't so 1990.' Blech."

I couldn't suppress a grin, because he was so right.

"She told me the other day that she thought I was so brave, she admired me so much, for keeping on the trail of Ivy's killer, but then I'd always been brash and impulsive, hadn't I?"

"Harpy," Al said.

"Shrew."

"Vixen."

"Virago." I was on a roll.

"I'll have to look that one up. Witch."

"Or something that rhymes with 'witch.'"

He laughed and turned away to answer the phone. I went into my office, the green, white, and lemon space I found energizing, yet relaxing. My "desk" was a six-foot-long project table. A whiteboard with a huge calendar imprinted on it hung behind it and showed all our bookings going out two years. Yep, we already had three weddings and a family reunion on the books for two summers from now. Even though those far-off commitments sometimes fell victim to breakups or other disasters, it made me feel a bit more confident that Eventful! would survive when I looked at the whiteboard.

The interchange and mention of Ivy Donner dipped me into one of those puddles of sadness that seem to linger on life's path after a loss. Sometimes you could skirt them, edge past them by hanging out with friends, or losing yourself in work, but sometimes you fell into them and they were deeper than you imagined. My friend Ivy had been murdered three months ago, and it's not like I thought about her every minute of every day, but when her name came up, or something reminded me of her, I felt my mood go from sunny to wilted in a heartbeat. I could have done without the publicity that catching Ivy's killer had netted me, too, despite the fact that it brought a new stream of clients to Eventful! But the *Heaven Herald* had run a front-page piece on the arrest and my part in it, and I anticipated more publicity when the trial started up. It was still a couple of months away, but I'd have to testify and I wasn't looking forward to that, mostly because I'd have to think about Ivy dying every day.

Forcing myself to put aside the melancholy thoughts, I worked out a few details for Elysium's grand opening on Friday, including coordinating with a U.S. representative's scheduler about the congresswoman's attendance. She was in the area anyway for a fund-raiser in Grand Junction, and had promised to drop by. For Derek's sake I was pleased, because that meant the likelihood of more publicity. And all publicity was good publicity, as the maxim went, and Ivy's death had proven in a distasteful way. The afternoon flew by in a flurry of phone calls, e-mails, and a meeting with a Heaven Parks and Rec official to see if he'd authorize painting the gazebo at Lost Alice Lake pink for a client's wedding, as long as she bore the cost and repainted it white after the event. He looked flummoxed by the request and said he'd have to put it before the town council.

"You sure come up with some off-the-wall ideas, Ms. Johnson," he said, shaking his head.

"Amy-Faye," I reminded him. "And don't blame me for this one. It's all the client's idea. Thinks pink is her lucky color and her marriage is doomed if the ceremony doesn't take place in a pink facility."

"Unless her groom's as nutty as she is, the marriage is doomed anyway," he said. "I'll get back to you as soon as I talk to the council."

"The wedding's not till next April, so no hurry." Thanking him, I crossed the meeting off my list—there's almost nothing more satisfying than striking through a to-do item—and headed for home to change into bartending gear.

Chapter 2

The pub's staff uniform for female employees was jeans with an orange shirt that tied at the waist and plunged to show cleavage. Not the real me. The men had a simple orange Polo shirt. The top had an embroidered harp—for "Elysium"—over the employee's name. In my case, the name was "Sam" because I was wearing her uniforms, not having time to get one of my own. Since I didn't intend to return to bartending as a full-time career, I was okay with being "Sam" for a few nights, until Derek and Gordon could hire a replacement. As I French-braided my hair to keep it out of the way, I grimaced at the way the orange shirt clashed with my hair and sallowed my clear complexion. Oh well.

When I pulled up at the brewpub parking lot, I noticed two women tucking flyers beneath the windshield wipers of parked cars. Hustling past them so as not to get caught up in a discussion of their cause or business—whatever it was—I entered the pub to find a scattering of customers downing Angel Ale and Exorcise Your Demons IPA. Even though the grand opening wasn't until Friday, the pub had been open for business for almost two weeks on a limited basis as Derek and Gordon trained their staff and finalized their menu.

Derek was behind the bar and he looked frazzled, even though the customer load was light. A twenty-something with a soul patch slouched between tables, taking orders.

"Thank goodness you're here," Derek greeted me. "Bernie's late and I need to be in the kitchen. Kolby's on the floor. It's all yours. You can figure it out, can't you?"

He disappeared on the words and I entered the circular bar through the hinged section and familiarized myself with the bar stock, sink setup, glasses, and draft choices. The grid beneath my feet was still firm, not squishy from years of being marinated in beer and alcohol, like the place I worked at in Boulder. Being behind the bar made me feel like I was back at CU, sacrificing sleep for money and grades. Hmm. Ten years on, my life hadn't changed all that much, only now I was giving up sleep to run my own business and I didn't have to worry about finals.

Kolby bellied up to the server's station and said, "Hey. A pitcher of Angel Ale, a Coke, and three Demons. Is your name Sam, too?" he asked, nodding toward my shirt.

He was kidding, right? "Nope. Amy-Faye. Derek's sister. Temp help. Just a couple of days until they replace Sam."

I studied Gordon's son. He was more slender than

his dad but had the same dark blond hair and blue eyes. He shifted from foot to foot while I filled a pitcher, waited for the suds to subside, and topped it off.

"Lucky you," he said. "I wish I could say the same. My dad's making me work here the rest of the summer. And he's not even paying me! Slave labor. He'd make me work here year-round, I'll bet, except I'm going back to Ft. Collins next month. I was planning on doing some rafting—the rivers're still running really high—but my dad nixed that." He sounded aggrieved.

I figured if his dad was paying his tuition, that counted as a salary, but I didn't say so. I added the Coke to his tray and gave him a noncommittal smile.

"Maybe we could hang out sometime," he suggested, eyes roving over me in a way that told me the apple hadn't fallen far from the tree. "I've always liked redheads."

"Who doesn't?" I agreed, not bothering to tell him I didn't routinely "hang out" with whiny, underemployed men ten years my junior. My taste ran more to well-seasoned cops and a certain blond lawyer . . .

"Hey, that's a good one." Kolby's laugh had a neighing quality to it.

Without wanting to side with Gordon on anything, I found myself agreeing with him about his son's loserhood. I immediately felt bad about the thought, since I'd only known the kid for two minutes. *Sometimes that's long enough,* my unkinder side said.

"Looks like your table's getting impatient," I hinted, eager to get rid of him. I blew out a long breath as he finally sauntered away.

"Hey, what's a gal gotta do to get a brew around here?"

"Maud!" I swung around happily at the sound of my friend's whiskey-and-cigarettes voice. An original member of the Readaholics book club, Maud Bell held a brew menu at arm's length and squinted.

"Don't get old, Amy-Faye," she advised, pulling rectangular reading glasses from a pocket of her camouflage pants and perching them on her nose. "It sucks."

"Noted. What'll you have? The Exorcise Your Demons IPA is my fave."

"Give me one of those." She slid the menu down the bar.

Sixty years old and six feet tall, she had a wiry build and weathered skin that testified to her summer and fall occupations as a hunting and fishing guide. In the winter, she fixed computers and designed Web sites. All year round, she posted regularly on her conspiracy-theory blog, Out to Get You. Her hair was an au naturel mix of silver, white, and iron, currently blunt-cut to chin length, and her upper lip was a shade fuller than her lower, overhanging it by a smidge, like she was perpetually about to drink from a straw. She wore a tan camp shirt tucked into her camo pants. "Have you finished *Orient Express*?" she asked, taking a long drink of the beer I set before her. "It's good."

I wasn't sure if she meant the book or the brew. "Yeah, but we can't talk about it without the others."

"Brilliant book. There's a reason that Christie woman has sold more books than anyone else on the planet, although that Poirot is an arrogant arsehole, as the Brits might say."

"Of course you liked it," I laughed. "It's about a con-spiracy."

Her lopsided smile pressed wrinkles into her cheeks and acknowledged my hit. Before she could respond, Bernadette "Bernie" Kloster slipped under the bar without bothering to raise the hinged section. "Sorry I'm late. The sitter was late. If I had a buck for every excuse she comes up with . . ."

A sprite of a woman barely five feet tall with sandy hair that tended toward frizzy, Bernie had gone to school with Derek, five years behind me and Brooke and Ivy. She married straight out of high school, had a couple of kids, divorced, and was trying to earn a teaching degree while taking care of her boys and working two jobs. On top of that, she bartended for my events sometimes. I tried to steer work her way whenever I could. She had her orange shirt knotted higher on her midriff than mine (showing off a tiny waist I couldn't help envying), and as I watched, she undid an extra button, exposing more bony chest. She was cute and even sexy in a pixieish sort of way.

"I need the tips," she explained matter-of-factly. "Seen Gordon this evening?"

Something airy yet tense in her voice caught my attention. "Nope. Just Derek. Why?"

"Good. I don't need another ass-chewing for being late. That man's always been unpredictable, but these days he's verging on psychotic. When he asks you out, you should say no."

"Already did, but why do you say that?"

"Trying to pay it forward and save other women

from making the same stupid-ass mistakes I made." She grabbed a damp rag and wiped the bar hard, as if trying to erase Gordon rather than sop up a splash of beer. "I'm pretty sure there isn't a woman in a five-county area he hasn't hit on."

"Not me," Maud put in with a twinkle.

I introduced the two of them, and Bernie said, "Count yourself lucky. Listen to me. Going all negative on you. I'm sorry. I'm not usually a whiner. Put it down to not enough sleep, too much studying, unreliable babysitters, and Billy getting lippy now that he's turned eleven. Says he doesn't need a 'baby' sitter anymore. If he hadn't broken his ankle playing Spider-Man on the roof three Sundays back when I left him alone, I might almost believe him. They talk about teenage girls having mouths on them, but so far I'd back Billy against any of them, and he's still two years away from thirteen. Gawd."

We laughed. A gaggle of customers came in and kept me busy for a while, drawing beers and mixing margaritas. Luckily, I still practiced that particular skill at home, especially when the Readaholics met at my place, and I whipped up a batch with ease. Bernie worked the floor with Kolby, turning on the smile and sass and earning some healthy tips, I was sure. Maud left after the one beer and said she'd see me tomorrow night at Brooke's house for the Readaholics meeting.

Shortly after seven, the happy hour crowd dwindled and Kolby took off, saying he had "plans." It wasn't my place to supervise him, so I didn't ask if his dad knew he was skating off so early. Bernie and I exchanged a glance that said we were both happy to see him go. I was washing mugs in the sink when a burly man with a beard approached the bar. Without introducing himself, he asked, "Gordon or Derek around? Need to talk to one of 'em."

"I'll find them," I said, knowing from his tone that he wasn't here to tell them they'd won the Publishers Clearing House sweepstakes. Wiping my hands on my jeans, I signaled to Bernie, who took my place behind the bar. "Can you hold down the fort a sec?"

"Sure." She gave the man a smile and slid a coaster in front of him.

Happy to escape the bar for a few minutes, I poked my head into the kitchen, but the workers said they hadn't seen either man in over an hour. Mounting the stairs to the third floor, I looked in their offices but found no one except the janitor—Foster? Forrest?—who was emptying Gordon's trash can. I'd never been in Gordon's lair, and I looked around curiously. A wooden desk with cubbyholes and a simple glass-front bookcase were centered on a rug with a worn floral pattern. Framed photos and blueprints of the building in its early days hung evenly on one wall, peopled by men in turn-of-the-century work clothes. I suspected the furnishings were left over from the building's factory days. I could totally see a waistcoated man in Edwardian garb putting his bowler on the iron coat tree that currently held Gordon's golf Windbreaker and umbrella. A laptop computer and high-end ergonomic desk chair struck anachronistic notes. I wondered if Gordon had gone through all the desk's cubbies looking for secrets, or routine invoices or notes from a bygone era. Somehow I didn't think so; he didn't strike me as the type.

"On the roof," Foster said, even though I hadn't asked him anything. "Smoking." His wrinkled nose said he disapproved.

"Thanks." Skipping the elevator, since I hadn't gone to yoga that morning, I jogged up another flight and paused by the door that led to the roof. It was closed, but I could hear the yelling through it.

"—can't do that, Gord. You'll sink the pub."

Derek's voice, sounding angry and desperate.

"—whatever the hell I want to . . . my money—"

Gordon, sounding implacable and arrogant. I hesitated, not wanting to walk into their fight, and not wanting to go away in case Gordon turned violent with Derek, as he had with Susan this morning.

"—don't try to stop me," Gordon bellowed. "If you do, I'll ruin you."

"—handle this through an arbitrator," Derek said.

Gordon answered with a string of curses. I bit down hard on my lip.

"—won't let you—"

"—can't stop me, you f—"

The thud of flesh against flesh had me barreling through the door. I burst onto the roof, a long expanse of weathered boards with a waist-high masonry wall, vents and air-conditioning compressor, planters, and a small shed. I found the two men locked together, trying to land punches without letting go of each other. It was still plenty light enough to see them clearly. Blood spotted Derek's shirt, and Gordon's pants pocket was ripped. They knocked against a planter and it rocked, the dwarf spruce inside it swaying. They were muttering and swearing at each other in guttural voices, words indistinguishable.

Gordon landed a punch into Derek's gut and he crumpled forward. From that position he wrapped his arms around Gordon's knees and took the bigger man down with him. They landed with a thud and began rolling across the rooftop, neither one gaining an advantage. I dithered about what to do, pulling out my cell phone to call for help—was I going to call the cops on my own brother?—but then remembered Derek's fury when I'd summoned a teacher to keep him from getting beaten up on the playground when he was in fourth grade and I was in sixth. I put my phone back in my pocket and started toward them as Gordon, who outweighed Derek by a good forty pounds, ended up on top, straddling Derek's chest. Both men were breathing hard and the punch Gordon threw at Derek's face lacked power and skidded off his cheek. I thought about throwing myself on Gordon's back and peeling him off Derek, but then I saw a better way.

A hose for watering the potted plants lay neatly coiled by the faucet and I turned it on full force and directed the cold water at the fighting men. As the stream splashed into his face, Gordon leaped up with a curse. Derek rolled away and staggered to his feet, bent over with his hands on his knees. They were good and soaked, I saw with satisfaction, which was what they deserved for behaving like a couple of middle school hooligans. Gordon shook his head and water droplets sprayed from his longish hair. He had a scrape on his face, and the buttons were torn off his shirt so it gaped open, displaying a furry torso. Blood dripped from his elbow and nose. He looked confused, like a man waking up from a nightmare, or someone trying to listen to a far-off voice. I don't know why, but I felt sorry for him, even though he'd just been whaling on my brother.

"Amy-Faye, what are you—?" Derek started, his voice verging on angry, but his expression embarrassed.

"There's a man downstairs who needs to talk to one of you," I said calmly, even though my heart was beating fast. *Idiots.* "Sounded important." Crossing to the faucet, I turned off the water. Not waiting for a reply, I marched toward the door, reasonably confident they weren't going to resume their fight. In fact, Gordon was pulling out a cigarette and heading toward the wall by the time I reached the stairs. A match flared. The way he hunched his shoulders said "keep away" and I was glad to comply. I glanced over my shoulder and saw Derek coming toward me, limping.

When he drew even with me, he shot me a sidelong look. "Leave it," he said, forestalling my questions.

The door closed behind us as we started down the stairs. "Derek, what—"

"It's none of your business and you can't help anyway."

As much as I wanted to help him, I knew his moods well enough to clamp my lips together. Sometimes brothers didn't want big sisters' help. In fact, *usually* brothers didn't want sisters weighing in on their activities, choice of friends, love lives, work, or drinking habits. At least, Derek didn't. I could still hear him yelling at our youngest sister, Natalie, last Christmas that she had no right doing an Internet search on his girlfriend of the moment, now ex, largely because of the info Nat gathered. Re this current crisis, he'd tell me when he was ready. Or not.

When we reached the third-floor landing, he peeled off, saying, "Tell whoever it is I'll be there in a minute. I've got a dry shirt in my office."

"Sure."

The door snapped shut and I wasn't sure he'd even heard me. Pinning a smile on my face, I walked down the last flights and emerged into the pub, now largely deserted except for the bearded man at the bar flirting with Bernie, and a couple of women dawdling over piña coladas in one corner.

"Everything okay?" Bernie gave me a look that told me I looked rumpled or pissed off or both.

"Derek will be here in a minute," I told her and the bearded man.

"Better be," he grunted.

"Wow, Don, I could take that the wrong way. You're not enjoying our conversation?" Bernie asked archly, with the suggestion of a wink at me.

Smiling gratefully, I grabbed a bar cloth and began swabbing down tables. Derek emerged two minutes later, greeted Don, and escorted him up to the offices. I wondered whether Gordon was there or if he'd left.

"Any idea what that was about?" I asked Bernie, nodding toward the disappeared Derek and Don.

"Nonpayment of bills." Worry creased her brow.

"Don told me all about it. The pub's ninety days in arrears with what they owe him for hops. I hope I'm not going to have to find another job again. This one suits me fine. Works great with my school schedule. I so do not want to have to job-hunt again. Gawd."

"I'm sure it's not as bad as that," I said, not sure of any such thing. I was ashamed that my first thought was for the nest egg I'd invested in Derek's pub, and not for Derek's disappointment if the pub failed. "Once Elysium is really open, after the grand opening Friday, this place'll be packed with people. I'm sure it'll be turning a profit in no time."

Bernie looked unconvinced but said nothing. Hefting a tub of dirty dishes, she carried it into the kitchen, bumping the door open with her hip. I tried not to think about how long it had been before Eventful! showed even a tiny profit margin. It was still hit-and-miss some months, four years in. When Bernie returned, I told her I was taking off and she nodded.

"I'll hang until Derek comes out. I'm on the clock until ten o'clock tonight anyway." Gesturing to the now empty pub, she added, "I think I can handle it on my own."

With a laugh, I said good night and left, emerging into a cooling Colorado dusk. A line of light on the western horizon tattled on the just-set sun, and an owl hooted. Pulling a flyer off the van's window, I crumpled it without reading it and tossed it into the passenger seat. Trash. I relaxed into the seat with a sigh. I'd forgotten how physically exhausting bar work could be. I was beat and the bar hadn't even been that busy. I was grateful I was supervising the grand opening festivities and not bartending Friday night. On my recommendation, Derek had already taken on extra help for the occasion, everything from kitchen workers, to servers, to janitorial staff. Cranking the ignition, I headed for home, a long bath, and bed.

Chapter 3

Client meetings kept me busy the next morning, and I was pleased as punch to land a December wedding ("We're not bringing a shotgun, but we ought to be, if you know what I mean," the bride's father told me grimly) and a family reunion.

"We're going to have to take on more staff now that you're getting better at signing up clients," Al said when I told him. Today's bow tie had clown fish printed on it. We were standing in the reception area, absently watching a window cleaner hired by the building manager squeegee the panes in the French doors.

" 'Getting better'?" I raised my brows.

"Yeah. You used to come across as way too desperate. Scared people off. You're more relaxed now."

I was half affronted, but I finally laughed. "Desperate? And here I thought that only applied to my love life. Glad to hear I no longer come across that way to clients. Maybe you'd like to come on full-time when you graduate," I said. I hadn't intended to broach the idea with him so soon, but since the opening was there . . .

Al blinked. "Really? Wow. Let me think about it."

"Did you have something else lined up? Other plans?"

"No. Nothing definite. I always figured I'd move to Denver or the Springs, maybe even out of state, and get a job in marketing with a big company or a nonprofit. I planned to sign up for some interviews through the college's career office." He tugged on his fishy bow tie, a habitual gesture when he was nervous.

"Well, let me know. If you want to stay, we can look into getting another intern from Mesa when you graduate." I didn't want to pressure Al, but I'd come to rely on him over the past months and I hoped he'd decide to sign on permanently with Eventful! "You're still available to work the pub opening Friday night, right? We'll definitely need all hands on deck for that."

"Aye, aye, Captain!" He saluted.

Rolling my eyes, I returned to my office to work on invoices until lunchtime. Twice, I picked up the phone to call Derek and twice I put the phone down again. If he needed my help, he'd ask for it. If he didn't want to share what was going on between him and Gordon, that was his prerogative. On impulse, I pulled my laptop closer and punched "Elysium Brewing," "Gordon Marsh," and "Derek Johnson" into a search engine. The first article that came up was from the business section of the *Denver Post*. TROUBLE IN PARADISE? ran the headline. I skimmed it.

"Trouble in Paradise, or rather Elysium? Recent reports suggest that Elysium Brewing, the latest in a long line of craft breweries opening around the state, may not be on solid financial ground. Venture capitalist Gordon Marsh has suffered reversals lately, including the failure of his Grand Junction nightclub Moonglade (see our June 7 article "Moonglade Bankruptcy") and damages assessed in a recent court case. He may be forced to liquefy some assets, and his stake in Elysium Brewing, located in Heaven, Colorado, is low-hanging fruit. This would leave first-time entrepreneur and award-winning brewmaster Derek Johnson high and dry without the capital to sustain the new venture. The craft brewing scene would be the poorer for such an outcome, in this reporter's opinion, because Elysium Brewing's Angel Ale is fit for, well, the gods."

Guilt niggled at me for invading Derek's privacy, but nothing reported in a major newspaper counted as "private," did it? At least now I knew what Gordon and Derek had been arguing about. Gordon wanted out of their deal. Anger burned in me. How could he do this to Derek? Owning the pub was Derek's dream. Gordon had no right to back out at the last second, just as the pub's doors were opening for business. I sympathized with Derek wanting to beat him up; if Gordon had been standing in my office, I'd have punched him myself. I wondered how far it had gone, if Gordon had already severed their partnership, or if he was only contemplating it. Surely their contract protected each of them against this kind of possibility? Maybe that was why Derek had mentioned arbitration. I felt so sad for Derek. Here he was, so close to having his dream come true, and Gordon was pulling the rug out from under him. I wished I knew another venture capitalist, or had a fairy godmother inclined to grant wishes, so I could help him out. But I'd already invested every penny I could afford (and some I couldn't) in the pub.

I reached for the phone to call Doug Elvaston, my former boyfriend who was a top-notch corporate lawyer. Then I remembered he was still on a leave of absence from his firm, crewing his way around the world on a friend's yacht. His bride had left him at the altar in May and he'd taken it hard. I'd gotten occasional postcards from him this summer, from places like Pago Pago, Manila, and Christchurch. They were blandly impersonal, although humorous, talking about the weather, the rigors of sailing, and the exotic sights he'd seen. One had ended with "Wish you were here," and I wondered wistfully if that was true, or if it was just standard postcard-speak. I shook myself. At any rate, Doug wasn't here to explain the legal ins and outs of partnership contracts to me.

With three birthday "events" scheduled for the next two weeks, plus a corporate retreat for five hundred and a retirement party, I reluctantly put Derek and his troubles out of my mind to concentrate on work. With any luck, the grand opening would be such a huge success that the pub would succeed even without Gordon's money. If not, well . . . we'd cross that bridge when we came to it.

That evening I parked between Maud's battered Jeep and Kerry Sanderson's Subaru Outback in front of my best friend Brooke Widefield's McMansion. Her in-laws had bestowed it on Brooke and Troy when they married and I knew it sometimes felt more like a prison than a home to Brooke. Her mother-in-law, Miss Clarice, conducted regular inspections to ensure that the house was immaculate. Not really, but that was how it felt. Brooke wore herself to a frazzle cleaning, straightening, and decorating the place anytime she had warning that Miss Clarice was coming over. The Widefields didn't want Brooke to work outside the home because that didn't convey the right "image," whatever that meant. Troy, something of a wet noodle who worked for Troy Sr.'s auto dealership, didn't have enough backbone, in my opinion, to tell his parents to find someone else's marriage to meddle in.

I entered the house without knocking and was greeted by the tantalizing aromas of cumin and oregano. Mmm . . . Brooke had made her special chili. Yum. My mouth watered and I realized I'd skipped lunch. "Hey," I called out as I entered. The formal entryway with its travertine floor, plaster walls, and crystal chandelier was cavernous and I wouldn't have been surprised to hear an echo, but if there was one, Brooke drowned it out. "In the kitchen, A-Faye."

I followed the tantalizing aroma to Brooke's gourmet kitchen, where I found Brooke at the stove, sampling the chili, and Maud and Kerry at the table, noshing on chips and guacamole. The kitchen was the least intimidating room in Brooke's house. It reeked of expensive the way budget kitchens smelled like old grease sucked into the paint and curtains—acres of granite, appliances with foreign names I couldn't pronounce, and extras like warming drawers and a second oven and a walk-in wine cooler—but it was homey, too, with redbrick around the stove and floral cushions on the chairs. The table in her breakfast nook looked out on a landscaped backyard, and three copies of *Murder on the Orient Express* lay on it, next to a galvanized bucket loaded with ice and beer. Brooke smiled her lovely Miss Colorado smile and came over to give me a hug, holding her spoon at arm's length so she wouldn't drip chili down my back. I was glad our relationship was back to normal after some stiffness when I insisted on investigating our friend Ivy Donner's death a few months ago, even after Brooke said we should give it up. Jointly rescuing Doug from his wedding fiasco had made us comfortable with each other again.

"I didn't buy it," Kerry Sanderson announced, scooping a gob of guac onto a chip. Her short gray-flecked brown hair barely twitched when she shook her head. She raised the chip to her aquiline nose with its flaring nostrils and sniffed at the guacamole, trying to identify an ingredient, perhaps. "No way."

We stared at her, puzzled.

"The book, the book," she explained, waving her copy of *Orient Express*. "No way did twelve people get together, hash out the plan, and come to consensus on jointly killing that Ratchett man. I've sat through enough meetings to know that it's virtually impossible to get more than five people to agree on a completely noncontroversial course of action at any one time. Murder? Never happen. Have you ever been to a town council meeting? They go on so long they make me murderous. I'll grant you that." She bit into the chip with a loud crunch.

We laughed. Kerry made her money as Heaven's most successful Realtor, but she was also the town's part-time mayor. Coming up on fifty, she was brusque and competent, and had bulldozed a bunch of initiatives through the town council that had boosted the town's economic development and made it an even more appealing tourist destination. She preferred police procedurals, maybe because her ex was Heaven's retired chief of police.

The front door squeaked open and closed gently, and we chorused, "Hi, Lola."

"Mew?"

I leaned down to pick up Misty, now half-grown, as she butted her head against my ankle. I'd rescued her in May and bestowed her on Lola, who owned a plant nursery and had a more pet-friendly schedule than I did. Misty purred loudly as I scratched under her gray chin, and tried to investigate the beer bottle I'd pulled from the bucket.

"I guess I'm the last," Lola Paget said. She stood in the doorway, a petite but sturdy woman with a gentle smile. With espresso-colored skin, a short Afro, and wire-rimmed glasses, she looked like a scientist, and had majored in chemistry at Texas A & M before returning to Colorado and opening the nursery. She always picked a more literary mystery when it was her turn to choose a book. "I hope you don't mind that I brought Misty. I had to keep her cooped up all day while we were spraying pesticides, and she was lonely."

"Of course not," Brooke said immediately, although I knew she'd be vacuuming up gray hairs and spraying disinfectant around the moment we left. "Maybe Clarice will go into anaphylactic shock the next time she comes over."

"Is she that allergic to cats?" Lola asked, brow creasing. "I'll put Misty in the car."

She reached to take the cat from me, but Brooke intervened. "No, no. I'd rather have Misty as a guest than Clarice." Putting a hand to her mouth, she asked, "Did I really say that?"

We laughed at her exaggeratedly comic expression, and I set Misty on the floor so she could explore. Helping ourselves to chili, we got down to the business of the evening: eating, drinking, and talking about our book. When I first formed the Readaholics, five years ago, we met in the library. When our membership settled at our current number, give or take a couple of women who drifted in and out, we began meeting in one another's homes. Much more cozy. And the addition of beer, wine, or margaritas led to more . . . spirited discussions of the books.

"Joe's traveled on the Orient Express," Maud said, lounging with one elbow on the back of the chair, and her legs straight out in front of her, crossed at the ankles. Her scuffed work boots looked alien against Brooke's highly polished Brazilian cherry floor. Joe was her partner, a wildlife photographer who was more often bundled up against the weather photographing Arctic foxes, or slogging through the Amazon getting pictures of piranhas, than hanging out in Heaven. Their frequent separations seemed to suit him and Maud.

"Went from Venice to Budapest, oh, twenty or twenty-two years ago," she continued. "Joe's client, the publisher of one of the mags Joe freelances for, rented the entire train for a celebration of some kind and hired Joe to do photographs of his guests. The flowing champagne, high-end sheets, and over-the-top luxury made him uncomfortable, I think. Too much. He'd rather have donated the cost of his ticket to a bird sanctuary."

"What an opportunity," Lola said, an uncharacteristic whiff of envy in her voice.

As the sole proprietor of Bloomin' Wonderful, and supporter of her grandmother and teenage sister, she didn't get the opportunity to travel often. I suspected money was tight in the Paget household. I swallowed a mouthful of chili. "You know," I said. "I didn't get into the book as much as I expected to. I mean, I enjoyed trying to figure out who killed Ratchett, but I didn't feel connected to any of the characters, and none of them felt connected to each other, except maybe the count and his young wife."

Kerry nodded briskly. "I react that way to most of Christie's books. They feel emotionally . . . flat."

"I knew that they were all in on it before I started reading—I saw the movie years ago," Maud said, "but I was interested to see how Poirot would figure it out. He should have smelled something fishy when two or three of the characters all admitted having ties to that kidnapping. First rule of conspiracies: There are no coincidences." She pursed her lips in disappointment at Poirot's slowness.

"How did you feel about Poirot concocting that story at the end to let them all get away with it?" I asked.

Lola shook her head slowly. "That was wrong. Yes, Ratchett was despicable, but murdering him was wrong, too."

"You don't think there's ever a situation when it's okay to kill someone?" Brooke asked. She rose to put the now empty chili pot in the sink to soak.

Lola considered, as she usually did. Lola was not like me—she didn't often say things in haste and immediately regret opening her mouth. "Maybe in self-defense, or in defense of someone helpless. Not in cold blood like in the book."

"They say revenge is a dish best served cold," Kerry said.

"It's best not served at all," Lola said with surprising tartness.

"Whoa, Lo," Brooke said. "That's easy to say, sitting around this table, but what if someone kidnapped and killed your child and the police couldn't catch them? Wouldn't you want to see them get theirs?" Elbows on the table, she put her chin in her hands and leaned forward to gauge Lola's reaction.

"I might want to see them punished, but I hope I wouldn't do anything illegal or immoral to make it happen." Lola creased her brow.

"Were they all equally guilty," Kerry asked, "or just the ones who struck the early blows that actually killed Ratchett?"

"Interesting," Maud said, dipping her chin to study Kerry.

The discussion swirled off in new directions and it was almost ten when we broke up, making plans to watch the movie version of *Murder on the Orient Express* next Thursday, a week from today.

"I hope you're all coming tomorrow night," I said as we took our dishes to the sink and got ready to leave. "Well, all except you, Misty," I said to the kitten, who was trying to decide if a sliver of corn chip was edible. She eventually disdained it and stalked, tail straight up, to Lola.

"Wouldn't miss it," Kerry said, scraping the leftover guacamole into the trash as Brooke approached with the cling wrap. "You don't want to keep this, Brooke, not after we've been double-dipping." She tucked the plate into the dishwasher. "Always good for the mayor to be seen supporting local businesses. And I'm happy to do my part," she said with a self-sacrificing air, "especially when it involves beer."

"That's why we voted for you, Ker," Maud said. She rose to her feet, yawned, and stretched long arms over her head. "I'll be there. Joe's in town, so I'll drag him along."

They left and Lola followed them, saying she and her grandmother would be at the opening. Since they were teetotalers, I appreciated the gesture. When it was just me and Brooke, we each grabbed another beer and settled into the squashy, loden green leather chairs in her family room. In the winter, there'd be a cheery fire crackling in the stone fireplace, but it was too warm for one now.

"Where's Troy?" I asked.

"Doing campaign strategy with his dad and some county movers and shakers," Brooke said. She was seated sideways on the chair, her knees draped over the armrest, and one foot kicked restlessly.

"Are you okay with it, that he's running for state senator?"

She shrugged. "I'm not against it, if it's what he really wants. Trouble is, I don't know if it's what *he* wants, or what his parents want. I've been married to Troy for ten years, and with him for almost fifteen, and I still have trouble sifting out who he really is sometimes, from who his folks want him to be. I think that's because he's not sure." She took a long pull on her beer.

I didn't know what to say to that. My taste had always run toward men who were sure of who they were—for better or worse—and I'd never understood Troy's attraction. Yeah, he was good-looking, rich, and a decent enough guy, but he kowtowed to his parents too much for my taste, let them decide where he was going to college (CSU), what he was going to study (business), and where he'd work afterward (Daddy's car dealership). Marrying Brooke was the only time he'd defied his parents. That he'd loved her enough to go against them had made me feel more warmly toward him for a while, but that feeling had worn off earlier this summer when he accused me of investigating Ivy's murder because I was an attention hound.

"Anything new on the adoption front?" Against her in-laws' wishes, Brooke had talked Troy into starting the adoption process after ten years of marriage and six years of trying unsuccessfully to have children.

"We've got someone coming to do a home survey on Monday. If we pass that—"

"When." Brooke kept the cleanest house in Heaven and had already baby-proofed every inch of it.

"—the agency will put our profile in their book of prospective parents who are interested in talking to pregnant girls—women—who are considering putting their babies up for adoption."

"Did they say how long it'd take?"

Brooke wrapped a piece of hair around her finger. "Same old story. A week, a year, never."

I could see she was trying not to get her hopes up and didn't want to talk about it anymore. Giving her an encouraging smile, I changed the subject, telling her about the fight I'd witnessed between Gordon and Derek and the article I'd pulled up.

"I'm so afraid for Derek," I said, voicing fears I hadn't even acknowledged to myself. "I don't know how—or if—he'll handle it if the pub goes under."

"Hey, Derek's a levelheaded guy," Brooke consoled me. "He wouldn't do anything drastic."

"What about the time he ran away from home after the incident at A. J. Lingenfelder's birthday party—"

"He was four!"

"—or the time he spray-painted 'CHEATER' on the Zooks' garage door, or—"

"Amy Zook *did* cheat. She Sparknoted the answers to—"

"—when he got arrested for vandalizing the signs and for that bar fight?"

"They dropped the charges when everyone said the other guy started it. He's older now," Brooke said. "Less impulsive."

"Hmph." I set my tone to "unconvinced."

"We could have Troy's announcement party at the pub," Brooke suggested.

"That's a great idea," I said gratefully, "if the pub lasts that long." The announcement was timed for mid-January of next year.

She leaned over to put her hand on my arm. "It'll be okay, A-Faye. He's a big boy. He's smart, he's resourceful, and he makes darn good beer. Things'll work out for him."

"Thanks." I smiled, thinking that only-child Brooke didn't understand. I'd been watching out for Derek all my life. Yeah, he was an adult now, and he made his own decisions and lived with the consequences, but I still wanted to help all I could.

On the drive home, I decided that the only way I could help at the moment was to produce the best-ever grand opening party, and that was what I determined to do. Not that I'd been planning a ho-hum grand opening, but I vowed to clear my calendar tomorrow and spend the day at Elysium Brewing overseeing every teensy-weensy, minute detail.

Chapter 4

Friday dawned crisp and clear, with the possibility of afternoon thunderstorms. Typical weather for this time of year. I said a little prayer that the storms would hold off, since we were counting on using Elysium's patio space to keep the crowd under fire marshal–mandated levels. Then I headed off to yoga, figuring I needed a little meditation if I were to survive this day mentally intact. Feeling limber and relaxed after class—held in Yael's studio on the third floor of the building where my ground-floor office was—I descended the stairs past the law firm on the second floor to the Divine Herb, which had the street-front space. Standing in line for a coffee, I overheard a cluster of suited men talking about coming to Elysium tonight and it made me smile.

"You look like the cat that ate the canary," said a voice behind me.

A happy glow spread through me. I turned to see Detective Lindell Hart smiling at me. The police detective was attractive without being handsome, although the longer I knew him, the handsomer he got. Hmm. He had ever-so-slightly receding, curly brown hair, a nose that had clearly been broken at least once, and a tan that testified to his time in a softball league and fly-fishing. He was almost a foot taller than me, maybe six-four, so I had to look up. "Hi. No canaries. I'm going to settle for a yogurt parfait and a large—a very large—coffee. Busy day."

"I'll bet. Everything ready?"

"It will be," I said with determination.

"I know you hired a couple of our off-duty guys to help with traffic control and security," he said. "Good move."

"Never hurts to have a cop on hand." I accepted my coffee, yogurt, and change from the clerk and moved to the condiments ledge to dump in some cream. Hart held my parfait for me while I tamped the lid back down on my cup.

"See you there at seven?"

"Come for the preopening party at six," I invited him impulsively. "It's for family and the area's movers and shakers."

"Which am I?" His brown eyes gazed into mine, humor and something else lurking in them.

"Neither. You're *special*." I gave the word a droll twist.

He grinned. "I've been waiting months to hear you say that."

Was he serious? He sounded like he was joking, but . . . I pondered the way his smile made my pulse race a bit, and wondered if it might be nice to be Lindell Hart's special someone. He'd moved here from Atlanta in April, and we'd gone out a few times this summer, but he'd been at a Homeland Security training session for almost two months, and my job tied me up most weekends, so we hadn't been able to spend a lot of time together. Then there was Doug.

I shook my head slightly to dislodge both Hart and Doug. I didn't have time to sort out my love life. Not that I really had a love life. I had two attractive men on the periphery of my life, one of whom had dumped me two years earlier and become engaged to another woman this past year, and another I barely knew. I needed to focus on the grand opening. Focus, focus, focus.

Hart and I parted on the sidewalk in front of the tea shop. "Gotta run," he said. When he handed over my yogurt, his fingers brushed mine and I felt that tingly glow again.

"Criminals keeping you hopping?" I asked.

"Staff meeting. I'd prefer the criminals."

I laughed, waved, and headed for my van as he walked down the block and turned the corner toward the police department.

I crunched into Elysium's gravel parking lot half an hour later, near nine o'clock, having taken a two-minute shower, pulled my hair into a ponytail to keep it out of the way, and shrugged into jeans and a tank top. Today was about work, not impressing potential clients. I'd sneak home before the actual party started and change clothes. Opening the van door to let the morning's cool breeze in, I spooned up my yogurt and scanned my to-do list. It was lengthy. It ranged from directing the caterers (for the preopening party—we were serving the pub's food during the grand opening), banner hangers, and cleaning staff, to making sure the extra chairs arrived and were arranged attractively in the second-floor pool table area for the preopening party, to checking stocks of toilet paper and towels in the bathroom, confirming with the valets, off-duty cops, and other extra staff, picking up the Elysium Brewing T-shirts we were handing out to the first hundred guests, and a couple of dozen more things. Where was Al?

On the thought, he drove up and stopped beside my van with a puff of dust from the gravel. "Reporting for duty, boss," he said.

"Don't call me 'boss,'" I told him for the millionth time.

"Where do you want me to start?"

A delivery truck from the party rental company in Grand Junction turned into the lot just then, so I sent Al upstairs with their team to supervise the transformation of the pool table loft. I headed for the kitchen, hoping the catering staff would show up before too long. Bernie was there, sponging a spot off the front of her uniform shirt. I said hello and peered out the kitchen's open back door. A produce delivery van was offloading while a kitchen worker kept track by marking items off on a clipboard. Two industrial-size Dumpsters yawned open behind the van, already half-filled with pallets and bulging trash bags stuffed with kitchen refuse, I guessed from the smell. Gordon Marsh, looking much more together today in pressed khakis and an orange Elysium Brewing golf shirt, a Band-Aid on his cheek, stood beside a Dumpster, apparently arguing with a zaftig blonde who used her hands as she talked. She looked familiar . . .

Bernie appeared beside me, probably curious about what I was staring at, and I asked her, "Is that Gordon's sister?"

She shrugged thin shoulders. "Wouldn't know. I've never met his sister. I think she's a step-, though, so you can't tell anything by looking at them." We studied the quarreling pair, who hadn't noticed us.

I put it aside, not interested in Gordon's love life, and too pissed off at him for what he was doing to Derek to say good morning. I checked with the head chef to make sure everything was okay in his domain. He gave me an "okay" sign with circled thumb and forefinger, and I left the kitchen in time to meet the janitor coming through the front door.

"Thanks for coming early, Forrest," I greeted him.

"Foster. Don't worry about it." He gave a small smile when I winced at getting his name wrong. "You were close. Most people don't think janitors have names. I've discovered in the past few months that we're an invisible breed."

Even though he was smiling, his tone was bitter. Wearing a white coverall, he was medium height with a sturdy build. Gray-flecked black hair with Roman-style bangs capped a face with an olive complexion and incipient five o'clock shadow I suspected reappeared ten minutes after he shaved. He wore Mizuno athletic shoes and looked to be in his late fifties.

"You a runner?" I asked, gesturing to his shoes, trying to make a connection.

"Used to play racquetball," he said. "Can't afford the club anymore. Might as well use the shoes to mop in. If you'll excuse me, I've got to get started. Busy day. Tilers didn't seal the grout in the bathroom when they put in the handicapped stall a couple months back and I need to bleach it. Gets dirty fast if it's not sealed."

I sidestepped out of his way. "I appreciate your attention to detail."

"Came in handy when I was an account manager."

From white-collar worker to janitor? Hmm. I didn't have time to get into it, although his tone invited me to ask. "I'll bet. Open a window. I can find a fan if you need one." The last thing we needed was the pub reeking of bleach. "We'll have a cleaning crew in tomorrow to help with cleanup," I assured him.

With a twist of his lips that could have meant anything from "Thanks" to "Who gives a damn?" Foster moved off, shoes squeaking slightly on the wooden floor.

The day passed in a whirlwind of activity with Derek, Gordon, Bernie, Kolby, and the rest of the pub staff working as hard as Al and I. Derek sent them all home in the early afternoon, with directions to be back half an hour before the party kickoff. I ate a sandwich on the run for lunch, munching down bites as I helped the banner company position the ELYSIUM BREWING GRAND OPENING banner, a symphony of dark brown and orange, along the roofline of the old building. I didn't get a breather until midafternoon, when I left the pub briefly to fetch the T-shirts from the shop in a strip mall on the far side of Heaven. It was while I was waiting in the T-shirt shop that I remembered where I'd seen the blonde talking to Gordon that morning. She'd been one of the two women distributing flyers in the parking lot on Wednesday. Why were they talking? He might have been chewing her out for soliciting his customers, although it had looked to me like *she* was haranguing *him*. When I got back to the van and dumped the T-shirt boxes in the back, I picked up the crumpled flyer from where I'd tossed it. Smoothing it out, I read:

Women Outing Serial Cheaters (WOSC) vs. Gordon Marsh

    If you're one of the hundreds of women screwed (literally and figuratively) by Gordon Marsh, join your sisters in woe at Elysium Brewing during its Grand Opening on Friday, 4 August. Thought you were alone?

    You've got lots of company. Have a beer on him and talk about busting his balls this Friday.

    Check our Web site for next month's target and to nominate future cheating subjects for outing and payback.

I reread the flyer, openmouthed. Really? There was an organization that identified and got revenge on cheating men? No way. This had to be a joke. But if it wasn't . . . That was all the grand opening needed—a pack of out-for-blood women looking to humiliate Gordon the way he'd humiliated them. Under some circumstances I might have admired the chutzpah of whoever had organized this, but not when it was my brother's livelihood at stake. Did this group get violent?

I called Maud. She was the computer whiz. If anyone could get the scoop on this organization quickly, she could. When I explained what I needed and read her the URL, she laughed.

"Happy to check 'em out for you," she said. "What a hoot!"

"I'd find them a lot hootier if I weren't worried they're going to wreck the party tonight."

"Don't worry," Maud said. "If it looks like they're dangerous, or even destructive, you can tell your detective and he'll take care of them for you."

"He's not my detective," I said, but the thought that Hart was going to be nearby cheered me up. "Thanks, Maud."

I climbed into the van, noticing that the sky was getting darker and the wind picking up. Just great.

Derek and Gordon feuding. Women maybe planning to teach Gordon a Lorena Bobbitt–style lesson. Thunderheads moving in. If troubles came in threes, this party was already at its limit and the first guest hadn't even arrived.

Chapter 5

The evening's attire was informal—it was a pub, after all—and I wore a yellow halter-neck cotton sundress with a fitted bodice and a flared skirt that simultaneously showcased my waist, hid my not-so-slender thighs, provided relief from the heat, and gave me two large pockets for my cell phone and other miscellany. I'd learned early on that pockets were invaluable to the event organizer. Derek looked handsome but nervous as the clock ticked closer to six, constantly swiping his hair back from his forehead. He wore olive slacks, an open-neck shirt, and a brown tweed sport coat.

"It'll go great," I assured him. "Nice duds."

"Mom picked them out," he admitted. He looked around and glanced at his watch. "Bernie's late again. If she can't find a reliable babysitter, I'm going to have to let her go."

I picked lint off his lapel. "We've got enough extra staff on—it's no big deal," I said, even though his personnel decisions were none of my business. I liked Bernie and didn't want to see her canned because of a flaky babysitter. Derek started to reply, but Gordon walked up, looking dapper in pale tan slacks topped with a well-cut navy blazer that took ten pounds off him. He moved like an athlete and smelled like expensive cologne when he bent to kiss my cheek. "You look like a million bucks, Amy-Faye," he greeted me, his smile charming and, for once, free of lechery.

I reluctantly admitted that I could understand why some women found him irresistible.

"You've worked miracles getting this place ready today. I'm surprised the army hasn't snapped you up to plan invasions."

"Hmm . . . I'm always up for expanding my business."

"Seriously, there's a place for you at GTM Capital anytime you want it. We can always use someone with your abilities and your"—he searched for a word—"unflappability."

I was taken aback and flattered. I liked the image of myself as unflappable. "Uh, thanks, Gordon, but I like running my own business."

He nodded. "I get that, but keep it in mind. We've got excellent benefits."

I opened my mouth to ask if his company was even going to be around a couple of months from now, but closed it without saying anything. I did not need to get this evening off on the wrong foot by pissing off Gordon and reminding Derek of his financial woes.

A Prius turned into the parking lot, followed by a

large SUV. A line of cars approached from both directions. "Battle stations," I murmured. "Here they come."

Things went well to start with. The turnout was beyond my expectations, with all of Heaven's leading citizens, a smattering of politicians from around the state, the billionaire owner of a nearby ski resort, and the aging rock star currently staying (or hiding out, depending on what tabloid you read) at the resort, and a couple of society and business reporters from Heaven and Grand Junction. As the special guests arrived for the preparty, they mounted the stairs or hopped into the elevator to get to the pool table room on the second floor. Many of them carried umbrellas, anticipating the storm that was clearly going to break before too long. The caterer had done a bang-up job, the pub's brews were widely acclaimed, and conversation noise soon rose to "this is a great party" levels. My parents and my oldest sister, Peri, and her husband, Zach, had been among the first to arrive and they were talking to Congresswoman Green and a woman I'd checked off the guest list as Dr. Angie Dreesen, Gordon's sister, at a table near the window. Her husband got held up at work, she'd said, but would be along soon.

The Widefields Senior, Brooke's in-laws, arrived early, and Brooke and Troy came soon after. My best friend looked stunning in green linen Bermudas and matching jacket with a slithery silver tank beneath it and metallic wedges that made her six feet tall.

"You've done it again," she said, giving me a hug. "Great party."

Lindell Hart showed up with his boss, Chief Uggams, a longtime poker pal of my dad's. I exchanged a few words with them before the caterer grabbed my elbow to ask a question.

"Later," I promised Hart with an apologetic grimace. "Mingle."

"C'mon, Hart," Chief Uggams said, plowing through the crowd. "I see Mayor Sanderson. I've got a bone to pick with her about—"

I never heard what he wanted to argue with Kerry about because the crowd closed around them. Fifteen minutes later I was able to take a minute to myself and I surveyed the happy crowd with pride. It was all going well. I let myself hope that Elysium Brewing would soon be on solid financial ground, and Derek could lose the worried look that seemed permanently stamped on his face. Fat chance. Things started going wrong as soon as the preparty wound up and the public began pouring in for the grand opening.

The first hint of trouble came when Derek, Gordon, and I went downstairs to throw open the pub doors at seven o'clock. There should still have been an hour of sunlight left, but the approaching storm had brought dusk forward. Four women marched across the parking lot against a background of gunmetal gray thunderheads, carrying a hand-lettered banner that read WOMEN OUTING SERIAL CHEATERS CONDEMN GORDON MARSH. Holding one end of the banner was the blonde who'd been distributing flyers. I didn't recognize the two in the middle. At the other end was Susan Marsh, chin jutting forward defiantly.

The three of us froze for a moment, gaping at the oncoming women who were arousing quite a bit of interest, confused looks, and laughter from people heading to the pub.

"Oh my God," Gordon muttered. "I need a smoke." He ducked back into the pub and I knew he was headed for the roof.

"Get rid of them," Derek whispered to me.

"How do you suggest—?" I glared at his cowardly and departing back. The women were almost to the door now, and they looked menacing, but I wasn't afraid of them. Maud had gotten back to me earlier and told me WOSC had never been known to use violence.

"They're into embarrassment and humiliation," she said, "not property damage or worse. Listen to this report of their 'outing' last month. 'Eight women, including two of his ex-wives, all betrayed by Samuel Asperlitz over a period of three years, gathered at his Grand Junction printing shop on Tuesday, July 15, to sing "Your Cheatin' Heart" and distribute T-shirts printed with a montage of photos showing how the target earned his nickname, "Assperlips."' I'd say it's adding insult to injury that they got the shirts printed by one of his competitors."

"'Assperlips'? I don't even want to know," I said. "La, la, la."

Maud laughed the gravelly laugh that always made me wonder if she'd been a smoker in her youth. "It goes on to talk about customers' reactions, his apology, yada yada. How many women must he have cheated on if they were able to round up eight to go public and 'out' him? I'll bet it's like the iceberg phenomenon, where only ten percent shows above the water. That would mean he cheated on eighty women. He must have something to offer that doesn't show in a head shot, if you know what I mean, because he looks like a nebbish," she added.

If Maud's theory held water, then Gordon had cheated on forty women, of which the approaching delegation was a small sampling. How did he have time to run a company? Deciding that confronting the women would only make a bigger scene and tempt the reporters to write about something other than how wonderful the pub was and how delicious the beer, I welcomed them and stood aside for them to enter. If they got out of line, I'd sic our off-duty cops on them. It was possible that a part of me didn't actually mind seeing Gordon Marsh get a taste of what he deserved, not when he was making Derek so miserable.

"Oh, gross, the toilets are overflowing!" A woman popped out of the restroom near the bar and made her announcement like she was calling a Rockies game and needed to be heard by everyone at Coors Field. I sent Al, hovering at my elbow, to find Foster and get it taken care of.

Then came the pitchers of beer Kolby "accidentally" spilled on the congresswoman and the billionaire (in separate incidents), the rumor that a drowned rat had been found in the brewing vat, and the kitchen fire (immediately extinguished, but not before smoke drifted into the main bar and sent people running for the exits). The deluge of rain that finally broke was like the curtain coming down on a really, really bad play. Of course, it drenched everyone who evacuated when the fire alarm went off and many of them opted to hop into their cars and call it a night. It was only a little after eight.

Derek's shoulders sagged when he saw how many people never came back in after the fire scare, and he trudged upstairs around eight thirty, looking defeated. My heart ached for him. Some of the staff looked equally ground down and slump-shouldered. I hadn't seen Gordon around in a while, not since he spotted the WOSCers—WOSCettes?—advancing across the parking lot. His sister and her delayed husband had left together ten minutes ago, dashing for a gold Lexus without even bothering to unfurl their umbrella. The WOSC contingent was still in place, singing along with the piped-in alternative rock music, perhaps waiting to have it out with Gordon, and Bernie seemed to have joined them. She'd finally arrived, apologizing profusely and ranting about car trouble, and worked twice as hard as anyone else for a while as if to make up for her tardiness, but now she was chatting with the WOSCers. The occasional clicking of pool balls told me a few people remained on the second floor. A handful of others hung on in the main bar for the free beer, but pretty much everyone else had gone, including my family, the Readaholics, and the VIPs. I couldn't blame any of them. I encouraged the stragglers to depart by declaring the bar closed. That wasn't part of my usual event organizing responsibilities, but this was for Derek. It seemed the least I could do, given what a disaster the evening had

turned into. The WOSCers, Bernie in tow, left with umbrellas aloft, two of them sharing. From the door, I
watched them dodging puddles and squealing about
their hair as they dispersed to their cars.

I'm a silver linings kind of person, but even I was
having trouble spotting any hint of silver in the series
of catastrophes that had plagued this party . . . until the
shrill screams ripped the air. At least there was no one
left to hear them, I consoled myself, running toward
the kitchen to see what new calamity had occurred.

I skidded on the kitchen's tile floor, still wet from various kitchen workers flinging water around to put out
the fire that apparently started in one of the microwaves, if its melted door and the charring on the wall
around it were any indication. Catching myself with a
hand on a stainless steel counter, I pulled myself up.
Drat. I'd twisted my ankle. Limping, I made my way to
the back door, which gaped open, and the screaming,
which was ongoing in bursts, sounding like a cross between a donkey and an air raid siren. "Heaw. Heaw.
Heaw."

With the rain still pouring down, it took me a moment to recognize the figure standing near the Dumpster, blond hair plastered to its head, mouth wide as it
continued to scream. The sounds were hoarser now,
less loud, as his throat gave out. The raindrops drumming on the metal garbage bin almost drowned them
out. I plunged through the rain to Kolby Marsh and
grabbed his arm.

"Kolby! What's the matter?"

Nothing.

I shook his arm. It took him a moment to focus on me. He stopped midscream and relief rolled through me. "It's okay," I said stupidly. "What's wrong?"

He blinked away the raindrops caught in his lashes and pointed to the Dumpster's open lid. I got a creepy feeling, like a hundred spiders were crawling up my arms. Shaking them, I approached the Dumpster, stepping around muddy puddles of rainwater and who knew what effluvia from the garbage. The rain actually beat down some of the odor, or maybe it clogged my nose so I couldn't smell anything. Either way, it wasn't as noxious as earlier in the day. I wasn't tall enough to see into the bin, but a couple of wooden pallets lay on the ground and I stacked them and climbed atop them. Careful not to touch the rim—ick—I peered in.

At first, I didn't see what had disturbed Kolby. The bin was half-full of swollen green garbage bags, glossed by the rain. There were the broken wooden pallets I'd noticed earlier, and what looked like a toilet tank. Rain dripped into my eyes and I blinked. I was turning back to ask Kolby what I was supposed to be looking at when I saw it. Him.

The back of his head was toward me, which was why I didn't see him sooner. The dark blond hair was matted and wet. One arm was flung over his head, the hand resting against the creamy porcelain of the toilet tank. His torso slanted down toward the back of the bin, draped over pallets and bags, and I couldn't see his legs. A sense of urgency flushed through me. No longer worried about the ick factor, I put my hands on the rim and levered myself up. He might not be dead. He could still be alive. I had to help him. He had to be alive.

"Call nine-one-one. Get help," I yelled at Kolby. I wasn't going to be able to get Gordon out of here on my own. Even the two of us couldn't do it. Balanced on my stomach with the metal digging into my flesh, I leaned forward and reached for the hand nearest me. I could see if there was a pulse . . .

My hand closed around Gordon's cold, clammy wrist. I yelped involuntarily and jerked my hand back. He was—

"My dad's dead," Kolby said. He had come up behind me and stood with his hands at his sides as I slid backward, one foot reaching for the pallet. "It's true, isn't it? My dad's dead."

He wasn't looking at me; his gaze was fixed on the Dumpster. "I'm so sorry." I started to pat his shoulder to comfort him, but then remembered where my hands had been. Looking down, I saw that my yellow dress would never be the same. It was smeared with heaven knows what kind of filth, including red streaks that might have been blood. I wasn't the swoony type, but this was too much. I felt light-headed.

"You two gettin' it on out there, or what?" a laughing voice called from the doorway. "Haven't you noticed it's rainin' cats and dogs? Ever heard of motel rooms?"

Kolby and I walked toward the kitchen worker, whose eyes widened as we got closer. "What have you got on your—?" His hand brushed up and down in front of his chest. "Is that blood? Jesus, Mary, and Joseph." He crossed himself.

"Call nine-one-one," I said, pleased to hear that my voice sounded calm. *Unflappable.* Thinking the word made tears spring to my eyes. "There's been an accident."

Chapter 6

I was in the kitchen, washing my hands in the deep sink, scrubbing and scrubbing, letting the hot water and the lemon-scented soap wash everything away, when I heard Hart's voice. Not five minutes had passed since we called the police. I swung around, surprised.

He strode in, looking so solid and dependable that I wanted to throw myself against his chest. I didn't, of course. I was sopping wet and there were too many people around. But I couldn't help smiling with relief. "Hart!" My voice caught. "Thank goodness. How did you get here so quickly?"

"I was upstairs knocking pool balls around when I got the call. I was waiting to take you home." His brown eyes swept over me and I felt as though he saw past my veneer of okayness to the confused and quivering mess underneath. He stepped closer. I could tell he wanted to put his arms around me, but the presence of Kolby and a handful of kitchen crew restrained him. "You're soaked. Are you all right?"

I nodded automatically. "Pretty much. It's Gordon. He's—" I didn't want to say *dead*. "In the Dumpster."

"I'll take a look. You." He pointed at the oldest worker, a mature man with sun-bronzed skin and crinkles at the corner of his eyes. "Find her something dry to put on."

The man nodded.

"Have you got any plastic garbage bags?"

"Here." The teenager who'd laughed at me and Kolby proffered a box. That made me think of Kolby and I spotted him slumped on an overturned bucket, head in his hands.

Hart stripped two from the roll and handed one to me. "Put your dress in this when you take it off."

When I drew my brows together, he said, "Preserving possible evidence." Holding the other bag over his head to stop some of the rain, he stepped through the still-open door and splashed toward the Dumpster.

By the time I had stripped off my dress, wrung out my hair, dried off on one grand opening T-shirt and put on another, and donned a pair of too-big men's gym shorts lent by someone, my brain was working a bit better. Where was Derek? My sandals were a slimy write-off, so I put them in the bag with the dress and wedged it under a sink where no one was likely to disturb it. Leaving the second-floor bathroom where I had changed (avoiding the first-floor women's room with the overflow issue), I took the stairs to the third floor. It was dark except for a bar of light shining from beneath one door. I padded barefoot down the hall and knocked.

At first, there was no response. When I knocked again, Derek's muffled voice yelled, "G'way."

Translating that as "Go away," I pounded with my fist. "Derek, open the door. Something's happened." I rattled the knob, but it was locked.

For long moments there was no response. Then I heard footsteps trudging toward the door. The knob clinked as Derek manipulated the lock, and the door swung inward six inches. A slice of Derek's face and one bleary reddened eye showed in the crack. A blast of alcohol fumes nearly knocked me down. *Oh no.* He was drunk.

"Know what'sh wrong," he slurred. "Pub's going down the toilet. Ka-flush." He raised his arm high and mimed flushing a toilet. "Gone. G'way, A-Faye. Hey, that rhymes. G'way, A-Faye, g'way, A-Faye," he repeated in a singsong voice. He started to close the door.

I stiff-armed it open and he staggered back a step. "Hey!"

I marched in. His office was longer than it was wide, with a battered wooden desk at one end and a tired couch at the other. A large potted plant flourished by the only window, and a sixteen-by-twenty framed photo of our family (a Christmas gift from our folks—each of us kids got one three years ago) hung on the wall next to a print of dogs playing poker. Tasteful. There was a closed laptop on his desk, along with a litter of file folders and an autographed Broncos football. The place smelled like a distillery, which was ironic, given that we were in a brewpub. He was clad only in a golf shirt and plaid boxers, his pale, hairy legs ending in bony bare feet. "What happened to your clothes?"

"Wet." He pointed to a heap of clothes half-hidden by his desk and a golf bag propped in the corner.

Blowing out an exasperated breath, I said, "You've got to pull yourself together, Derek. Gordon's dead." It wasn't the way I'd have chosen to break the news, but only shock tactics were going to pierce the alcohol force field he'd put up.

"If only," Derek said. He turned and started toward his desk, where a half-empty bottle of vodka stood.

"Stop it." I grabbed his arm and forced him to look at me. "Gordon Marsh is dead. Really dead. In the Dumpster out back."

He blinked three times slowly, looking owlish. "Dead? Gordon's dead? Gordon Marsh?"

I nodded with increasing impatience in response to each question. "Yes. Gordon Marsh is dead. We need to get some coffee in you." I knew coffee didn't make you undrunk, but it might sharpen his wits enough to make him coherent. There was a coffeemaker on a table behind his desk with a quarter-full carafe. Cold, sludgy coffee. Not exactly Starbucks, but it would do the trick. I turned the burner on to warm the dregs, poured the remaining vodka onto the robust potted croton, hoping it wouldn't succumb to alcohol poisoning, put the bottle in the trash, and turned back to Derek. "Do you have— Never mind."

I ransacked his desk drawer and found some aspirin. Pouring three into my hand, I gave them to him. While I was pulling bottled water from his minifridge, he chewed them and swallowed them dry. Looking at him, I knew they weren't going to make a dent in tomorrow's headache. I handed him the water and told him to drink it all. He did. "We need to get you cleaned up."

"Your hair is wet," he said, gaze wandering over me.

"So is yours."

A chill swept over me, raising goose bumps. Why were Derek's hair and clothes wet? I trotted down the hall to the bathroom, dampened a few paper towels, and brought them back. A pair of lime green golf slacks hung from a coat tree, along with an umbrella and a shirt in a dry cleaning bag. I grabbed the slacks and thrust them at Derek. "Put on some pants. Tuck your shirt in. Wipe your face." I handed him the towels. "Comb your hair."

He followed my directions obediently, running his fingers through his damp hair to comb it, and by the time he was looking marginally more presentable, the coffee was ready. I poured him half a mug and watched impatiently while he drank it. He was my baby brother and I loved him, but sometimes I wanted to beat him. If there'd been a pillow handy, I might have.

Tires crunched on gravel. Red and blue lights flashed through the window and striped the walls. Voices drifted up from the parking lot. Derek scrunched his eyes closed but then opened them, looking suddenly more alert.

"Gordon's dead," he said. His face went green and I thrust the trash can at him, afraid he was going to throw up. He controlled himself. "The police are here."

I nodded.

"Did you say he was in the Dumpster?"

I nodded again, beginning to feel like a bobblehead doll.

"How did he get there?"

"Good question."

We were silent for a beat, and then we said together, "We should go down."

I made Derek take the elevator, since I was afraid he would tumble down the stairs. When the doors opened on the ground level, we found all the lights on and the pub swarming with uniformed police officers. It looked like chaos, but I suspected there was a plan to their to-ing and fro-ing. Hart strode into the bar from the kitchen, face grim. When he spotted me in my too-big shorts and Derek in his lime green slacks, his face lightened momentarily. "Good thing the photographers already left—"

A flash interrupted him and proved him wrong. Derek and I flung our hands up to shield our eyes and a reporter I didn't know said, "Derek, how will a murder in your pub affect business?"

With a head jerk, Hart summoned a uniformed officer, who hauled the reporter outside, still shouting questions. With a beckoning hand, Hart fetched an officer, who took Derek's elbow and asked him to "Come with me, sir." She led him toward a booth on the far side of the bar.

When I started to follow, Hart's hand on my arm stopped me. "We need to keep you separate until we've interviewed both of you."

My eyes widened. "You think—?" Of course he thought we were potential suspects. I'd found the body—which I knew from reading crime fiction made me an automatic

suspect—and Derek was the dead man's business partner. I swallowed hard. "Was he murdered?"

"Well, I don't think he flung himself into the Dumpster and bashed himself over the head," Hart said.
"How did you come to find him?"

"Kolby found him," I said automatically as Hart
pulled out a small notebook. "His son. I heard him
screaming and went to see what was up."

"Kolby's the kid in the kitchen?"

I nodded. Almost before I realized I was thirsty, Hart
said, "Let me get you some water." He fetched a glass
from behind the bar and returned to me. While I drank
it, he led me up the stairs to the pool-playing area,
which was deserted. Balls and cue sticks lay on the
green felt tables. We sat at a high top with two stools.
Sticky rings decorated it from the mugs that had sat
there earlier. A collection of glassware covered the short
bar's counters, ready for washing. I wondered vaguely
who had bused all the tables.

"Now," Hart said, "when was the last time you saw
Gordon Marsh alive?"

I thought back and realized I hadn't seen Gordon after we'd opened the pub doors to kick off the grand
opening. I told Hart that. "He saw the WOSC women
marching across the lot with their banner, said he
needed a smoke, and disappeared." I was thankful Hart
had been at the party so I didn't have to explain what
WOSC was. "I don't think I saw him after that, not even
outside when we all evacuated for the fire." If I'd missed
Gordon earlier, gone to look for him, might he have survived?

My head dropped. I didn't feel that it was my fault, precisely, because I couldn't possibly have foreseen or prevented the night's disasters, but I still felt low. Hart's hand landed on my shoulder, heavy and comforting. "None of it was your fault," he said. "It was a great party, until . . ."

"Yeah. Right up until the women's toilets got clogged, the kitchen caught on fire, people started talking about rodents in the brewing vats, and my brother's partner got killed." I felt guilty for lumping Gordon's death in with the other events and started to apologize.

Hart's brown eyes narrowed. "You know," he said thoughtfully, "so many things going wrong almost sounds like sabotage."

My mouth fell open and I snapped it closed. "But who—?"

"Can you think of anyone who might not want this pub to succeed?" Hart asked. "Or who might have it in for Gordon or your brother?"

"The WOSC women," I said immediately. "I don't know who they all are, but they've got a Web site. And Kolby and his mother, Gordon's first ex-wife, were mad at him about money issues." I summarized their argument, complete with mug-throwing.

"And Derek?"

I shook my head, wet hair strands sliding against my neck. "I can't think of anyone who had it in for Derek."

"No, I mean did Derek have a beef of any kind with Gordon?"

I lowered my eyes, and used my thumbnail to scrape

at a crusty spot on the table. Should I tell Hart about the fight I'd seen? It would immediately make him suspect Derek. *He already suspects Derek,* my logical side said. It wouldn't take much research for him to discover Derek and Gordon were on the outs about money. I decided on half-truths. "They were having money issues," I said. "Derek didn't tell me the details." True.

Hart gave me a long look but didn't probe further. "Anything else?"

Images of Derek and Gordon rolling across the rooftop played in my mind. Derek had nothing to do with Gordon's death, I told myself, so the fight wasn't germane to the investigation. I didn't want to get my little brother in trouble, and I didn't want the police wasting time and resources by looking closer at Derek when they should be searching for the real murderer. I recognized the rationalization, but still said, "No."

Hart spent another half hour taking me through the evening step by step, trying to get me to remember who I'd seen talking to Gordon at the preparty, and where I'd seen him. "You said he walked away about seven, when the party started, that he said something about having a cigarette. That would be on the patio?"

Shaking my head, I said, "No. The roof."

"Show me."

We traipsed up the two flights of stairs and pushed through the unlocked door. It was full dark, only the glow from the pub's windows and a sickle moon lending a little light. I hadn't realized before how isolated the pub was, with no buildings close by. Lights from a residential area two miles north were the closest signs of habitation. The rain had stopped, but puddles remained. Colder air had followed the rain into the region and I shivered in my borrowed shorts and T-shirt. Wrapping my arms around myself, I said, "He used to stand by the railing." I pointed.

Hart headed for the section of wall I indicated, not bothering to avoid the puddles. After a moment, I followed him, stepping carefully in my bare feet. Grit stuck to my soles. Hart stopped close enough to the wall to see over it, but didn't touch it. Shifting two feet to his right, he peered at the wall and then leaned over it to inspect what lay beneath.

"What?" I asked, coming up beside him.

"Look." He pointed.

I craned my neck and he caught me around the waist as I threatened to bump against the wall. With his strong hands on either side of my waist, burning through the T-shirt's thin fabric, I looked down. The Dumpster sat directly below where I stood, three floors down, illuminated by a portable light the police had brought in, I imagined. Police personnel in protective coveralls were bent over, searching the ground around the Dumpster, and some vehicle had gouged ruts into the mud.

Hart tugged at me and I stepped back, finding myself pressed up against him for a moment. "Sorry," I said, flustered.

He gave my waist a quick squeeze and for a moment I thought—hoped?—he was going to turn me around and fold me into his arms. But he released me and stepped back. He was investigating a murder, I reminded myself, and I was a suspect. At least on paper.

I drew in a long breath to regain my equilibrium. "So," I said, relief flooding through me, "he fell?"

Hart was shaking his head before I finished speaking. The humidity had made little curls stick up all over his head. "Not without help." He stood beside the wall. "This wall is waist high on me and nine or ten inches wide. No way could someone trip or stumble, even drunk, and fall over accidentally. But look at this." He used a pen to point at faint grooves and scrapes that were lighter than the surrounding masonry. "These happened recently. My money's on tonight. I've got to get a crime scene team up here."

He herded me away from the wall and made a call. Waiting, I shivered and wrapped my arms around myself again. The breeze raised goose bumps on my bare arms, and my beginning-to-dry hair flapped around my face. I was cold, miserable, worried, and even a little sad. I hadn't liked Gordon—he'd been a grade-A jerk in many ways—but no one deserved to be heaved off a roof into a Dumpster, to lie there broken until he quit breathing.

When Hart hung up, I stayed quiet as he shepherded me downstairs. He gave me a supervised moment with Derek, sequestered in a booth. He looked pale and ill, hunched over the table and holding his temples as if his head would explode if he let go. He didn't notice me at first.

"I can wait for you, Derek," I said when he looked up, bleary-eyed. "I can drive you home."

He started to shake his head, thought better of it, and said, "Go home, Amy-Faye." His voice was drained of all emotion, expressionless. "Just go home."

"I'd rather wait and drive—"

"Go."

I hesitated, but then nodded. "I'll call you tomorrow."

He didn't say anything and after another moment of hesitation, I let Hart pull me away.

"I wouldn't call him too early," Hart said.

My gaze flew to his face. Why? Were they planning to arrest Derek?

"He'll have the mother of all hangovers," Hart explained.

He ushered me out to the parking lot. It was choked with police cars and vans, including a K-9 vehicle, an ambulance—too late—and the coroner's van, which left as I watched. Tree limbs shivered with the wind's gusts and sent eerie shadows chasing one another across the gravel. Raindrops beaded on the hood of my van. My limbs suddenly felt heavy and it was all I could do to hold my eyelids open. Reaction. Exhaustion.

"Want me to have someone drive you home?" Hart asked, eyeing me with concern. "I'd do it myself, but I can't—"

"It's okay," I said. "I'm good."

He laid his hand against my cheek. "You're not good."

"Well, maybe I've been better." His hand felt good, big and warm, and I put mine over it for a moment.

"We'll talk tomorrow."

I knew he'd have hugged me if there weren't so many cops and official folks around.

I bit my lip and nodded.

"Come to the station when you get a chance so we can make your statement official. I may have a few more questions once I talk to Derek and Kolby Marsh." He opened the van door, closed it when I got in, and banged the side as I started it up. I watched him return to the pub and walk under the now sagging ELYSIUM BREWING GRAND OPENING sign.

I couldn't make myself leave. Not until I knew Derek was okay. I sat in the van and cranked up the heat, which dried me out eventually. The windows steamed over. I turned the van off until the chill got to me again and I turned it back on. Over the next hour, a handful of pub employees trickled out, having been interviewed by the police, I assumed, until only Derek's car and the police vehicles, including Hart's Tahoe, were left in the parking lot. The rain started again, a gentle *tinking* on the van's roof. Finally, Derek came out, escorted by a uniformed officer. They walked to a police car and for a heart-stopping moment I thought Derek was under arrest. I started to open the van door. Then, when the officer let him into the front passenger door, I realized he was giving Derek a ride because he was drunk. Good idea. Should I offer to drive him? No, he'd already told me he didn't want me to stick around; I didn't want him to think I was mother-henning him. Letting the police car have a thirty-second head start, I pulled out after them and started for home.

Chapter 7

A night's rest and Saturday morning's brilliant sunlight brought perspective. It also brought a loud and insistent knocking on my door. Eight twenty-two. Derek? The police? I sat bolt upright, flung back the sheets, and stumbled to the front door in the oversize "Run, Ralphie, Run" CU T-shirt I used as pajamas. Conscious of my scanty attire, I peered out before opening the door. Brooke stood on the stoop, clad in Athleta yoga gear with her dark brown hair in a high ponytail, holding a steaming cup in either hand. Coffee. I'd have opened the door for a zombie or a chain-saw-wielding maniac bearing coffee. I undid the locks.

Before I even had the door all the way open, she was saying, "I heard about Gordon. Did you really find the body? Are you okay? Here, I thought you could use this." She thrust the coffee at me and came in when I stood back. She gave me a hard, coffee-juggling hug. "Are you okay?"

I was touched by her concern. I nodded and took the

first, sublime sip of coffee. There's nothing quite like that first taste of coffee in the morning. "Thanks. I'm okayish. Better than last night. On your way or already done?" I indicated her yoga togs.

"Done. That's where I heard about Gordon's murder—Susan Marsh was there, spilling the beans to everyone. Apparently, Kolby got home at one a.m. and woke her to tell her all about it and the grilling he got from the police. Tell me everything."

"Let me get dressed."

She followed me back to the bedroom and plopped onto the unmade bed. My room was unabashedly girlie with pale lemon walls and lots of white eyelet in the curtains, ruffled bed skirt, and accent pillows. The framed family photo identical to the one in Derek's office hung near my dresser, the blond maple one I'd had since childhood. Two garage sale bedside tables bracketed my full-size bed, the one on my side holding a ceramic lamp made by my college roommate, a clock, and my to-be-read pile of books, including the latest Louise Penny, Michael Connelly, Catriona McPherson, and Nancy Pickard novels, and two well-worn classic Dick Francis paperbacks, the "comfort" reads I reread when I felt stressed. A seven-foot-tall bookcase held many of the books the Readaholics had read, a shelf of classic mysteries, and diet books, reference, and miscellaneous others. I'd grown up in a house that was wall-to-wall books, so I prided myself a bit on keeping my book habit under control and only having one bookshelf in my bedroom.

I told Brooke about last night as I put on a clean T-shirt and denim skirt, and then brushed my teeth and hair. The latter was all wonky, since I'd fallen into bed with it still damp last night, and I wet my brush to smooth out the kinks. Giving up, I reached for a ponytail elastic.

"I'm so sorry you had to go through that," she said as I twisted my thick hair into a messy topknot. "It sounds awful. I'm sorry Gordon's dead, of course, especially like that, but he was kind of a jerk. He cornered me last night, you know, tried to kiss me."

I spun around from the bathroom mirror. "No way! With Troy there?"

Brooke shrugged one shoulder with the casual "What can you do?" attitude of a beautiful woman who was always getting hit on. "I think he was drunk. He was weaving when he walked."

"Where was this?"

"On the third floor. I'd gone up to use the bathroom up there because the one on the main level was, you know—"

"What time was it?"

"Um, a little after seven? The big party was just kicking off and I wanted to use the bathroom before it got icky—you know how they get when there's a crowd—so yeah, a bit after seven."

That was before the fire, and after the last time I'd seen Gordon. "The police might want to know," I said. "I think they're trying to put together a timeline."

"Like Hercule Poirot," Brooke said, getting up and beginning to straighten the bedclothes automatically.

"Making the list of who was where when, and what time they last spoke to Ratchett."

"Quit," I said.

She stopped midpillow plump. "Oh," she said, realizing what she was doing. "Habit. Sorry."

Brooke had never been such a neatnik until she married Troy, and his overbearing mother, Miss Clarice, took to dropping by unannounced to criticize Brooke's housekeeping.

"Detective Hart wants me to sign my statement this morning," I said. "We could go together."

"I'm not going like this," Brooke said, indicating her skintight lavender capris. "I'll call him later. I'd better get home and shower. You're sure you're okay?" Her green eyes searched my face.

"Shoo," I said, with a grateful smile.

There was no hint of a smile on Derek's face when I arrived at his duplex fifteen minutes later. It was a narrow house in an area of similar 1940s–era shotgun-style houses, and his door was only five feet away from his neighbor's door. They shared a rickety veranda with house wrens nesting in the eaves in four places, if the white streaks down the wooden siding and on the veranda floor were any indications. I'd stopped for bagels and coffee on the way, but Derek didn't reach for either when he opened the warped screen door to me. His pale face had the same flat affect as last night, and his dark auburn hair stuck up like a hedgehog's quills. From the muddy circles under his eyes, I guessed he hadn't slept at all.

"The police think I did it," he said once I was inside and had forced him to take one of the coffees. I trekked back to the kitchen with its cheap white appliances and cherry-dotted wallpaper that had probably gone up when Air Supply was in the Top Ten.

"I'm sure they don't," I said, smearing cinnamon cream cheese on a wheat bagel. "They've only just started their investigation."

"Yeah, well, you should have heard them grilling me last night. Where? When? Lay it out for us again. Account for every minute of my time. Were we fighting over money? Did I follow him to the roof? Did he take a swing at me? Was it self-defense? If I got mad and lost my temper, I should just tell them. Perfectly understandable, your hard-ass boyfriend said."

"Hart's not my boyfriend," I said automatically, inwardly a bit angry at Hart over what seemed like an unnecessarily harsh interrogation. I saw the fear beneath Derek's veneer of control. I sat at the round kitchen table, pushing aside a stack of beer brewing magazines, what looked like financial documents, and a pizza box with two petrified slices of pepperoni left in it.

He took a carton of orange juice from the fridge and glugged from it. Wiping the back of his hand across his mouth, he said bitterly, "I can hardly wait until they hear about the partnership insurance."

My fingers tingled with cold, despite the warm bagel I was holding. "What insurance?"

"We were both insured—Gordon and me—for a cool one mil. He insisted on it, actually—said it was a standard clause in all his contracts. A lot of the start-ups he underwrote were highly dependent on the ideas and entrepreneurship of a single individual and he said the insurance mitigated the risk of losing that key person. It was a five-year-term policy, just long enough for the pub to either succeed or tank. I argued for a similar policy on him."

I chewed a bit of bagel while I processed this. Not good. Even a doting sister like me could see that Derek had a million reasons to do away with Gordon, the investor who was going to yank his financial rug out from under the pub. "You didn't tell them?"

"I wasn't thinking clearly last night," Derek said. Leaning against the counter, he ran a hand down his stubbled face. The refrigerator compressor kicked on with a metallic whine that said Derek would need to buy a new fridge before long.

"You were loaded."

"Can you blame me? Everything went wrong. Everything!" He opened a drawer just so he could slam it closed.

"Hart suggested maybe it was sabotage. Is there anyone who would want to ruin the pub? Or hurt Gordon or you?"

"Well, obviously someone wanted to hurt Gordon," Derek pointed out. "I mean, not to sound ugly, but who didn't want to hurt Gordon? I certainly did—well, you saw me punch him. Those weirdo women from last night looked like they wouldn't have minded clawing his face off. Then there's Susan, Kolby, his sister—"

"Why his sister?" I asked, intrigued by new information.

"She and her husband blame Gordon for their daughter's death. She died three months ago. Car accident."

"I don't see—"

"She was drunk, well, over the limit anyway. Just barely, from what Gordon told me."

"I still don't see how that's Gordon's fau—"

"She got that way at Moonglade, his nightclub in Grand Junction."

"Oh."

"He hosted a twenty-first-birthday party for her and a bunch of her college buddies."

"Oh," I said again. It sounded as though Gordon had been trying to be nice. How tragic.

"Other than that—" Derek shrugged. "I must admit the thought crossed my mind. Not for real," he added hastily when I choked on a bite of bagel. "Just, you know, in the way you think, in the heat of the moment, how things would be better or easier or whatever if someone was . . . gone. I would never have actually *planned* something."

Something. *Murder.* I totally knew Derek didn't have it in him to cold-bloodedly plot to murder someone, not even Gordon, but I remembered the fury with which he'd gone after his partner on the roof. Had he been up there with him last night? Had Gordon said something that sparked another fight? Had— I made myself stop thinking along those lines.

"Why were your clothes wet?" I asked.

"What?" His brows drew together in puzzlement.

"Last night, when I came upstairs to get you and you were drunk, you were only wearing your boxers because your slacks were wet. So was your hair. Why?"

"Not because I was up on the roof pushing Gordon off!" he yelled. "What do you think I am?"

"Chill," I said, exasperated with his histrionics. There was a good word for Al. *Dramatics, hysterics, over-the-top emotionalism.* "I don't think for one minute that you killed Gordon. I just want to know what you told the police about being wet."

Still glowering, Derek said, "I had to go out to my car. I'd promised Troy Widefield I'd give him a six-pack of the new lager I'd developed here"—Derek had a pretty sophisticated brewing operation in what should have been the guest bedroom where he made small batches of new recipes—"and I got drenched going out to get it."

"That's okay, then," I said, relieved. "I'm sure Troy will confirm that for the police."

Derek squirmed. "Brooke and Troy had left by the time I got back inside and went looking for him. I took the lager up to my office. Drank most of it before starting on the vodka."

No wonder he looked so ill.

"I'm in trouble, aren't I?" His hazel eyes, so like mine but with longer and darker lashes, which was completely unfair, were shadowed with worry.

"You should maybe get a lawyer," I said, rising. I tossed my empty cup into the trash can under the sink. "I'd call Doug, but—"

"I've already got one. One of my basketball buddies is a lawyer. No one you know." He paused, and almost gulped. "I'm scared, A-Faye. What if they arrest me? Who will run the business? Even if I don't get convicted, the pub will go bust and I'll be bankrupt. If they do convict me—"

"Shh." I wrapped my arms around him and hugged tightly. He was stiff at first, but then he crumpled in and buried his face in my hair. "It's not going to come to that," I said.

He squeezed me for a moment, and then broke away. "Big sister will take care of it, huh?" he said with the ghost of a smile. "Make the bad policemen leave her baby brother alone?"

"Something like that," I said, glad to see him attempt some humor. I punched his shoulder. "Get dressed, go to work, and get the pub cleaned up. No moping."

"I don't mope."

"You mope."

"This may look like moping, but it's actually a hangover," he said, gesturing to his drawn face with its bloodshot eyes and stubbled cheeks. "A freaking hellacious hangover like I haven't had since my frat days."

"Whatever." He didn't need sympathy. He needed someone to kick him in the butt and keep him from awfulizing about how bad the situation might get.

"I can't go to Elysium. The cops have it sealed off as a crime scene. They said maybe tomorrow." His shoulders slumped.

"Oh. Well, go hang with the folks, then. Mom'll feed

you pie. Rhubarb's good for hangovers." I had no idea if that was true, but it sounded plausible.

His eyes brightened at the thought of Mom's strawberry rhubarb pie. "What are you going to do?" he asked.

"Work. And figure out who really killed Gordon."

He snorted gently as if I'd said I was going to design a time-travel machine or come up with a Middle East peace plan. "Yeah, well, thanks," he said.

I kissed his scratchy cheek, trying not to recoil from his morning breath, and left.

Chapter 8

I really did have work to do. Saturday nights were almost always booked with an event. Tonight's was a
roast—the make-fun-of-someone kind, not the edible
kind—to celebrate the retirement of the school superintendent. It was being held at the high school so they
could use the stage for skits and such like, and the caterers were setting up in the cafeteria. I'd arranged for
the gym to be decked out in promlike decorations and
a DJ was set to play for dancing. The whole thing was
rather sweet, and I'd had fun putting the event together, but now I needed to concentrate on Derek's
problem.

Sitting in my van outside Derek's house, I called Al
and asked if he could fill in for me this afternoon, getting everything set up. He agreed, saying he didn't
have much homework this weekend. I thanked him,
assured him I'd be there by five, and hung up. I really
did need to think about hiring another part-time assistant. I'd still need to be at the high school tonight, but

now I had a few hours to try to sort things out for Derek. Where to start?

Coffee. I'd start with coffee. Caffeine would kick-start my thought processes. I drove to the Divine Herb and got a cranberry orange muffin to go with my jumbo coffee. Sugar would amplify the coffee's effect. Scoring a small table by the window, I pulled my phone out and began making notes, nibbling on the muffin. I'd only gotten as far as (1) Talk to WOSC women and (2) Talk to Susan/Kolby when Hart's voice interrupted me.

"You didn't tell me about Derek and Gordon having a fight on the roof."

I looked up, feeling a guilty flush climb up my neck. Hart stood looking down at me, mouth firmed into a straight line, holding a cup with steam escaping through the lid vent. The mingled accusation and disappointment in his eyes lanced through me like a needle. *Damn it.* Derek must have told him.

"I'm sorry." I gestured toward the chair, but he didn't move. "I *am* sorry. He's my brother. I know he didn't kill Gordon." My eyes pleaded with him to understand.

He shook his head slightly, denying my mute appeal. "I thought I could trust you to be truthful with me, Amy-Faye."

"You can! I am. I told you they were having money issues. I just didn't—" I stopped, ashamed of my legalizing, of my lie of omission. "You're right. I should have told you about the fight." It hurt more that he was disappointed in me than that he was angry.

"Tell me now."

He finally sat across from me and I let out a relieved breath. His foot bumped mine under the table, but he withdrew it. I told him in as much detail as I could recall about Derek's fight with Gordon and what they'd said. Hart's lips twitched when I got to the part about turning the hose on them. He didn't say anything, though, just took a few notes, and asked, "Is that everything?"

"Yes." I nodded once, firmly.

He flipped the notebook closed and stood, startling me.

"Wait. Do you have the autopsy results yet? Have you talked to Kolby or Susan Marsh? Is—"

There was a trace of regret in his voice when he said, "You're too close to this one. I can't talk to you about the case. We'll see you down at the station sometime this morning to sign your statement, right?"

"Right," I whispered. The day seemed gray and chilly all of a sudden, even though the sun shone brightly through the window beside me, highlighting a gleam of white I took to be shaving cream beneath Hart's left ear. I wanted to wipe it off. "I'm really sorry."

"I know." He seemed about to say more, but then he swallowed the rest of his coffee, put the cup gently on the table, and walked away.

I watched him go, his back straight and shoulders squared, curly brown hair lit with gold by the sun. Overnight a wall had gone up between us and it hurt. It hurt a lot. I blinked back tears and made myself return to my list. If I was going to cry about anything, it should be Derek, who was facing ruin and a potential prison sentence. Unable to concentrate, I put my phone away and pushed my chair back with an ugly scraping sound. If Detective Lindell Hart wasn't willing to share any of the case details, I'd find out for myself.

My office was at the back of the building housing the Divine Herb, but for once I didn't feel like making lists. I needed to *do* something. Hurrying to my van, I pulled away from the curb, not sure where I was going. My incomplete two-item list came to mind and I determined to talk to the ringleader of the Women Outing Serial Cheaters. They had a clear motive for wanting to kill Gordon, and opportunity as well, since they were at the pub last night. Maud had researched them yesterday; she'd know where to find them. I headed for Maud's house.

As I pulled into the circular driveway of Maud's timbered one-story on the outskirts of town, I saw her hosing down the boat near the garage-cum-shed. She stood with her feet braced wide, the way she always did, shoulders squared, like she was on the deck of a ship, riding out a storm. I guess it's helpful to have a grounded stance when shooting at elk or trying to land a fish. She turned off the hose and made a visor of her hand to watch me as I approached. Wearing a white T-shirt tucked into multi-pocketed khaki shorts, with work boots and a bandanna around her head, she looked as if she'd just come back from a fishing charter. The large orange bucket of flopping trout seemed to prove that.

"Client had to catch a plane back to D.C.," she said

when I eyed the fish. "Gave them to me. Joe'll smoke 'em tonight. Delish. What's wrong?"

Words poured out of me as I filled her in on what had happened after she left the grand opening. She'd heard about Gordon's murder—no one knew more about what was happening in Heaven than Maud—and she listened carefully as I told her about lying to Hart, being worried about Derek, and wanting to find Gordon's killer to keep my brother out of jail.

"Sounds like your brother's in a pickle," she said when I finally ran out of words, "but it's nothing the Readaholics can't sort out. You call Brooke and I'll get hold of Lola and Kerry. We figured out what happened to Ivy when the police wanted to call it a suicide—we can darn well figure out what happened last night. The police might want to play 'I've got a secret'—they never want to share information with the citizens who pay their wages—but nothing happens in this town that I can't ferret out."

My muscles went limp with relief and I almost dropped my phone when I pulled it out to call Brooke. When I gave her a short explanation, she said she'd be right over. Lola was busy with Bloomin' Wonderful, her plant nursery, which wasn't unexpected on a beautiful Saturday morning, but Kerry told Maud she'd come by as soon as she finished a house showing. It warmed me that my friends were willing to drop everything to help out. When Maud lobbed a sponge at me, I set to washing her boat with gusto, ready to let the sunshine and physical labor drive away the worry and sadness I'd been feeling since talking to Derek and then to Hart.

Half an hour later, the four of us minus Lola were scrubbing Maud's boat and making plans. Brooke, wiping down the surfaces inside the boat, spoke from above us. When she found out we were doing manual labor, she gamely twisted her dark hair into a messy bun and tied the tails of her royal blue shirt at belly button level, kicked off her fashionable metallic sandals, and clambered into the boat with a rag and a spray bottle. She still managed to look like a supermodel.

"I think you're right about those WOSC women, A-Faye," she said. "We should check them out."

"Why in the world would they talk to any of us?" Kerry asked. She clutched a sponge in both hands and used her whole upper body to move it vigorously across the boat's underside. Soapy water dripped down her arms to where she had her sleeves rolled at the elbows. Her open-neck white blouse was not looking as crisp as when she'd arrived.

"Maybe," I suggested slowly, thinking the idea through, "one of us contacts them to say she dated Gordon and is so sorry she couldn't be at the pub opening to 'out' him—because of work or illness or something—and wants to know how it went?"

"I'm not saying I dated Gordon," Brooke said, straightening. "That would not go over well with Troy."

"Joe would think it was a hoot," Maud said, smiling broadly, "but I don't think anyone would buy the idea that Gordon was dating a woman ten years his senior, especially not a string bean like me. Judging by the other night, he liked his women on the rounder side." She looked at me.

"Hey," I protested.

Kerry gave me a "get over it" look. "Face it, everyone's rounder than Maud."

"Fine, I'll do it," I said.

"You knew him better than the rest of us, so you'll sound more plausible," Brooke said. "While you're checking up on the WOSCers—do you s'pose that's what they call themselves?—I'll see if I can find out the scoop on his niece's death."

"And I'll get hold of the autopsy report," Maud said.

The three of us turned to look at her with varying degrees of surprise.

"I have sources," she said, pleased with our reaction, but trying to act as if it was no big deal. "You don't think I just make up the stuff on my blog, do you? I work damn hard ferreting out the truth about political shenanigans and other conspiracies in this town. No offense, Kerry."

"None taken," our part-time mayor said. The way she dropped her sponge into a bucket with a soggy plop belied her words.

Maud finished rinsing the boat and turned off the hose. "I've cultivated a lot of sources over the years. You'd be surprised how many people want to be whistleblowers but can't afford to risk losing their jobs. People who work for the government—and not just the minions, either, in medicine, insurance, for nonprofits, the schools. Corruption and conspiracy are rampant in all sectors. They're happy to pass info along to me so that the truth gets out there. I'm looking into a conspiracy now involving the National Forest Service and that corporation that wants to develop—"

"You're a public servant, Maud," Kerry interrupted with a sour look.

I jumped in. "Where do I find WOSC headquarters, Maud, if there is such a thing?"

After consulting her smartphone, she told me that the Web site only listed a post office box. "No physical address," she said. "And the contact e-mail isn't in anyone's name. It's just WOSC at Gmail-dot-com. Conspiracy rule number two: When people try to hide their identity, they've got something to hide."

I pondered that, wondering how I could get hold of whoever was in charge of WOSC. I'd have to send an e-mail and wait for a reply, I guessed.

"I'll ask the police chief for an update on their investigation. There are some perks—damn few—to being the mayor of this burg, but finding out what's going on with city funds—from police investigations to buying a new snowplow—is one of them. Let's get together on Monday evening to see what everyone's found out," Kerry, ever the organizer, said. "We can do it at my house. Six thirty?"

We all agreed and tramped back to our cars, a bit wetter than when we had arrived. Brooke caught up to me as I was getting into the van. "How's Derek holding up?" she asked, worry putting a line between her brows.

"Not so well," I said, grateful for her concern. "He's worried that he'll lose the pub and end up in jail. He looked awful this morning when I talked to him; I sent him over to Mom and Dad's."

"If there's anything Troy or I can do . . . Troy Sr. knows some good lawyers."

Troy Sr. had enough business irons in the fire to keep a whole herd—pack? flock? pod?—of lawyers gainfully employed. *A murder of lawyers* . . . I liked that. "Thanks, Brooke, but he's already got a lawyer."

She hugged me. "Tell him to hang in there. No one with half a brain could think he killed Gordon. It sounds like he'd have had to stand in line to get to him, as many people as Gordon pissed off. Like Ratchett in *The Orient Express*."

"I don't think Gordon was as bad as Ratchett," I protested. "He didn't kidnap and kill children."

"You know what I mean." She stood back so I could close the door.

"Have a good rest of the weekend," I said. "Thanks for worrying about Derek. Call me if you find out anything. Otherwise, I'll see you at Kerry's Monday night."

She agreed, and with a brief toot-toot of my horn, I drove off.

With some reluctance, I reported to the police station to sign my statement. The Heaven Police Department building was red brick, separated from the street by the sidewalk, and one block off the downtown square between Mike's Bikes and A World Apart, the new travel agency. Pink and purple petunias frothed from planters outside the building, getting leggy and tired-looking as summer raced toward fall. A skateboarder careened down the sidewalk, ignoring signs prohibiting the activity, and forced me to jump against the glass door that didn't quite go with the building's facade.

Inside, it was cool and dry. The reception area consisted of a counter, molded plastic chairs, and what might have been the building's original tile floor. I'd never been in here before this summer, but what with Ivy's murder and now Gordon's, I was spending more time here than some of the town's repeat offenders, I was sure.

"Amy-Faye Johnson. Detective Hart told me to expect you."

Mabel Appleman was in her seventies and had been the police dispatcher forever, starting back in the era of typewriters, carbon paper, and party lines, as she liked to remind people. She wore blue-framed glasses that perched halfway down her roman nose, and had tightly permed gray curls. Double-knit polyester was her fabric of choice, and today's short-sleeved powder blue jacket had brassy buttons the size of fifty-cent coins. She occasionally came to Readaholics meetings when we were reading a police procedural.

"I heard you've gotten mixed up in another murder," she greeted me.

"I wouldn't say 'mixed up,'" I protested.

"Well, if you aren't yet, you will be," she said, digging through an in-box and retrieving a couple of pieces of paper stapled at the top. She thrust them at me. "Here. You're supposed to sign this." She pointed to the signature line and slid me a pen she pulled out of her tight curls.

I took it, disappointed that I wasn't going to see Hart. I started to read the statement.

"What are the Readaholics reading now?" Mabel asked.

"*Murder on the Orient Express.*"

"Ah. That was the first Agatha Christie mystery I ever read. It seemed very clever to me then, the way Christie built up to the climax with Poirot interviewing the suspects one by one, and then gathering them together and revealing all." Mabel spread her hands wide on the last word, as if performing a magician's trick. "And the elegance of that train, oh my. Of course, it doesn't work like that in real life." She gestured to our surroundings. "Crooks don't work together, and if they do, one of 'em rats the others out." She eyed me sideways. "Heard anything from Doug Elvaston lately? I hear he's sailing around the world. Any idea when he'll be back?"

I didn't need her prying into my private life. Not that Doug and I had had anything to be private about since we broke up more than two years ago. I didn't lift my gaze from the page I was reading. "Nope."

"I hear tell your brother could use a good lawyer," Mabel said.

That brought my head up. She blinked at me innocently from behind her lenses.

"Have you heard something?" I whispered. "Are they going to arrest him?" I resisted the urge to add *He didn't do it.*

"How would I know that? Chief Uggams and Detective Hart don't check with me before they go off and make an arrest," she said, her expression inviting me to probe further.

"No, but you might overhear something, *accidentally*." I could just picture Mabel lingering in the hallway outside the chief's office, or taking note of indiscreet conversations between the uniformed officers. They should probably put suspects in an interview room with Mabel, I thought, who could coax information out of a spaghetti squash.

"Well." She leaned forward so a brass button clicked against the counter, pushed her glasses up her nose, and looked around. "I did get the impression Lindell—Detective Hart, I should say—and the chief were pretty excited about something they found in the vic's phone records. And the chief and Jackie Merton, the DA, left at lunchtime for a couple days' fishing up at the chief's cabin, so I wouldn't expect an arrest before they get back on Tuesday, at the very earliest. But you didn't hear that from me," she said, sitting back.

"Thanks, Mabel." I signed the statement and handed it to her. "We're thinking about reading a Michael Connelly book for next month. Want to join us?"

"Harry Bosch or Lincoln lawyer?" she asked, tucking the pen back in her hair.

"We haven't decided. Do you have a preference?" I expected her to go for the cop series, but she surprised me.

"Lincoln lawyer," she said. "Then we can watch the movie. That Matthew McConaughey has got It with a capital *I*."

I laughed, tickled that Mabel was still interested in

"It," and told her I'd let her know what book we picked out.

Emerging onto the sidewalk, I dodged the skate-boarder again and bumped squarely into Detective Lindell Hart. I recognized his smell before my eyes told me who it was. His arms caught me at the waist automatically and steadied me. His palms burned through my thin blouse to my skin. Was it my imagination, or did he hold on a few seconds longer than necessary?

"Sorry," I said, stepping back. "Someone should give that kid a ticket."

Hart smiled, like he'd forgotten he was disappointed in me, and said, "Officer Bradford talked to him. The kid's here with his parents for a week. Tourists. The town council has asked us not to discourage tourism, so . . ."

"I signed my statement," I said, then could have hit myself for reminding him that he was mad at me.

No anger showed on his face. The breeze riffled his brown curls. "Thanks."

"I'm really sor—"

"Over and done with," he said, not letting me finish another apology. "I might have done the same if it was my brother."

I didn't believe that, but happiness bubbled through me, making me feel lighter. I smiled. "Over and done with," I agreed.

"What do you have going on tonight?"

"A retirement for the school superintendent," I said regretfully. Was his question a precursor to asking me out? "If you're not doing anything tomorrow, I could make you dinner," I heard myself offer before I thought it through. What was I thinking? I wasn't much of a cook. He'd think I was too pushy. We weren't—

"Sounds great," Hart said immediately. "No job talk, though. Nothing about your brother, or the case."

"Cross my heart," I said, making the familiar gesture.

Taking me by surprise, he leaned forward and kissed my cheek. "I'll bring the wine."

Before I could react, he disappeared into the building, whistling.

Chapter 9

The retirement roast Saturday night went off without a hitch, thank goodness. Eventful! couldn't stand another evening like last night. As Al and I watched from the back of the musty-smelling auditorium while various teachers and principals shared anecdotes about the superintendent, I told Al that I'd changed my definition of "successful event."

"No dead bodies," I whispered. "That's it. We can cope with anything else, but no dead bodies."

"What about a hostage situation?" Al asked, obviously trying to poke holes in my new definition. "One with gunmen and a SWAT team and huge media coverage?"

"As long as there are no dead bodies, I'm good with it," I maintained. "The media coverage might draw in more business."

"What if it goes on for months, like in Iran?"

I gave him a "now you're just being silly" look. "If it

goes on for months, then it's not part of the event we contracted for, so it doesn't count."

Al choked back a laugh as a man in the back row turned to frown at us. "I'm going to check on the caterers," I whispered, making my escape.

My heels clicked on the school's linoleum floor as I walked. It felt weird to be back in the high school as a grown-up. The walls had obviously been painted over the summer, since the odor still lingered and they were glossy and pristine. The top half of the walls was white and the bottom half a crimson red, the Heaven High School colors. The lockers hadn't been replaced, it didn't look like, not if the dents were anything to go by. Just before reaching the cafeteria, I came to my old locker, 214. On a whim, I dialed the combination, which came back to me as if I'd been stuffing my history and biology texts in there yesterday, rather than twelve years ago. The door popped right open, emitting a too-sweet fragrance I recognized from my last visit to Bath & Body Works. I found myself staring at myself in a mirror attached to the inside of the door and automatically smoothed my copper hair and dabbed a fleck of mascara from my lower lid. Pictures of a callow-looking teenager were taped to the door, and basketball jerseys, shoes, texts, folders, pens, cosmetics, hair paraphernalia, and other gear were jumbled together. A film of pink powder that might have been a broken blush covered it all. How could it be such a mess this early in the school year? When this was my locker, it had been a model of neatly shelved texts and clearly organized folders and notebooks, color-coded by class. Even in high school, I thought, closing the door with a clang, I'd been headed for a career based on organizational skills.

With a reminiscent smile, I stepped into the cafeteria, happy to see that everything looked to be on schedule. The high school choir stood on risers at one end of the long room, ready to burst into song when the superintendent appeared, and nets secured hundreds of balloons to the ceiling. Tables set—check. Food ready—check. I let out a long breath, relieved that nothing was on fire and no one was screaming about rats or overflowing toilets.

"About ten more minutes, I'd guess, before they wrap up the roast," I told Alana Higgins, owner of the catering company I favored for large events.

"We're ready," she said, and we chatted for a couple of minutes, before I saw Bernie Kloster, in the black slacks and vest, white shirt, and black bow tie that made up her bartending gear, emerge from the kitchen carrying a tub of ice. I'd forgotten she would be here.

"Let me help you with that, Bernie," I called, moving toward her. Taking one end of the tub, I helped her carry it to the bar set up at the back of the cafeteria.

"Thanks, Amy-Faye," she said.

Her face was pale and pinched, and even her exuberant hair seemed limper tonight. She'd hinted that she'd dated Gordon and that they'd broken up; I wondered if she'd really cared for him.

"You heard about Gordon?" I asked tentatively.

She nodded and bit her lower lip. "Yeah. I couldn't believe it when Billy told me this morning. He's always up before the rest of us on a Saturday and he was looking for the funnies page when he saw it in the paper. He hobbled in and knocked against my bed and I swear to God I thought the house was on fire, the way he was carrying on. When I finally got him to calm down, I didn't believe what he was saying, not until he showed me the front page with Gordon's picture. 'That's that guy who liked you,' Billy kept saying, jabbing at the page so hard he tore a hole in it. 'The one with the Camaro.' He's mad about cars, Billy is. Gordon took him for a spin once and Billy didn't talk about anything except that car for a week. Supercharged this, direct injection that, Bluetooth and navigation system." She smiled thinly.

"I'm sorry, Bernie."

She waved a would-be dismissive hand as she began setting glassware up on a table behind the bar. "I didn't love him . . . At least, I don't think I did. Not really. He was exciting, and handsome, a good lover, and he had money. I know that shouldn't matter, but when you're barely scraping by, a guy who can take you out for a nice steak dinner seems nicer and smarter than the guy who can't even manage a bucket from KFC." Her voice was tinged with matter-of-fact self-knowledge. "It's the shock of it, more than anything. That, and I feel bad that I was hanging out with those women who were bad-mouthing him all night. He wasn't a saint, but he didn't deserve that." She sniffed.

I dug a packet of Kleenex out of a pocket and offered them to her. "Did you know any of them?" I asked after she blew her nose. "Had you met them before?"

I helped her align liquor bottles atop the bar's table-cloth-covered surface. I knew it wasn't the first time liquor had been present in the high school; Allen DiDomenici and some of his pals had spiked the punch at the prom our senior year.

She shook her head. "Well, I knew Susan Marsh, of course. She had no business there, I'll tell you. The pot calling the kettle black."

It took me a moment, and then I clinked two bottles together in surprise. "You're saying Susan cheated on Gordon?"

"Uh-huh. She had a fling with one of Kolby's teachers, Gordon said. Even though it was years ago and they've been divorced forever, I could tell he was still hurt by it."

"Huh." I didn't know what, if anything, to make of that. "What about the other women? Did you get their names?"

"The blond with the big boobs was Guinevere Dalrymple. I mean, how do you forget a name like that? Her parents should be shot, don't you think? Gawd. She seemed to be in charge. I think one of the other gals was Sally something. I was pissed, so I don't remember like I should. The opening was a disaster with the fire and all, and I was sure I wasn't going to have a job in a week, so I drank a bit more than I should have." She busied herself pushing the cartons the liquor bottles had been in beneath the table, and I guessed she was ashamed of getting drunk on duty.

I committed the name to memory. There shouldn't be too many Guinevere Dalrymples, if I Googled it. The sound of voices headed our way told me the roast portion of the evening was over. I needed to get back to work. Saying a hasty good-bye and good luck to Bernie, I gave the choir director the high sign and they began a rousing chorus of "For He's a Jolly Good Fellow" as the super and his family came through the door. Crimson and white balloons cascaded from the nets secured to the ceiling, and people gasped with pleasure. Everyone joined in the singing and I let myself take pride in how well things were going. It was balm for my wounded professionalism after last night. Maybe I still had a future in the event-planning biz.

Chapter 10

It was already hot when I got out of bed Sunday morning and readied myself for church. I didn't go all the time, but I felt the need after the week's events. My parents would be at St. Luke's and I suspected they'd drag Derek along if he'd spent the night with them. I was right, I discovered, when I slid into the pew beside them two minutes after the service started. I never seemed to get to church exactly on time. I'd long ago decided there was something psychological about that, since I could make events at a party happen with the crisp timing of a Sousa march.

Mom scooted over to make room for me, and I whispered a compliment on the hibiscus-patterned muu-muu that swathed her bulk. Its pink background rosied her magnolia-petal complexion, the envy of every woman north of forty in the entire town. Her naturally curly hair was pinned up under a straw hat with a rolled brim. Sheena at Sheena's Hair Jungle was responsible for dyeing it back to its original chestnut every month or so. Her eyes were hazel, like mine, and she had a wide mouth slicked with a pink lipstick that matched her dress. She patted my thigh, smiled in her good-humored way, and faced forward to listen to the minister.

My mathematician dad, built like a lumberjack with a graying beard, loomed on her other side. He waggled his bushy eyebrows at me in welcome. He'd exchanged his usual plaid shirt and jeans for his church attire of short-sleeved shirt and belted slacks. Dad had no interest in clothes. Zero. Keeping Dad dressed appropriately for his job as a professor at the university was kind of a family hobby: Natalie gave him a couple of no-iron shirts each year, Mom supplied him with socks and underwear, and my other sisters contributed sweaters and the occasional tie. I gave him a new belt, reversible black/brown, every other year for Christmas as my contribution to his sartorial adequacy. Derek, not usually a churchgoer since he'd left home, gave me a look that said, *Get me out of here.*

It almost made me giggle, but I primmed my mouth and paid resolute attention to the service. After, we greeted the minister and some of our friends. Derek drew me away while Mom and Dad were chatting with one of the elders about the new capital campaign. "Let's get breakfast," he said. "I'm starving."

"Shouldn't we wait for Mom and Dad? They—"

"I've been mommed and dadded to death," he said, tugging me along toward his Subaru Outback, a venerable workhorse used to hauling all sorts of brewing, camping, and skiing gear. "Don't get me wrong—I'm grateful for them, they're sticking by me, and they let me hide out at the house yesterday—but I need a break. Mom kept wanting me to feel a lump on her arm and tell her if I thought she had liposarcoma, whatever the heck that is. I reminded her that she banged her arm on the car door."

I laughed in understanding. "Where do you want to eat?"

In answer, he put the car in gear and headed toward the Pancake Pig, where a chef-hatted pig held aloft a platter of pancakes from atop a tall pole. An Elvis number battered us as we entered the white, turquoise, and chrome interior, which wasn't as crowded as I expected. We must have walked in between the before-church crowd and the after-church crowd, and gotten lucky that the didn't-go-to-church crowd was out hiking or boating or otherwise enjoying the glorious day.

"I'm going over to the pub today," Derek announced after he ordered a Western omelet and I asked for my usual blueberry pancakes. "The police said they'd be done with it. I need to get started on cleanup."

"Good for you," I said, relieved that he seemed to be past the shell-shocked despair of yesterday. "Do you need me to help? I don't have anything going on this afternoon."

He looked grateful but hesitant. "Foster's coming— I'm paying him triple overtime—but if you have time . . ."

"I'll come out for a couple of hours." I told him that the Readaholics were all on his side and filled him in on our plan of attack.

He looked skeptical, as if he didn't think we could really help, but said, "Thanks. I appreciate your friends helping out." He went on to tell me about his discussions with his lawyer and what he'd heard about Gordon's funeral. "His mom's in a nursing home in Denver, so they're doing it there," he said. "His sister's putting it together. Angie, from the opening. Kind of surprising, actually, given that they never got on, even before Kinleigh died. Her mother was suing his dad, or vice versa—I couldn't keep it straight. Organizing the funeral might be her way of saying 'sorry.' I'll go, of course, if the police don't toss me in jail before then." He squirted Tabasco on his eggs with a splatting sound.

I hated to hear him sound defeatist. "Derek—"

"I know, I know."

"I'm happy to go with you, keep you company on the drive, if you want." Denver was a good four hours from here.

"Thanks, but I've got business in Denver, too. With GTM."

Gordon's company. I didn't pry into the details beyond asking, "Will you be able to keep Elysium open?"

He chewed and swallowed before answering. "If I don't go to prison. Gordon's death doesn't change GTM's contractual obligation to Elysium. He was going to pull out of the deal, but there were several iterations of lawyers and court dates and arbitrators to wade through before that got finalized."

So Gordon's death benefited Derek even more than I imagined. A million dollars of insurance. Freedom from the worry that Gordon was going to pull the plug on their partnership. I didn't say so aloud. There were others who had benefited by Gordon's death; there had to be.

The standard August afternoon storm clouds scudded across the sky as I arrived at the pub around three o'clock. It looked so much like the way it had on Friday that I repressed a shiver. The gravel in the lot was churned up and the grand opening banner sagged sadly from one side of the building, tangling with yellow-and-black crime scene tape that had been torn down but not removed. Derek's Subaru and a Honda Accord I took to be Foster's were the only other vehicles in the lot. Squaring my shoulders, I walked into the pub, determined not to let the atmosphere get to me.

"Where shall I start, O captain, my captain?" I asked Derek, who was collecting glassware in a plastic tub. My perky attitude and smile were intended to lift his spirits.

"Stop with the poetry stuff, okay?" he said semiirritably. "We weren't all lit majors." He thrust the tub at me and I took it automatically. Its weight strained my biceps.

"Wow. We weren't all music majors, either—does that mean we never listen to music? And we didn't all study art, so does that mean—?"

"Just get the glasses into the dishwasher, okay?" he said. "Foster's working on the bathrooms. I'm going to start upstairs."

"And we weren't all dishwashing majors, but we still do dishes," I called after him as he headed up the stairs. I thought I heard a snorted half laugh from him, so I was happy.

The kitchen was a disaster. Between the fire and all the police marching in and out in the rain, tramping in mud, it looked like a herd of drunk mastodons had held a convention in it. My gaze went to the back door, but it was closed. Relief sighed through me. I didn't have to look at the Dumpster where I'd found Gordon's body. I set to work loading the glassware into the industrial dishwashers, and made three trips into the bar area and the pool lounge to collect more before setting the dishwashers to run. They started with a satisfying gurgle and were soon emitting a brisk lemony scent that made me feel efficient.

I began making a list of what else needed to be done; I couldn't help myself—lists pour out of me like words from a novelist or stock market figures from a broker. The microwave needed to be replaced and someone brought in to repair the burned dry wall and paint it. The—

Tuneful whistling sounded behind me, making me whirl. Foster came in, black bangs sweat-glued to his forehead, coverall damp in spots. He stopped whistling midtune when he caught sight of me, and used the mop to push the wheeled bucket into the kitchen.

"You startled me," I said.

"Sorry. Bathrooms are done. Not much point in mopping in here yet, I guess." He looked around at the chaos and smiled.

I realized it was the first time I'd seen him smile and it seemed weirdly inappropriate in the circumstances.

Maybe he was happy to be making extra money. "Uh, thanks for coming in on a Sunday," I said. "I know my brother appreciates it."

"Seemed like the least I could do," he said with a nod of acknowledgment. He opened the louvered door of a storage closet and slid the bucket in, hanging the mop on a rack.

"You mean because of what happened? Gordon dying?"

"Tossed off a roof: Couldn't have happened to a more deserving guy," Foster said with simple pleasure. He banged the door closed.

I hadn't expected him to be grief-stricken, but his reaction was several shades off normal. I backed up a step. "Come again?"

"Gordon Marsh was a bottom-dwelling, scum-sucking lowlife," he said, a hint of venom twisting his smile. "If I had any balls, I'd have killed him myself. Bully for whoever did it."

I stared at him, speechless for a moment. The clinking of glasses in the dishwasher and the churn of the machine filled the kitchen. Clearing my throat, I finally said, "I take it you knew him?"

"We didn't hit the links together, if that's what you're asking," he said, crossing his arms over his broad chest and leaning back against the counter. The fingers of his right hand tapped incessantly against his left biceps. "GTM—Gordon—bought out my company a year ago. Before the ink dried on the contract signatures, I was out on my ass. All the leadership team got canned because Gordo wanted to bring in his own team. He fired me personally. Looked me in the eye and told me I didn't have the skill set the company needed, that I didn't fit with the new management philosophy, that I was a dinosaur. I spent twenty-six years with that company, and suddenly I don't fit in?" Ruddy patches flared on his olive skin, and the pulse in his neck beat like he'd run a four-minute mile.

"I'm fifty-four—not exactly highly employable in this economy. We had to sell our house and move into a crummy apartment. We're living upstairs from a pair of high school dropouts who smoke dope, sleep all day, and play crappy music all night, and next door to a loser who stocks shelves at City Market. That's not who we are. We used to live in Redlands Mesa in Grand Junction. My wife stuck by me, but she had to go back to work—she's teaching preschool for a pittance. You don't think it kills me that I can't support my wife? Most of our old friends are embarrassed by our circumstances— we don't see much of them anymore. It's not like we can invite them to dinner; we don't even have a dining room. My son—my twenty-six-year-old son!—offered us money to tide us over."

"That was nice of him," I ventured, thinking that Foster had a darn good motive for murder (if there was such a thing). He'd also had opportunity . . .

"A father's supposed to take care of his children, not the other way around," he yelled.

His fury brought home the fact that I was trapped in the kitchen by the man who might have murdered Gordon. He was between me and the door leading to the pub. I was closer to the back door, but if it was locked,

I'd have to fumble to open it and he'd catch me, if he wanted to. He didn't have a weapon, but he was a burly guy and since I'd neglected to add hand-to-hand combat skills to my résumé, he could probably take me down without even breaking a sweat. Resolving to sign up for a krav maga class if I got out of this kitchen alive, I held up my hands in a placating gesture. "How did you end up working here?"

Almost absentmindedly, he picked up a scrubbie and began to scour the counters. That knocked my tension level down a notch; a scrubbie wasn't as threatening as a knife or an Uzi.

"I had a lot of time on my hands, what with no job and only the occasional interview for something for which I'm hugely overqualified, so I started following Gordon's buyouts and investments. I was looking for an opportunity, an opportunity to do to Gordon what he'd done to me. I was a bouncer at Moonglade for a while, but then that went out of business. I had nothing to do with it, but I counted it as a win. I took home a bottle of champagne that night and celebrated with my wife. Oh, she thinks I'm obsessed and I should just let it go, but how do you just give a pass to the guy who ruined your life?"

I was afraid he was going to wear a hole in the stainless steel counter. After a moment, he took two deep breaths and moved to the sink to rinse out the pad. "Then I heard about Elysium. I checked out the hiring Web site and here I am." He spread his arms wide. The scrubbie dripped on the floor.

He wasn't a threat to me, I realized. He wanted me

to be his audience, to applaud his ingenuity and planning, to rejoice with him in Gordon's downfall. Oops. Bad choice of words.

"You sabotaged the grand opening," I said, understanding and fury rising in me. "The bathroom? The microwave?"

He gave a mock bow.

"You were willing to crush my brother's dream, to cost him his life savings, to lose people like Bernie Kloster their jobs—all to get back at Gordon?"

For the first time his self-assurance faltered. "He deserved—"

"Derek doesn't deserve to lose the pub!"

Foster turned sulky, his mouth pulling down at the corners. "If he's going to get into bed with an asshole, he's got to expect—"

"What? That a disgruntled jerk like you is going to show up and try to ruin everything he's worked for his whole life?" I was breathing so fast and hard it was making me dizzy. I forced myself to take a slower breath. "You're just like Gordon. Worse. At least Gordon was trying to make money for his company and employees. You . . . you just wanted revenge and you didn't care who got screwed. Bernie has kids to support."

"Screw you, lady. I don't need to listen to this," Foster said, unzipping his coverall with a quick motion and stepping out of it. His foot got caught and he hopped awkwardly.

Resisting the urge to push him over, I asked, "Do the police know about your connection with Gordon?"

Balanced on one foot, Foster raised his head and gave me a slit-eyed look. "I told you I didn't kill him. Kudos to the guy who did, but it wasn't me. I was in the ladies' bathroom half the night, pretending to clean up the mess I caused by stopping up the toilets, and then I was hanging around in here, waiting for my chance to set off my little incendiary device in the microwave. I never went near the roof. I left when everyone evacuated for the fire and I never came back. The cops can ask my wife what time I got home."

"I'm sure they will," I said, planning to call Hart and offer up Foster as a suspect replacement for Derek.

I sidled past Foster, out of his reach, while he was still trying to drag the coverall over his shoe. He made no move to stop me. When I reached the stairs and started up to Derek's office, I heard him yell, "And you can tell your brother I quit! I'll be in tomorrow to pick up my paycheck."

A door slamming told me he'd gone out the back way, past the Dumpsters.

I charged up two flights of stairs to the offices on the third floor. "Derek!" I ran down the hall, calling my brother's name. A chair scraped, his door squeaked open, and his head popped out.

"What's the matter?"

I skidded to a stop and began to pour out the story of my encounter with Foster. "Your janitor—he might have killed Gordon," I babbled.

"You're not making sense." Derek drew me into the office. "Calm down and start over."

The sight of the office knocked the words out of me.

The clothes that had been there were all gone, as were Derek's computer and the papers that had cluttered his desk. "Where'd everything go?" I asked.

"The police."

"They can't just march in here and take your stuff," I said, incensed. I stalked from one end of the room to the other, trying to figure out what all was missing. The family portrait and the tacky dogs still graced the walls.

"They can with a search warrant. My lawyer was here with me. Everything was by the book. If you think this looks bad, you should see Gordon's office." Derek ruffled his auburn hair, seeming resigned rather than pissed off. "What were you saying about Foster?"

"Oh yeah, right." I filled him in on my conversation with the erstwhile janitor. "He's been sabotaging the pub all along," I said, "because he's got a gargantuan grudge against Gordon. He says he didn't kill him, but I wouldn't bet the house on that. I mean, it's one thing to admit to clogging the toilets and exploding something in the microwave, but—"

"He did that?" Derek took a hasty step toward the door, as if he was going to have it out with Foster.

I stopped him by saying, "He's gone. And yes, he put an 'incendiary device,' as he called it, in the microwave. Seemed proud of it. Anyway, he admitted the sabotage but said he didn't kill Gordon. I think we should tell the police."

"Damn right we should."

"Oh, and he says he quits and will be in for his check tomorrow." Foster's chutzpah in blithely assuming Derek would hand over a paycheck after what he'd told me would have made me giggle if I weren't afraid that he'd killed Gordon.

"There won't be much left of it by the time I subtract out the cost of the microwave and repairing the damage in the kitchen and bathrooms," Derek said wrathfully. "If it isn't just like Gordon to hire a guy who hates his guts." He pulled out his cell phone and called the police, putting the phone on speaker.

Lindell Hart wasn't in the office, but the officer who answered the phone promised he'd pass along the message. "Detective Hart will call you back tomorrow," he said.

"I guess criminals don't work on Sundays," Derek said as he hung up.

In all fairness, there wasn't much crime in Heaven as a routine thing, and Hart was a detective shop of one. I didn't plead his case with Derek, though, and I didn't mention that I was going to see Hart tonight. Nothing would make me bring up any aspect of the case this evening, not after promising that I wouldn't. Hart could get Derek's message in the morning and ask me about Foster then. An image of the janitor fleeing to a South American hideaway worried me for a sec, but I dismissed it; he didn't seem to have the funds to jet off to a nonextradition country, and nothing he'd said made me think he would take off.

"I've gotta go," I told Derek. I still needed to stop by the grocery store and shower, and Hart would be on my doorstep in just over an hour. "I've got company coming."

Chapter 11

The thought of seeing Hart tonight made me anxious to leave. Anticipation simmered in me, making my skin extrasensitive to the cold spray in the produce area of the City Market, and my nose susceptible to the heady scent of roses and the herbal tang of the carnations as I passed through the florist section. Throwing together a quick marinade for the salmon steaks when I got home, I shoved them in the fridge and hopped in the shower. I dithered over which top to wear—the lacy tobacco-colored tank top that made my copper hair glow, or the loden green peasant blouse that greened my eyes?—and had barely slipped the latter over my head when the doorbell rang.

I opened the door. For a split second, I expected to see Doug, and the realization that I hadn't cooked dinner for a date since breaking up with Doug made me widen my eyes. I needed to move on. I was moving on, I told myself, inviting Hart inside and taking the bottle of white wine he offered.

"From Two Rivers Winery, right down the road," he said.

He looked good. And he smelled better, with a fresh, woodsy scent that made me think of hiking through the trees bordering Lost Alice Lake in the fall. His slightly receding hair curled crisply around his ears, and his eyes smiled down into mine. I smiled back, truly happy to see him, and he reached for me, his hands on my waist pulling me toward him until we were pressed together from chest to thigh. "Can we just get this out of the way?" he murmured, and kissed me.

His lips were warm and firm against mine. Tendrils of heat uncoiled from the pit of my stomach, and warmed every inch of me, especially the inches mashed against Hart's solid body. His hand at my waist snugged me more firmly against him as his mouth plundered mine. I moaned and went to put my arm around his neck, clonking him on the head with the wine bottle I still held.

"Ow," he said, as I gasped, "Sorry!"

He rubbed a spot above his head. "That's the first time I've been beaned by a wine bottle for kissing a woman." He smiled, his gaze falling to my swollen lips. "I've been thinking about doing that for three months."

We'd only known each other for three months. Possible replies zipped through my head: "Don't wait another three months before doing it again" and "Was it worth the wait?" Both sounded stupid inside my head, which meant they'd sound worse if I actually said them. I stood mute, feeling flustered and aroused, trying desperately to come up with something that would be lighthearted yet not dismissive, meaningful but not OMG-you're-going-to-turn-into-a-stalker. Finally, I said, "Are you hungry?"

"Oh yeah."

The look he gave me left no doubt about what kind of hunger he was referring to, but I had some of my equilibrium back and I headed for the kitchen, saying, "You can open this"—I hefted the wine—"while I put the asparagus in to roast."

The house I'd bought six months ago was 1980s vintage and small (what Realtor ads called "cozy"). That held true for the galley kitchen, where it was impossible for two people to work without bumping into each other. Luckily, Hart and I were okay with bumping into each other. I found him the corkscrew and he levered the cork out of the wine while I spread the asparagus on a cookie tin, rolled it in olive oil, salt, pepper, and garlic, and put it into the oven, which had preheated while I showered. Hart had found the wineglasses and now poured the wine into them. It was a lovely pale gold color—like angel hair, I thought fancifully.

"What shall we drink to?" Hart asked, raising his glass.

"Heaven, Colorado," I said, maybe because I had angels on my mind.

"Possibilities," Hart countered.

"Both." We clinked our glasses and drank. The cool crispness of the wine slid down easily. "Yum."

"What can I do to help?"

"Set the table." Like Foster's apartment, my house didn't have a dining room. (Unlike Foster, I did not feel resentful over the lack.) I pushed all thoughts of Foster out of my mind. The options were tray tables in the den or hunching over the glass-topped coffee table in the sunroom. I loved the sunroom, so I handed Hart woven place mats, napkins, and utensils and pointed him in the right direction. Moving the asparagus to the lower rack after five minutes, I slid the salmon under the broiler and set the timer. Hart returned when it dinged. My body sensed his presence before I turned around; he emanated a magnetism that pulled me toward him. My distraction made me careless and I burned my wrist pulling the salmon out.

"Oh!"

My involuntary gasp brought Hart the two steps to my side. "Run cold water on it," he said, grabbing a pot holder and taking the broiling pan from me.

I ran water on the pink line creasing my wrist. It throbbed a bit, but it wasn't bad. I told Hart as much, but he insisted on raising my wrist to inspect it. "I think you'll live," he said. He drew my wrist to his mouth and said, "A kiss will make it better." His eyes met mine, and then he bent his head and gently touched his lips to the burn.

I swallowed hard and fought the urge to rake my fingers into his hair. If that happened, we'd end up in the bedroom and I was not, not, not going there. Not tonight. Not when Hart might arrest my brother on Tuesday. Reluctantly, I pulled my hand back. He might have been thinking the same way, because he let go immediately and took a step back so I wouldn't have to brush against him to reach for plates in the cupboard.

I took a deep breath to steady myself and told my hormones to go back into hibernation. "Salad's in the fridge," I said, dividing the fish onto the plates and using a spatula to dish out the asparagus spears. The dark green made a pleasing contrast to the salmon's pink flesh and I added a slice of lemon to each plate because I liked the yellow with the other colors. The effect made me smile. I carried the plates into the sunroom while Hart followed with our wineglasses.

The peace of the sunroom settled over me as I put the plates on the mats. Furnished with wicker chairs upholstered in bright floral cotton, the room had floor-to-ceiling windows that looked out to the front, side, and back yards. Sunlight slanted in, striping the celadon-colored ceramic tile with gold. A profusion of plants that I'd bought from Lola grew happily from window-sills, large ceramic planters, and hanging baskets. Adjusting the blinds to cut the worst of the glare from the setting sun, I sat.

"This is excellent," Hart said after a mouthful of salmon. "I was going to offer to cook for you next time, but all I can do is burn meat on a grill. And veggies. Dessert comes out of the freezer."

"Sounds like fun," I said, glad we were already talking about a next time. "You know, I don't even know where you live."

He told me about his rental condo on the south side of town, up against the mountain. "A bear got into my trash last week," he said. "Not a problem I had in Atlanta. I don't put the cans out for collection until the morning now."

"Are you liking Heaven, despite the bears, now that you've been here awhile?" I nibbled on an asparagus stalk.

"I like Heaven *because* of the bears and other critters, and the sky, and the clean air, and no gangs, and friendly people," he said. "There aren't nearly so many people killing each other here, either."

The specter of Gordon rose between us. I dropped my gaze to my plate and pushed at some salmon skin with my fork.

"Damn. Sorry. Didn't mean to bring that up," Hart said, wincing. "It's one of the biggest contrasts with Atlanta; I was getting burned out, catching three to four homicides a month. You can only marinate in the juices of people's inhumanity to each other for so long before you get—"

He broke off and finished the wine in his glass in one long swallow.

"Is that why you left? You were burned out?"

He hesitated a second and then said, "I left because my partner got shot. Killed. We were on the scene of a domestic, where a uniform had had to shoot a man whaling on his wife with a shovel. The EMTs were loading him into the bus when Sarah and I arrived. The wife, a little-bitty thing, was on a gurney, head bleeding, IV in her arm, about to get taken to a different hospital in a separate ambulance. I wasn't even out of the car when she pulls out a .32 and begins spraying bullets around, yelling that the cops had murdered her husband. One of the bullets ripped through Sarah's right eye. She died. The man and his wife both lived."

"That's awful," I said. I finished my wine, horrified by this glimpse of his life before Heaven. Something about the way he said his partner's name made me wonder if their relationship had gone beyond the workplace.

"I kept at it for another six months. When my air force brother came home on leave, he took one look at me and told me to quit the job. He had the distance, the perspective, that I didn't have right then. I was too close to it. As soon as he said it, though, I knew he was right. I became a cop because I wanted to make a difference, but I began to see that I couldn't make a difference in Atlanta. Collar one pusher, another takes his place before you snap on the cuffs. Put away a gangbanger, knowing that at the same moment some ten- or eleven-year-old kid is getting initiated, sucked into a way of life that will have him laid out on a slab or in prison before he's sixteen. I turned in my badge the day Philip flew back to Germany, took some time off to fish and think, ended up here." Hart smiled ruefully. "I didn't mean to get all heavy and depressing on you."

"I'm glad you told me. And I'm glad you chose Heaven." I leaned over and kissed him gently on the lips, then stood and gathered our plates. "Dessert comes out of the freezer here, too," I said. "Vanilla or Moose Tracks?"

"Some of both?"

"You got it. With Kahlúa on top?"

"Heck yeah!"

I laughed.

He stayed another hour and we deliberately kept the

conversation lighter, talking about books, movies, and music we liked, about high school memories, and childhood pets. When the last bit of sun had almost faded from the room, and the floor lamp I'd turned on cast plant shadows on the floor, he stood to go.

"Good thing we took care of that kissing thing up front," he said at the door, "so we don't have to stand here and feel awkward, wondering if—"

I shut him up by pulling his head down to kiss him. Fifteen minutes later he tore himself away and jogged down the sidewalk to his car. I closed the door behind him, leaned against it with my eyes shut, still tasting him and feeling his hands on my body, and thought how much it was going to suck if he had to arrest my brother. It made me determined to redouble my efforts to find out who had really killed Gordon Marsh.

Chapter 12

Monday morning at the office was busy, as Al and I completed our usual "lessons learned" drill about each of the weekend's events and prepared and mailed billing statements. Al eyed me as we worked.

"You seem to be in an unusually good mood, boss," he said. "Cheery."

"Full of joie de vivre."

"No fair using foreign words. Jovial."

"Merry."

"Like you got— Oops." Al blushed and hid it by bending to look for something in his desk drawer.

I pretended I hadn't heard him, although I suspected I was blushing, too. Pointlessly, since I hadn't, in fact, gotten laid. But I'd come a lot closer to it than I had in a very long time, and the prospect was still out there, tantalizing, energizing. *Work. Focus on work.*

The phone rang. Al picked up. "Detective Hart for you," he said.

Happiness bloomed in me. "I'll take it in my office,"

I said. I knew my smile aroused Al's curiosity, but I couldn't help it.

"Good morning," I said, picking up the phone.

"Good morning back."

I heard the smile in Hart's voice, but then he turned businesslike. "Foster Quinlan. Tell me about him."

I felt a bit deflated. He was calling about the message Derek had left yesterday, not because he couldn't bear to start his day without talking to me. I made my tone match his as I recounted everything I could remember about my conversation with Foster. "He said he didn't kill Gordon," I admitted, "but I didn't believe him. He really had it in for Gordon. Blamed him for losing his job, his friends, his house, and his dining room."

"What?"

"Never mind."

"We'll talk to him. We're talking to other people, too. Your brother wasn't the only one with a motive for killing Gordon Marsh."

"Thank you for that," I said.

He lowered his voice. "I had fun last night."

"Me, too."

"I wish you weren't involved in this case."

"Me, too," I said fervently. Because that would mean Derek wasn't implicated.

"I'll be in touch."

We hung up and I wondered if his last words meant professionally or personally. I rolled a pencil across the desk so it dropped off the far side. Having to keep our lives compartmented into personal and professional boxes because of Gordon's murder was frustrating. I rejoined Al in the front office, trying not to look self-conscious and failing miserably if the grin on his face was anything to go by.

"I need to put some time in today on the triathlon," I said. "I'm not happy with the Web site." The event wasn't until next summer, but the Web site I'd had a designer working on for two months needed to go live within a couple of weeks and it still had too many glitches. Shades of Obamacare. Giving Al a list of tasks to complete before he left for class at noon, I closed myself in my office and worked steadily for a couple of hours. When I came up for air and a coffee break, I settled back at my desk and typed "Guinevere Dalrymple" into a search engine.

And there she was. The zaftig blonde who'd been arguing with Gordon the evening he died. I guessed organizing Women Outing Serial Cheater events didn't pay the bills because the Linked In head shot that came up made it look like she owned an online dating service. Was that how she and Gordon had met? Oh, the irony. Her office was in Grand Junction, forty-five minutes away. I had at least three folks I needed to talk to in Grand Junction, meetings I'd been putting off, and I suddenly decided that this afternoon was the perfect time to squeeze them in.

Since Al had already left for class, I turned on the answering machine and locked up. Another reason to get another intern: I didn't like leaving the office unattended. True, event planning didn't lend itself to a lot of walk-in business, but still. The trip from Heaven to

Grand Junction, although only about forty miles, was like descending from heaven to Hades, at least in terms of temperature at this time of year. At eighty-two hundred feet, Heaven's altitude and forests and nearby lake kept us cool, even in August. Grand Junction, much lower, and practically in Utah, was broiling hot. Ninety-eight degrees, in fact, I noted, as I passed a bank displaying time and temperature. At a stoplight, I wriggled out of the shrug I was wearing over a sleeveless blue blouse and tossed it in the passenger seat, netting an appreciative honk from the grinning guy in a pickup in the next lane.

I conducted my meetings as quickly as possible, touring a new caterer's facilities and talking to the young couple who ran the business about their training and rates (I was getting more and more work in Grand Junction), watching a magician's act and deciding he was too lame to book for any of the kids' parties I organized, and sitting down with the Web site designer to explain the problems I was having with the triathlon Web site. Between the magician and the Web site designer, I grabbed two tamales at the hole-in-the-wall Mexican joint I loved so I was ready to tackle Guinevere Dalrymple by two.

The online dating service, Mutual E-ttraction, was located in a strip mall between a pet-grooming parlor and a bowling alley. Keeping in mind that Guinevere might have seen me at the pub, I loosed my hair from its French braid and shook it around my face so I looked as different as possible from Friday night. Getting out of the van, I approached the business. It looked reasonably prosperous, with the name in navy blue script, sparkling clean windows, and square planters on either side of the door brimming over with geraniums, greenery, ice plant, and other blooms. A sixteen-by-twenty-inch poster in the window was headed WOMEN OUTING SERIAL CHEATERS in bold typeface, and listed upcoming "events." This was definitely the right place. I scanned it quickly but didn't recognize any of the men's names. Mentally reviewing my story, I pushed through the door, which announced my presence with a deep *binng-bonng*.

Two desks faced me, both empty, with two closed doors behind them. Three computers sat on a long counter that ran down the left side of the room. Comfy chairs on castors sat before each terminal, and a stack of brochures poked from the top of a wire container affixed to the wall. Everything was some shade of green: spring green on the walls, moss green carpet, tweedy green upholstery on the chairs, lime green organizers on the desks. The only nongreen item was the listless corn plant in the corner, trending toward an "I give up" tan. I felt as if I'd wandered into a jungle.

"Green is the color of hope, of birth," a woman's voice announced. I turned to see Guinevere Dalrymple emerge from the right-hand door. She shut the door on the sound of flushing and moved toward me. "We're about the birth of new relationships here at Mutual E-ttraction, so it seems wonderfully apropos, don't you think? I'm Guinevere and I'm so happy to meet you . . . ?"

"Faye," I supplied.

Her voice was low-pitched and musical, practically hypnotic. She should have been a radio host or a ser-monizing minister. Her ample bosom swelled beneath a thin apricot sweater, and a wide white belt defined her waist. An ankle-grazing skirt did a good job of slimming full hips. Blond hair cascaded in an expen-sively highlighted tumble to her shoulders, and her suspiciously full lips gleamed with a peachy lipstick. Her plumpness minimized facial wrinkles, but I guessed she was in her mid-forties, maybe even push-ing fifty.

"Are you looking for a relationship, Faye?" she asked. "We can get you started right now." She gestured to-ward the computers.

Grasping for the script I'd mentally prepared, I said, "No, actually I'm here because of an earlier relation-ship." I gestured toward the poster in the window. "My ex cheated on me. With lots of women. I don't even know how many." I worked a sob into my voice.

Guinevere glided over and patted my shoulder. "Oh, my dear, we've all been there. Some detractors have taken issue with my running both a dating service and Women Outing Serial Cheaters, but we've got to face reality, right? Numbers don't lie. The vast majority of men are going to cheat on their wives or girlfriends. It's biology. I'm not excusing them, not at all, but it's the way they're wired. The good Lord just plumb screwed up when he gave men testosterone." She launched into a scientific-sounding bunch of claptrap about why men couldn't help cheating.

I fought down the urge to giggle and wished Lola,

the chemistry major and science whiz, could be here to laugh at this with me. "I'm sure you're right," I said. I couldn't help asking, "Do you have a science degree? You know so much."

"That's kind of you to say, dear. I've made this aspect of biology a life study, but my degree's in marketing."

Ha! No surprise there. "How did you end up starting a dating service?" I asked, genuinely curious about her and momentarily losing sight of my mission.

"Oh, everything in my life seemed to draw me toward this," she said, plumping down in a chair and gesturing for me to do the same. "Growing up on a ranch where I learned the value of selective mating; my time in college observing dating rituals and breakups; working in advertising and sales, which are all about relationships, right?; and, of course, my own marriage and divorce from a serial cheater. I knew if I could help people find their way to healthy relationships, I would be doing the world—well, at least, Grand Junction—a service. We do such a good job of matching people at Mutual E-ttraction, and for a very reasonable rate, that I think I can say with certainty we've cut down, way down, on the instances of cheating." She gave a modest little smile.

"Despite the biological imperatives," I couldn't resist saying.

"Indeed." Her smile got tight, and she swiveled to the computer, typing in a few quick commands. "Now, let's get your account set up."

"I don't think I'm ready for another relationship

yet," I said, dabbing at my dry eyes with a tissue. "Ever since I found out about Gordon and that—"

"Who?" She sat bolt upright and whipped around to face me. Her blond hair flew out and then resettled less artfully.

"Gordon," I said, widening my eyes innocently. "My ex-boyfriend. You 'outed' him on Friday, but I had to work so I couldn't participate, and I wanted to know—"

"You're talking about Gordon *Marsh*?"

"Uh-huh. And even though he's dead, I—"

Her chair went sailing across the room with the force of her explosion from it. "What? Dead? You're saying Gordo is dead? There's no way. I— Who are you?" She leaned over me, exuding clouds of Oriental-spiced perfume, and I stood up so I wouldn't feel at such a disadvantage. "What happened?"

Her surprise seemed genuine, as did her distress. I felt a pang of guilt at breaking the news to her so abruptly. "I'm sorry. I figured you'd know. It's been in the papers, on the news—"

"I don't pay attention to the *news*," Guinevere said, as if I'd accused her of being a Peeping Tom. "He can't be dead."

"I'm afraid he is. The police think someone pushed him off the roof of Elysium Brewing."

"Murdered. The bastard, the dumb bastard." She put the back of an index finger against her lower lid to stop the tears. "I always told him he'd push someone too far one day, but would he listen?"

I gazed at her in gathering astonishment. "Excuse me," I said, "but did you know him?"

"Know him?" She gave a bittersweet smile. "Who do you think invested in this place"—she gestured to the green room—"and helped me get it off the ground? WOSC was his idea."

Bam. I rocked back on my heels.

She didn't seem to notice my reaction. "When I divorced him for cheating on me—"

"You were married?" I yelped.

"I'm the reason he and Susan broke up," she admitted. "Wait a mo. I need a drink." Disappearing through the nonbathroom door, she returned moments later with a bottle of rosé wine. Unscrewing the top, she explained, "We host weekly get-togethers for our matches. Help them break the ice. Wine, beer, Chex Mix, blooming romance."

I had to stop myself from offering her ideas on how to make the weekly events more unique.

Pulling a Harry Potter mug off her desk, she filled it with wine. "Want some?" She offered the bottle.

"No, thanks. Driving."

"To Gordo." She lifted the mug in salute and then downed about half its contents. "We didn't last long. Only six months. I suppose I shouldn't have been surprised that a man who would cheat on his wife with me would cheat on me. But I was. I had at him about it, of course, and he promised it would never happen again, but I wasn't that stupid. Fool me once, shame on you, et cetera, et cetera. We got divorced, but managed to stay friends. 'Friends with benefits,' they'd call it today." She downed another long swallow of wine, refilled the mug, and said, "We went on a vacay to Acapulco a few years back, after he'd had another nasty breakup with some gal who pitched a hissy about his cheating, and that's when we dreamed up the WOSC idea.

"There were margaritas involved," she said with a reminiscent smile. "Lots of margaritas. We thought we were joking, but it still seemed like a good idea in the morning, so we made it happen. We've done plenty of outings in Denver, and been as far as Salt Lake City and Laramie, even to Birmingham once. You'd be surprised by what some women will pay to see men who cheated on them humiliated. In a completely legal and nonviolent way," she added with the air of one parroting a lawyer's phrases. She drank the mug's contents again, looked at it, and took a swig straight from the bottle.

"He was the first cheater WOSC outed, of course. He gave me the names of a dozen women he'd dated. I contacted them, and eight of them ponied up a hundred bucks to be in on it. We got some local news coverage, word of mouth took over, and pretty soon it was a nice little sideline. I wouldn't want to have to pay my mortgage off what I make from WOSC, but I redid my kitchen lasht year on the proceeds and took a nice cruishe." She was beginning to slur her *S*'s. "Damn you, Gordo. Why'd you have to go and get yourshelf killed?"

"I'm really sorry," I said sincerely, feeling like a heel for lying to her.

She blinked at me. "Who did you shay you are?"

"Amy-Faye Johnson," I said, coming clean. "Derek Johnson, the guy who owns Elysium Brewing, is my brother. The police think maybe he had something to do with Gordon's death, but I know he didn't. I came to see you today hoping you could tell me something about the women who were involved in the outing Friday."

"WOSC outed Gordon every other year or so," she said, smiling at the memory. Most of her lipstick was gone. "He was responsible for a lot of repeat business, although not as much as Lars Ingerholt."

I fought down the urge to ask about Lars. "What time did you last see Gordon?"

Guinevere blinked twice, trying to focus. "Um, I got there early Friday and talked to him about expanding Mutual E-ttraction. The pet salon next door is going out of business and I could take over that space. Wouldn't it be nice if we had a bigger space and could host bigger parties, maybe do some shpeed-dating events?" We both surveyed the room for a moment, envisioning forty or fifty singles mingling, eating, exchanging phone numbers.

"Sounds like a good idea to me," I said.

"I know, right? But Gordon wasn't having any of it. He said the numbers weren't what they should be for expansion and that I should table the idea for a year or two. Anyway, we had a little shpat—tiff—about it. Then I gathered up the gals who had come to out him and we did our thing. I think the last time I saw him was . . . hmm, maybe seven? He was headed upstairs for a smoke. Nashty habit." She made a face. The empty wine bottle slipped from her hand and rolled a foot before stopping.

"Who were the other women that were involved?"

"Well, Susan, of course—she comes every time. Wait. I shouldn't be telling you. It'sh confidential." Guinevere stood and walked to her desk, listing only a little. She put a hand on the desk to steady herself, removed a compact from a drawer, and began to poke at her hair and reapply her lipstick. She adjusted her belt. "Elashtic. Gotta love it. Got a potential client coming at four," she said. "You'll have to leave. Unless you want to meet him?" She scanned me. "Are you a Libra? He was definite about wanting to date a Libra."

"Aquarius," I said, rising. "Look, Guinevere, I saw you and Susan Marsh at the pub, and I know Bernie Kloster hooked up with you guys later on. Who were the other two women? Do you think any of them—Susan, or the others—were mad enough at Gordon to physically hurt him?"

"Who would want to hurt Gordo? He was smart and funny and generous. He didn't mean any harm. He couldn't help himself. Testosh . . . testosterone." Guinevere's eyes filled with tears and she suddenly crumpled into the desk chair. "Who am I kidding? I can't meet a client tonight. I'm closing up." Her voice shook as she called and left a voice mail for the man who wanted a Libra. Tears were streaming down her face when she hung up.

"Look, can I take you home?" I asked. She definitely shouldn't be driving.

"I'll call a taxi. Please leave." She weaved toward the door and managed to open it on the second try.

"I'm sorry for your loss," I said as I passed her.

She didn't seem to hear me. She didn't even close the

door, but drifted back toward her desk. I pulled the door gently closed, phoned for a cab, and waited in my van until it arrived and she got in. Then I hit the road for Heaven, eager to meet up with the Readaholics and hear what everyone else had discovered.

Chapter 13

I barely had time to skate by my house, down a yogurt and a hunk of leftover salmon, and change into shorts and a T-shirt before it was time to head for Kerry's house. I parked at the curb and walked up the flagstone walkway to the double doors. The strains of a song I recognized from childhood but couldn't name drifted from the open window of the garage apartment where Kerry's daughter, Amanda, lived with her two-year-old son. A ladder was propped against the side of the large gabled house Kerry had inherited from her parents, and a lanky figure with moplike black hair stood precariously on the highest step, dabbing salmon-colored paint on the gingerbread trim.

"Hi, Roman," I called up at Kerry's seventeen-year-old.

His reply, if you could call it that, sounded like "Uhn." I took it to mean "Hi, Amy-Faye. Nice to see you again." Teenish is such a succinct language.

When I knocked, Kerry answered almost immediately, and pointed me to the larger of the two living rooms, where my friends were gathered. She looked flushed. "I'm getting iced tea for everyone. Do you want some? No booze tonight because I've got to be out of here in an hour—I'm giving a talk about city government to a Girl Scout troop."

"Sure, thanks. Need me to help carry? Do you feel okay?" I asked as she fanned herself with both hands.

"Hot flashes suck," she said. "Women sure got the short end of the hormonal stick." She disappeared in the direction of the kitchen without waiting for me to answer and I walked into the living room, wondering what it was about hormones today. First Guinevere and her testosterone lecture, and now Kerry.

Lola, Brooke, and Maud were seated on the stiff Victorian-era furniture Kerry had inherited along with the house and couldn't yet afford to replace. Only Brooke looked natural there, sitting cross-legged on a blue horsehair (at least that was what it felt like the only time I sat on it) sofa. The sofa's high arms and the ornately carved wood rising in points from its back defeated Maud's attempts to assume her usual lounging position, and its height made Lola perch on the very edge of the tufted seat so her feet would reach the floor. She greeted me with a smile. "Hey. We were just talking about the autopsy report. But now that you're here, we can talk about your date last night." Gentle mischief gleamed in her brown eyes.

"How did—?" Why did I even bother asking? Total lack of privacy was one of the drawbacks of living in

Heaven, or any small town, I imagined. I sat on a low, tufted ottoman with feet like a lion's paws.

"One of my customers saw the HPD Tahoe outside your house last night and mentioned it to me this morning when she came in to pick up some barberry because she knows we're friends," Lola said, clearly tickled by my reaction. "So—"

"So, either you were being arrested—which apparently isn't the case—or you had a hot date with the hot Detective Hart," Brooke finished. She leaned forward so her mink brown hair spilled over her shoulders. "Tell all."

"We had dinner," I said. "Not much to tell. Salmon, asparagus, and—"

"We don't care about the *menu*," Brooke laughed. "Did you—?"

"We ate, chatted, and he *left*," I said, emphasizing the last word. "As the local spy might have been able to tell you if he'd cruised past around nine or so."

"No—" Brooke made smooching noises.

"What are we—fourteen?" I asked, blushing. I flashed on Lola, Brooke, and me sitting around in my bedroom with its bean bag chairs when we were in high school, dissecting one another's crushes.

"Aha!" she said triumphantly.

"What are you 'ahaing'?" Kerry asked, slipping back into the room with a pitcher of tea and stacked acrylic glasses, which she passed around.

Brooke took pity on me and changed the subject. "I read up on his niece's death," she said. "Her name was

Kinleigh Dreesen. There doesn't seem to be anything there, really. It's the—I hate to say 'usual'—the not *un-usual* tale of a girl who drank too much, partying with her college friends, and drove her car off the road into a tree. She died at the scene. Gordon was with her and he pretty much walked away from the wreck. Her friends say she was giving him a lift home because he had a 'dizzy spell.' " Brooke put air quotes around the words, as if they were a euphemism for "drunk." "Her parents, Gordon's sister and her husband, made a big fuss in the paper, alleging he and his club, Moonglade, were responsible, but the girl was of legal age and . . ." She shrugged. "They—the parents—accused Gordon of being the driver, and accused the police of a cover-up when they said a blood test showed he was sober. I guess he had tried to help the girl, who was thrown from the car, and there was some question about who was driving, even though a witness definitely said Kinleigh was driving when they left the club. The stepsister and her husband tried to bring a case, and he countersued for defamation of character. It was just ugly, a case of hurt people making a tragedy so much worse. Moonglade went out of business anyway a few weeks later. Troy and I went there once. It was nice. Classy. Definitely a step above most Grand Junction nightspots."

"What a senseless tragedy," Lola said. "You can see why the parents were looking for someone to blame. Gordon was there, so . . ." She let the thought die out, and then said, "Maybe we should get back to the autopsy report," she said. "Maud, you were saying?"

"Gordon was a big man with a big-time problem," Maud said, putting on rectangular cheaters and reading from her steno pad. "Six-one, two hundred twenty pounds, and in generally good health . . . except for the brain tumor." She peered over the glasses to see how we reacted to her bombshell.

"Brain tumor!" Kerry exclaimed.

"I'd've thought lung cancer, as much as he smoked," I said.

"Maybe he really was dizzy when Kinleigh drove him home," Brooke said, eyes widening.

"Poor man," said Lola. "Did he know?"

"Good question," Maud said, pointing at Lola. "I haven't been able to find that out yet. I talked to a friend of Joe's, though, an oncologist, and showed her the X-rays I got from the coroner's office. She said the tumor, a glioblastoma, was inoperable, terminal, and might have been affecting his speech, balance, and even personality."

"How so?" Kerry asked, seating herself in a rocking chair.

"Less executive function," Maud answered, referring to her notes again. "Unusual fits of anger or acting out. Not the way I want to go," she added, trying to lean back against the sofa and frowning at it when her head hit part of the wood carving. "Kerry, damn this couch. You should break it up for kindling."

"That explains a lot," I said, telling them about Gordon heaving a beer mug at his ex-wife and exploding at the least little thing. "I don't think Derek knew Gordon was ill."

"I'll bet the murderer didn't know Gordon was ill, either," Kerry said. "Why bother murdering someone who's already up against his expiration date?" Her flush had subsided and she was rocking gently back and forth.

"Maybe the tumor made him lose his balance and just fall off the roof," Lola suggested.

I wished that were possible, but I shook my head. "You haven't been up there, Lo. No way could anyone fall over accidentally—the wall is too high."

"Let me read you the rest of this," Maud said, abandoning the sofa to lean against the fireplace, cold and only faintly ashy smelling at this time of year. "And for heaven's sake don't mention this to anyone until you see it in the paper. We're not supposed to know this. I don't want my source getting in trouble, or refusing to help me out in the future." She cleared her throat. "The gist of it is that he was conked with the proverbial blunt object, got a fractured skull that was probably fatal, and was then tossed over the wall. There's lots of data about mortar that matches samples from the wall in the scrapes on his arms and face, antemortem bruising, blah-blah, and then a cracked cervical vertebra, supposedly suffered postmortem, that probably happened when his body hit the metal lip of the Dumpster."

Lola put a hand to her mouth. "That's just awful." She closed her eyes and I wondered if she was saying a prayer.

"At least he didn't suffer long," Kerry said practically. "He was dead before he landed in the Dumpster, it sounds like."

We sat in silence for a moment, chastened by the reality of violent death. I cleared my throat and said, "Let me tell you what I found out about Women Outing Serial Cheaters." It took me fifteen minutes, but I gave them a blow-by-blow account of my discussion with Guinevere Dalrymple.

"She was married to Gordon?" Kerry exclaimed. "How many ex-wives does he have?"

"More important," Maud put in, "do the police know? Maybe this Guinevere was madder at Gordon than she let on, or maybe she's in his will." She made a note and I knew she was going to do her damnedest to get hold of Gordon's will. "They can also get her to cough up the names of the other participants in the 'outing,'" she said. "What did Chief Uggams have to say about the investigation, Kerry?" she asked.

Kerry planted her feet and quit rocking. "That man! He's on a fishing trip until tomorrow. With a homicide case on his plate, he goes off after trout *and* takes the DA with him! Mabel put me through to Detective Hart, and he wouldn't say more than that the investigation was going well, they were collecting evidence and interviewing witnesses—a lot of them, since there were so many folks at the grand opening—and he hoped to make an arrest by the end of the week. Sorry, Amy-Faye." She shot me a look that said she assumed Derek would be the arrestee.

My stomach clenched, but I said, "He might have been talking about Foster." I told them about my run-in with the ex-janitor and his obsession with revenge on Gordon.

"What we need," I said when I finished, "is Hercule Poirot to march all the players in one by one and grill them about what they saw and where they were when, and then draw up a timeline."

Lola smiled faintly. "I don't think it's ever quite that easy for the police in real life."

"Maybe they were all in on it," Maud said, her eyes lighting up.

"All who?" Brooke asked. "In on what?"

"Gordon's murder," Maud said impatiently. "Maybe his exes and his son, and his sister, and the WOSC women, and the janitor, and everyone were in on it together. Like in *Orient*."

"Everyone except Derek," I quickly put in.

Kerry hooted derisively. "You have finally lost it, Maud. You left out the CIA and Sirhan Sirhan. These people don't know each other, and even if they did, how many people does it take to toss one man—even if he weighed two hundred plus—off a roof? You don't think someone would have noticed if half the party trooped upstairs to the roof and came back soaking wet?"

Maud made a disgruntled face, unhappy at having her conspiracy theory debunked so quickly. "I'm just saying it's possible."

Kerry, never one to let well enough alone, added, "Yeah, well, it's *possible* that the town's new ad campaign will triple our tourist business, but I'm not holding my breath."

Part of her earlier question had caught my attention.

"Does the autopsy report have a time of death, Maud?" I asked.

She scanned her notes. "Somewhere between seven and seven thirty. Seems to be based on stomach content analysis."

We all grimaced, and Brooke said, "Eww."

"Anyone remember when it started raining?"

They all shook their heads, but Maud said, "I see where you're going with this. I'll check with the weather service."

"It started raining before the fire alarm went off," Kerry remembered. "Everyone got wet from standing in the parking lot. I had to wring out my bra when I got home. I'll try the chief again when he gets back tomorrow afternoon. Better yet, maybe I'll set Chester on him." Chester was both the former police chief and Kerry's former husband. She looked at her big-faced watch. "I have to shoo you out of here. Can't be tardy for the Girl Scouts."

We thanked Kerry and left. I waved at Roman, still up on his ladder, trying to dab paint on the row of gingerbread shingles just under the eaves. His ladder rocked and he dribbled paint onto a windowpane. That would be fun to clean up. The Readaholics seemed more subdued than usual, I thought, saying good nights as Kerry pulled out of the driveway, tooting the Subaru's horn, and zipped down the street. If the others were feeling like me, it was because finding Gordon's murderer seemed hopeless. There were too many people we knew about who had grudges against him—

motive—and too many people at the grand opening who might have had the opportunity to kill him. And the means of death was readily available to anyone who took the time to climb to the roof. Wait . . . maybe not. Maud had said Gordon was hit with something. I wondered if the police had the weapon in hand, and what it might have been. Something available on the roof, or something the killer would have had to bring along?

I let go of my train of thought for a moment, catching up to Brooke before she got in her Mercedes. "How did it go with the home inspection today?" I asked.

She smiled. "Great, just great. The woman, Elaine, was very nice, and she seemed happy—impressed even—with the house, how clean it was and everything."

"Who wouldn't be?" There were operating rooms that weren't as clean as Brooke's house.

"Troy even came home from work to be with me when she came," Brooke added. "He's as committed to this as I am," she assured me.

"Of course he is." It was her parents-in-law that couldn't stomach the thought of their son adopting a child that didn't have Widefield blue blood trickling through his or her veins. "What happens next?"

"We do an interview, and then—keep your fingers crossed—we're in The Book. This agency gives The Book to expectant mothers so they can choose who they want to adopt their baby. They've got two new pregnant girls coming in next week to go through The Book."

"That's wonderful. Keep me posted."

"You bet," Brooke said with a grin. "And you keep me posted on progress with Detective Hot—I mean Hart."

I blew a raspberry and headed to my van as Brooke drove off. From behind me came a scraping sound, and a strangled yelp. I pivoted in time to see Roman's ladder list to the right, bang against the side of the house, and crash into the juniper shrubs. Roman flung his paint can, which tumbled end over end, spewing salmon-colored latex that spattered me from head to toe as I raced toward him, and tried to jump off the ladder, but it looked as though he'd caught his shirt in the ladder somehow and couldn't pull free in time. He tumbled headfirst into the shrubs. The branches quivered as he thrashed.

"Roman!" I called, skidding to a stop in front of the junipers. A rich evergreen scent arose from the crushed limbs.

"I'm okay," he mumbled, sitting up and spitting out the tip of a juniper branch. His moplike hair was messier than usual, and salmon paint streaked it and his face. He tried to push himself up, but cried out, "My wrist!"

"Let me see."

He held out his right hand. Even without an MD, I could see it was broken, already swollen and with a strange bulge that made me wince in sympathy. "I'm taking you to the doctor," I said, thinking quickly. At this hour, the only option was the urgent-care clinic on Paradise and Fourth Street. "Give me your other hand."

I helped pull him up, my hand lost in his bigger one.

He cradled his injured wrist in his left hand as I urged him toward the van. "How about you call your mom while I drive, okay? Do you think you can do that? She can meet us at the clinic."

Roman nodded, hair flopping. I helped him into the van and tried to drive smoothly so I didn't jar his wrist while he dialed one-handed. "Voice mail," he said after a moment. "She turns her phone off when she does speeches."

That might have been the longest phrase I'd ever heard him utter. "Do you know where she is, where the Girl Scout meeting is?"

Roman shrugged in the teenage boy way that could mean anything from a simple "No" to "Why are you bothering me with this?" to "I heard blah-blah-blah and thought I should act like I'm listening."

We were at Alliance Urgent Care now, and I turned into the nearly empty parking lot. I hoped that boded well for our wait time. Thank goodness it was Monday night, and not a weekend. I helped Roman out of the van, noticing his face was distinctly paler, and held the door for him. The space was brightly lit, linoleum-floored, and virtually empty. An elderly man sat at the farthest end of the waiting room, listlessly flipping the pages of a magazine. Some inane reality show played on the TV mounted in a corner. The middle-aged black receptionist greeted us with a smile and "Can I help you?"

I explained why we were there and Roman held out his wrist. The receptionist handed me a clipboard. "Mom, if you could fill out these forms, we'll get—"

"She's not my mom," Roman said at the same time I said, "I'm not his mother." At her confused and now suspicious look, I explained. The receptionist asked for Kerry's cell phone number, called it, and left a message summarizing the situation. "Dr. Dreesen will be right with you," she promised us.

Before I had time to figure out where I knew that name from, a door to the right of the reception desk opened and a petite woman in a snowy lab coat appeared. She had a stethoscope draped around her neck and her sandy blond hair in a low ponytail. I recognized Gordon's sister immediately. "Roman Sanderson?" she called crisply, looking right at us.

Sweat beaded Roman's forehead, which I took as a sign of increasing pain. "Do you want me to come back with you?" I asked, not sure of the protocol.

"Nah." He shambled toward where Dr. Dreesen waited and they disappeared through the door.

"The washroom's through there," the receptionist called to me, pointing.

I wasn't sure what she meant, but when I pushed into the restroom and saw the salmon speckles all over my face and clothes, I understood. Using paper towels and warm water, I scrubbed off most of the paint on my face and hands; my clothes and hair would have to wait until I got home.

The magazines on offer—*American Baby*, *Highlights*, and *Rider Magazine* (perhaps because motorcycle riders spend a lot of time in ERs?)—held no allure, so I occupied myself for the next forty minutes by alternately watching the reality show, which featured precocious brats being forced into beauty pageant slavery by their tyrannical mothers, and calling Kerry. She still hadn't answered when Roman and Dr. Dreesen reappeared. Roman sported a cast wrapped in traffic-cone-orange tape, and a woozy look that suggested they'd given him some effective painkillers. Dr. Dreesen beckoned to me.

When I approached, she gave me a sharp look. "I know you."

"Amy-Faye Johnson. I'm Derek Johnson's sister. We met at Elysium Brewing." *Where your brother died.* Up close, I towered over her, which doesn't happen often, since five-four doesn't often qualify as "towering." She couldn't have been more than five-one, and I'd bet she didn't weigh a hundred and five, dripping wet. She had pretty, delicate features, pinched with worry or exhaustion, and I put her at forty-five or -six. I wasn't sure whether or not to offer my condolences, given the circumstances, but I finally said, "I'm very sorry about your brother."

"Stepbrother. You found him." Her pale blue eyes searched my face.

I tried to read her tone or expression, but couldn't, so I simply nodded.

"I'm sorry. That must have been horrid for you."

Surprised, I nodded again.

"The police suspect your brother, Derek."

Tired of nodding, I stood, waiting to see where she was going with this. By my side, Roman scratched at a line of paint of his cheek.

"Roman, why don't you sit down while I write out a prescription for your pain meds?" she suggested.

When he was out of earshot, she scribbled on a prescription form, ripped it off the pad, and handed it to me. "I don't think your brother did it," she said, "and I told the police that."

"You did?" I failed to keep the surprise out of my voice.

"There was a line of people with much more long-standing"—she searched for a word—"grudges against Gordon, most of them family. You can't hate someone properly unless you're related, can you? Even by marriage. When my mom married his dad, we redefined 'dysfunctional.' My sister and I were furious about having to leave our house and friends to move in with Larry and Gordon. We took it out on Mom. Gordon was furious about being landed with two younger siblings he was expected to take care of, and took it out on us. The first year was torture and it got worse from there. When Larry cheated on Mom the first time, it all went to hell in a handbasket. By the eighth or ninth time, Mom spent more time with her lawyer than with us. Gordon had escaped to college by then." Her thin smile was a blade. "He killed my daughter, you know." She fumbled at the neck of her blouse and tugged on a thin gold chain. A locket dangled from it and she flicked it open with a thumbnail to show me the photo of a pretty girl with short brown hair and a broad smile. "That's my Kinleigh."

I got the feeling she had gone through the locket routine a thousand times since her daughter's accident. "She was beautiful," I said. That didn't feel like enough, so I added, "She looks kind."

The clinic door opened and I looked over, hoping it was Kerry, but a young mother came in, bouncing a crying toddler on her hip and promising him that the doctor would fix his ear. Dreesen had scanned the duo automatically, it seemed, and decided the child's problem wasn't life-threatening, because she didn't rush off. She nodded and tucked the locket away.

"You're perceptive. She was very kind. If it weren't for Gordon—" Her tone was as corrosive as sulfuric acid and I inched away. "I'm sorry. I'm not supposed to keep talking about it. Now, about Roman—"

She described the break, the X-rays, and the dosage for the painkillers. Before she could leave, I said, "When was the last time you saw Gordon at the party?"

Realization flashed in her eyes, and the thin smile reappeared. "Are you asking me for an alibi?" She held her hands out from her sides. "Do I look like I could heave a two-hundred-plus-pound man over a wall?"

She didn't look burly enough to strew rose petals. No way could she have pushed Gordon over the wall, not without a winch and crane. "Your husband—" I started.

"Wasn't even there by the time the police say Gordon died," she said with the air of someone who had told this story already, to the police, probably. "He was late leaving the office and then stopped to help someone with a flat tire. He didn't get there until we were all in the parking lot because of the fire. The police are satisfied with his alibi."

She was turning away, ready to help the earache boy, when I asked, "If you told the police you don't think

Derek was involved—thank you, by the way—did you suggest someone who might have done it?"

She hesitated, but then said, "My money's on Susan. Susan or Kolby. I might have hated Gordon more than they did, but they wanted his money in the worst way. Susan's never stopped trying to break the prenup. And Kolby . . . well, do you know Kolby?"

"We've met."

She nodded as if to meet Kolby was to despise him, which was pretty close to true. "He tried to kill Gordon once before, you know. Tried to run him over."

Before I could react, the clinic door burst open and Kerry rushed in. "Roman! Are you okay? How many times have I told you not to stand on the top rung? Thank you so much, Amy-Faye. Are you the doctor? Is he going to be all right? That's his pitching arm—when do you think—?"

I patted Roman's shoulder and said good night, not expecting a reply, but he surprised me. "Thanks for driving me over here," he said with a sweet smile. "You're the bomb. Want to be the first to sign my cast?"

Borrowing a Sharpie from the receptionist, I signed his cast, told him to take it easy, and escaped while Kerry was still interrogating Dr. Dreesen. I had a lot to think about.

Chapter 14

A crush of new business descended on me Tuesday morning, and I didn't get around to thinking about lunch until almost one o'clock. Three new jobs, I thought gleefully, labeling a blue file folder for the corporate offsite I'd just booked and entering it on my whiteboard schedule. I didn't think I'd ever landed three events in a single morning. Al—who had class on Tuesday mornings—would be amazed when he came in. From my office, I heard the front door open on the thought, and I called out, "Hey, Al, guess what."

"What?"

It wasn't Al's voice. I looked up, disbelieving, to see Doug Elvaston standing in the doorway, white grin splitting his tan face, sun-bleached hair falling across his forehead. He looked fit, and leaner than when he left, without the shell-shocked look that had made him seem fragile after Madison jilted him at the altar. His forearms, displayed by the madras shirt he wore, were corded with muscle. My mouth fell open. I scrambled up. "Doug! You're back."

He swept me into a bear hug. "I'm back. Miss me?"

The question brought me up short. I had missed him, but not nearly as much as I would have thought I would, I realized. Perhaps I was truly over him? The thought seemed traitorous, so I squeezed him extra hard and said, "Of course!"

He released me and held me at arm's length to study me. "You look great, Amy-Faye."

"So do you." His eyes seemed greener and his teeth whiter against the deep tan. "How long have you been back?" It couldn't have been too long or the local grapevine would have told me. "Are you working?"

"Four days, and sort of. Do you have time for lunch? I've got something I want to show you."

"Sure. I was just thinking about lunch. Let me grab my purse."

Four minutes later we were out the door and Doug was opening the passenger door of his Camry for me. We drove a quick four blocks north and stopped. There wasn't a restaurant in sight. This part of town was mainly residential, with a smattering of offices housed in converted homes. "What—?"

"You'll see." Doug parked at the curb and fairly dragged me out of the car. In front of a three-story Victorian house that reminded me of Kerry's place, minus the salmon-colored splashes on the window, he said, "Ta-da!"

I looked closer and saw a wooden sign gracing the

postage stamp front yard. DOUG ELVASTON, ATTORNEY-AT-LAW, it read in dark red script on white, to match the house's colors.

"You've left the firm," I breathed.

Doug threw up his arms. "I'm a free man!"

"What—? How—?"

"Let's get some food and I'll tell you all about it."

At the Salty Burro, only half a dozen tables had diners at the tail end of lunch hour, and a single waiter was trying to handle them all. Delicious scents of jalapeño and cumin filled the air. Doug munched on a tortilla chip in our high-backed booth, and said, "I had an epiphany while I was at sea, Amy-Faye. Madison did me a favor by dumping me."

I raised a skeptical eyebrow.

"No, really. If she hadn't left me at the altar, we'd be married now, splitting our time between Heaven and Manhattan, each of us so deep in the rat race of billable hours and fighting to make partner that we'd probably never see each other. It would probably have taken me years to see that that's not the life I want, if Madison hadn't made me see it."

"Let me nominate her for sainthood," I said drily, crunching hard on a chip. "She could at least have told you prior to the wedding day that she wasn't going through with it."

"Granted," Doug agreed. "I haven't really been happy—'fulfilled,' I guess, is a better word, but that sounds so navel-gazing and therapyish—since I got out of law school and joined the firm. I was excited that they hired me and about the money, but I don't get much say in my cases and the hours have been back-breaking. When I went into law, I wanted to make a difference, to help people, but the only people I ever see are opposing counsel—more lawyers, not real people who need help like that summer I did legal aid in Denver, remember?"

"I remember." My enchiladas arrived and I began to salivate. I was starving.

"So, one night at sea, I'm on the midwatch, and it's dark, but not fully, because the water always has a glow to it, phosphorescence or reflected stars, and I'm totally alone on deck, just me and the sea, and I realized I felt peaceful. For the first time in years. Since before I joined the firm, since back when you and I were together."

I tensed, but he didn't seem to be giving that last phrase any special significance, hinting at anything; he was merely stating a fact.

"And I got to thinking." He slurped a spoonful of chicken tequila soup, one of the Burro's specialties. "I got to thinking that a lot of the 'have tos' in my life weren't really. Have tos, I mean. They were self-imposed. I don't have to make the kind of money I'm making to be happy. I don't have to run my life in six-minute increments for billable hours. I decided that night that I was going to quit the firm and go it alone. I e-mailed my resignation from the yacht and started searching for offices to rent in Heaven whenever we were in port and I could get a wireless connection. When I got back Saturday, I went straight to the leasing office and signed a contract. Now I'm just like you—a self-employed small-business owner." He stretched his arms along the booth's back, and grinned at me.

"Welcome to penury," I said, returning his grin. "And if you think you'll be working fewer hours now that you're on your own, you're in for a big disappointment."

"Yeah, I know, but I'll be working for myself, on cases that interest me, and I think—I hope—that will make a big difference. I've already got two clients. So, what's new with you?" He leaned forward to spoon up more soup.

Lindell Hart immediately sprang to mind, but I said, "Well, Derek may get arrested later this week. For murder."

"What!" He practically spat a mouthful of soup at me.

Perversely pleased with his reaction, I gave him chapter and verse on everything that had happened since the grand opening on Friday. "If you'd come home a day earlier, you could have been there."

"Sounds like a good party to have missed." His brow wrinkled. "Does Derek have a lawyer?"

"Drumming up business?" I teased. Before he could reply, I said, "Yeah, some guy he plays basketball with."

"Well, if there's anything I can do, tell him to call. Completely pro bono, of course. Heck, I thought of the D-man as my future brother-in-law for a long time; I can't charge him."

I dropped my fork. Before I could say anything, a couple of women I knew said hello on their way to the door. By the time they'd passed, the moment seemed to be gone and I didn't react. There hadn't been anything portentous in Doug's tone, and he didn't look self-conscious now as he studied the bill and put twenty bucks down. It was a throwaway remark, not an invitation to resume a relationship that had been dead for two years and on life support a year before that, I told myself.

As he dropped me off in front of my office, with a peck on the cheek and a promise to call, a niggling thought arose: Maybe our relationship wasn't dead beyond hope of resurrection. An image of Lindell Hart smiling down at me made me smile involuntarily. Even if resurrection was possible, was I interested? That was the sixty-four-thousand-dollar question for which I didn't have an immediate answer.

When I walked around the building to the back garden and my office entrance, I saw two figures standing in the reception area: Al and Hart. A smile broke over my face at the sight of Hart and I entered with a cheery "Hello."

Hart's expression wiped the cheery right out of me. "Got a minute?" He gave a tiny head nod toward my office.

Closing the door behind us, but hovering near it rather than going to my desk, I asked, "What?"

Hart laid a hand on my shoulder. "Officers are arresting Derek as we speak. I wanted you to hear it from me. I don't have a choice, Amy-Faye. I shouldn't be telling you this, but we found Gordon's blood on a shirt in Derek's trash can."

I jerked away from his hand. "From the fight the other day, not from that night!" I exclaimed. "Gordon got a bloody nose. It got all over Derek."

"It's the shirt he was wearing Friday night. Witnesses ID'd it. The chief and DA got back from their fishing trip last night and issued the arrest warrant as soon as the lab tests came back this morning."

Hart's voice stayed gentle as mine became more shrill. "What about Foster? Have you talked to him? Or Guinevere Dalrymple? Did you know Gordon was married to her? She's the woman I saw arguing with him before the party. She was mad at him about money." I told him about my meeting with Guinevere, the words tumbling out of me. "And what about his other ex-wife and Kolby?" I asked, not giving him a chance to respond to my Guinevere story. "His sister says they've had it in for him for years, and that Kolby already tried to kill him once."

Hart's brows snapped together. "You talked to Angie Dreesen?"

"Long story," I said wearily. I walked to the window and placed my forehead against the cool glass, staring out at the garden. A hummingbird buzzed past, two inches from my nose. They'd be going south soon. Hart touched my shoulder again and this time I didn't shake his hand off. Instead I turned and burrowed against his chest as he pulled me in tightly.

"I'm sorry," he murmured against my hair.

"I'm mad at you," I muttered into his shirt.

"I don't blame you." His hand stroked my back.

I pulled away far enough to look up at him. "I'm

going to find out who really killed Gordon," I said. "You can't stop me from talking to people." My tone dared him to try.

His eyes serious, he said, "Be careful, Amy-Faye. Bring me anything you find and I'll follow up on it, I promise. In case we don't have the right guy—"

"You don't."

"I don't want you making a killer nervous with your questions."

"The killer better be nervous," I said, slitting my eyes, "because I'm going to find him. Or her."

Hart had to leave and as I closed the door behind him, Al asked, "Bad news, boss?"

"The worst."

"The Russians detonated a nuke over California? Ebola is clearing out Chicago? *Sports Illustrated* is abandoning their swimsuit issue?"

"Worse," I said, but a small smile peeped out. I got his point. "My brother's been arrested for murder."

Al actually clapped his hands to either side of his face, like that kid in the *Home Alone* movies. "No! No way. Get out. Derek might be a thoughtless boob sometimes, and obsessed with beer, but he's not a killer."

"My thoughts precisely," I said, half impressed and half irritated at Al's perception and honesty. Derek might, every now and then, be a thoughtless boob, but only I (and maybe my sisters) got to apply that label to him. Al frequently made me rethink the old saw "Honesty's the best policy." I marched past him to my office. "I need to let my folks know."

I dreaded calling my parents and couldn't decide whom I wanted to pick up the phone, Mom or Dad. Mom would cry and Dad would rant. Before I could make myself dial, the phone rang. I snatched it up. "Eventful!" I said in a tone that would discourage anyone considering hiring me to organize a cheerful celebration.

"I heard Doug's back in town," Brooke said, in her "let's dish" voice.

"The police arrested Derek for Gordon's murder."

"That's not funny."

"No, it's not."

"You're serious? Oh my God. When? Why? What can I do?"

Her instant and sincere concern and offer of help eased the tension in my chest. I drew a deep breath. "Nothing right now. I'll let you know if anything comes up. Oh, and I already knew about Doug. We had lunch today and he showed me his new office. He's quit the law firm and is going it alone. Gotta call my folks about Derek. I'll call you tonight."

I hung up on her demands for more information and forced myself to dial my parents' number. Their phone rang twice, but I hung up before they answered. News like this needed to be delivered in person. I managed to calm myself on the short drive to Mom and Dad's. Derek hadn't killed Gordon; ergo, Derek wasn't going to prison. He might spend a night in jail—how fast could his lawyer get him out on bail?—but that wouldn't kill him. Not in Heaven, where he'd probably be the only prisoner, except for maybe a drunk or two.

Pulling into the weed-choked driveway—Dad would rather stare endlessly at unsolvable math equations on his whiteboard than do home maintenance or yard work—I hesitated a moment before getting out of the van. Rarely had I returned with less enthusiasm to the rambling two-story I'd grown up in on the east end of Heaven. The house, with its flaking gray paint, overgrown yard with apple and peach trees, and detached, two-car garage was normally a haven, but not now. The winey-sweet smell of fermenting peaches, fallen from the trees and greatly appreciated by the squirrels, birds, and bears, clung to my skin as I climbed the veranda steps.

Dragging Dad out back to the table where Mom did her book reviewing in the summer, I broke the news of Derek's arrest. The hum of bees feasting on the fallen peaches was the only sound for a few moments after I said the *A* word. They were more stoic than I expected. Mom did, indeed, cry, but only for a couple of minutes before drying her eyes with her shirt hem and saying, "Derek's tough. This family is tough. We'll get through this. I hope the stress doesn't bring on a shingles attack, not that I've ever had shingles, but I'm pretty sure I had chicken pox as a child, so it's always a possibility. Did you know shingles pain can linger for *years* after the blisters have disappeared?"

Dad bellowed about police incompetence and their willingness to settle for the suspect that first came to hand, rather than putting time and effort into finding the real killer, and added that "Clarence Uggams better not show his face at Thursday night's poker game."

Then he, too, calmed down and we discussed the situation and whether or not to tell my sisters.

I had to admit I didn't know if Derek was allowed visitors, and we were on our way out the door to see when we stumbled over a tall young woman on the veranda, preparing to ring the doorbell.

"I'm Courtney Spainhower," she introduced herself. "Derek's lawyer."

When Derek said that a basketball buddy was representing him, I'd assumed it was a guy. Mentally slapping myself for my sexist assumptions, I shook her hand. "Amy-Faye Johnson. These are my folks, Norm and June. I guess you've heard?"

Courtney was at least six feet tall, even in flats, and dressed professionally in a black pantsuit with a white open-neck shirt. Her black hair was cut short, and she moved with an athlete's grace. She was attractive, I thought, rather than pretty, but there was something arresting about her—maybe the intelligence in her brown eyes or the way she seemed totally focused on the person she was talking to. I wondered if she and Derek were more than basketball buddies.

Mom invited her in and Courtney took us through the legalities of the situation, saying she was sure the judge would grant bail at the arraignment later in the day. "Derek's not much of a flight risk," Courtney said. "He doesn't have much money, he's got longtime ties to the community, and his business is here. They'll make him surrender his passport, of course."

I'd forgotten Derek even had a passport, but then I remembered that he'd spent time in Germany and Belgium, studying brewing a couple of years back. While my parents talked finances with Courtney, I first wasted time wishing the Readaholics were enmeshed in a Grisham legal thriller or a Scott Turow book, so I'd know more about what was likely to happen with Derek's case. Then I turned my mind to the practicalities of proving my brother innocent. It seemed to me that my next step should be talking to Susan and Kolby Marsh. Angie Dreesen knew them better than I did, and if she thought they were capable of bopping Gordon on the head and tossing him off the roof, they were worth talking to.

Courtney told us not to try to see Derek at the jail, but just to wait for his release. "I don't think he wants you to see him like that," she told my mom gently, when it looked like she'd insist on going downtown.

"Oh," Mom said, and for all her bulk, she seemed small.

"Orange isn't his color," I said, trying to lighten the atmosphere. "It's even worse on him than on me." When I escorted Courtney to the door a few minutes later, I joined her on the veranda and closed the door behind us. "If you've got a minute . . ."

I let her know about everything I'd seen and heard since Friday night and she took notes furiously.

"I work with an investigator, of course," she said when I wound down, "but she's got nothing on you. If you get tired of event organizing, give me a call." She grinned, which crinkled her nose in a cute way that made her look less intimidating. "There's enough reasonable doubt in what you've told me to fill a silo, which will come in handy if this ever gets to trial, which I don't think it will."

Buoyed by her words, I thanked her for helping Derek, watched her drive off in a utilitarian SUV, and headed for my van. I knew Gordon's ex owned a boutique downtown; if I left now, I would get there before closing. Time to channel Sharon McCone and do some PI-type detecting.

Chapter 15

I drove back into town and parked diagonally in front of Susan Marsh's boutique, West of Eden. The single display window framed a mannequin wearing fall attire of slim-fitting dark jeans that no real ranch hand could afford (or woman with real thighs wear), a corduroy jacket over a silk T-shirt, and hand-tooled ostrich boots that probably went for more than my monthly mortgage. A bell tinkled when I opened the door, and a butterscotch-colored Pomeranian yapped from a dog bed under the window.

"Marshmallow, hush," Susan said, dark head popping up from where she was arranging a boot display on a low shelf. She came toward me wearing half her inventory, to include a saucer-size silver-and-turquoise belt buckle around the slim waist of her denim skirt, and a smile that faded when she recognized me. Up close, her hair was a bit too dark to look natural against the slight crow's-feet and mouth brackets of a woman whose fiftieth birthday was a couple of years past.

"Your brother killed my ex," she greeted me. "Bianca Appleman was just in here, and she heard it from her husband, who heard it from his mom, who works at the police department."

Thanks, Mabel. "He didn't do it." Could I just have that tattooed on my forehead so I didn't have to keep repeating it? Marshmallow trotted over on tiny paws to sniff at my feet. He was unbearably cute with his lion's ruff of fur framing his pointy nose and ears.

"The police arrested him." Susan smoothed her feathered hair back.

I didn't feel up to going into the whole "innocent until proven guilty" thing, so I had started to ask her about Friday night when she cut me off.

"Don't get me wrong. He did me a favor. He did lots of people a favor. Gordon had a dark side that not everyone saw, you know? Hey, you want some herbal tea?" She swished to a counter behind the register, Marshmallow following with his funny straight-legged gait, and popped a pod into a Keurig machine without waiting for an answer. The scent of peppermint drifted to me.

"That doesn't mean he shouldn't do time for what he did," she said in a self-righteous voice that made me want to punch her, "but I'm happy to contribute to his defense fund. I can put a jar—you know, with a sign that has a photo of Darren and says something about paying for legal fees, blah-de-blah—for people to put change in, right here by the register." She patted the counter with a manicured hand with a thumbnail torn almost to the quick. "Opening stock boxes," she said, following my gaze to her nail and folding her fingers around her thumb.

"Derek," I said, accepting the mug of tea she handed me. "Not Darren."

"Sure, whatever." Marshmallow yapped once and she picked him up, cradling him in her arms and stroking his head absently.

"You know," I said, "I don't see what Gordon did to make people so mad. Yeah, he was a hound dog, and he had to make hard decisions as a businessman, but he didn't strike me as the kind of ogre lots of people say he was." I sipped the tea and tried to look unthreatening and only mildly curious.

"You weren't married to him."

Because I'm not that dumb, I thought about saying, but didn't.

"He was selfish and stingy. Why, he even quit paying his own son's college tuition. It's not like I could afford to pay it, not off what I make here." She flung out an arm to encompass her high-end Western merchandise. "This place barely pays for my utility bill and cable," she complained. "And he was going to stop the alimony payments when—" She broke off and continued with "I didn't mind so much for myself, but a mother's got to look out for her son, you know?" She set the dog down and he yipped a demand to be picked up again, which she ignored.

I wondered how she defined "look out for," and tried to assess how much muscle there was under her long-sleeved shirt. She was about my height of five foot four, and looked fit for a woman in her early fifties. Not as fit as Maud, who made her living slogging through the forest after game, or winching her boat on and off the trailer, but gym-fit. And she had a strong, healthy son . . . Good grief! I was getting as bad as Maud, seeing conspiracies all over the place. But the idea wouldn't go away. Both Susan and Kolby were at the pub Friday night, and Kolby had discovered his father's body. In many of the police procedural books the Readaholics had discussed, the cops made a point of suspecting whoever discovered the victim's body.

Leaving my mug on the counter, I drifted to a nearby rack and began to riffle through Western shirts with yokes and pearl snaps, pretending I might be interested in buying something to prolong the conversation. "So . . . I saw you with the WOSC group Friday night. Have you known those women long?"

"I don't know them at all," Susan said. She dinged open the cash register and began to tally receipts in preparation for closing. "Well, except for Guinevere, who stole Gordon away from me but who got hers when their marriage went belly-up in six months, and that bartender gal who worked for Gordon, Brenda."

"Bernie."

"Yeah, her."

"Were you with them the whole time on Friday?"

Her head came up at that. "You think one of them might have offed Gordon?"

Actually, I thought she might have, but I said, "It's a possibility."

She sucked on her lower lip. "I'd love to be able to point you at Guinevere, but there's no way she did it. She was still in love with him, the poor sap. I think she only organized the 'outings' because it gave her a chance to see him. If one of his floozies had been pushed off the roof, then, well, okay, I'd nominate Guinevere. The big green monster has her in its grips, but good. But Gordon? No way. Although she did go off looking for him soon after we got there," she mused, cocking her head.

If Guinevere was jealous . . . "How long was she gone?"

"I don't know. Ten, fifteen minutes?"

Long enough. I pulled a green shirt decorated with white embroidery off the rack and held it against my chest. Cute, but not worth the three-figure price.

"One of the other women—Sally? Cindy?—didn't leave the table all night. Must have had a bladder the size of a Volkswagen Beetle. And that Bernie, she didn't get there until late, and then she kind of came and went in between serving drinks."

I wandered back to the counter, where Susan had closed the register and given in to Marshmallow's demands to be cuddled. My phone vibrated with a text alert, but I ignored it, refreshing myself with peppermint tea. Unsure how to work the conversation around to Susan's own movements, but sure that Kinsey Millhone or Sharon McCone would have finessed more information from her, I tried another tack. "I heard you inherit everything," I lied, watching her over the lip of the mug.

"What idiot said that?" she asked indignantly, almost dropping the dog. She set him on the floor, and her face was flushed when she straightened. "Gordon wouldn't leave me his belly button lint. It all goes to Kolby. The market's down, and Gordon's been making some strange financial decisions recently," she groused, "but it should still be in the neighborhood of eight or nine million, all Kolby's."

And he would undoubtedly share generously with his mother, until she pissed him off, that is. "That should take care of his tuition," I observed.

"Oh, he's not going back to college, not now. There's no need." She looked at her watch.

Before she could kick me out, I said, "Is it true that Kolby tried to kill Gordon before? Before Friday night, I mean?"

She slitted her eyes and the warning about mother bears protecting their cubs came back to me. "That is total BS! It was an accident."

To keep my excitement from showing, I stooped to pet Marshmallow. My fingers sank deep into his plushy fur, and his little pink tongue licked at my chin. "Really?"

"Kolby had just gotten his permit. He was only fifteen and a half. Anyone can get 'drive' and 'reverse' mixed up, especially when they're first learning to drive. Gordon should have known better than to stand in front of the car. Kolby barely nudged him. Okay, yeah, he was pinned up against the garage door, but Kolby hit the brakes as soon as he realized it. It was Gordon's own fault that his back got all scraped up because he wouldn't let Kolby try to back up and made him hit the garage door remote to raise the door instead.

"Mrs. Goudge from next door, the old bi—busybody—was the one who called the police. She came outside to fetch her cat in—the nasty animal teases my poor Marshmallow and does his business in my iris bed—and saw the whole thing. She told the police it was attempted murder, but even the police knew that was nonsense. It wasn't the first time she cried wolf. Why, the year after we moved in, she called nine-one-one to say someone had broken into her house, when it was her own son, checking up on her because she wasn't answering her phone. And she reported a pack of kids with weapons one Halloween. It was Halloween, for crying out loud! They were in costume, trick-or-treating, or, at any rate, not doing anything very awful. Teenagers, you know."

She was breathing hard by the end of her recital, clearly still upset by the incident. "Gordon was fine, perfectly fine," she added, "but Kolby was so traumatized by the incident that he refused to get behind the wheel for at least six months. He didn't get his driver's license until he was seventeen, the last of his friends to get one."

Oh, the tragedy of being the last kid with a driver's license. "Huh," was all I could think to say. The way she spun the incident, it certainly sounded like an accident, but what would have happened if the neighbor hadn't come outside?

Susan didn't give me time to think about it. She checked her watch again and said, "Hey, I need to close up. So, if you're not going to buy anything . . . The jeans over there"—she nodded to neat stacks on shelves by the fitting room—"come in a curvy cut."

Hmph. "I don't have time to try them now," I said. "Maybe later in the week."

She followed me to the door to turn over the Closed sign. Marshmallow frisked around her feet, clearly knowing that a walk or ride was forthcoming shortly. "Let me know about that jar," Susan said as I left, "for your brother."

"Will do." Under no circumstances could I see Derek tolerating the humiliation of people slotting dimes and pennies into a jar to pay his lawyer, but I didn't want to spurn Susan's offer outright. Ten steps from the store, I brushed against a mustached man wearing a cowboy hat who rapped at the West of Eden door Susan had just locked. I paused, pretending to answer my phone, and watched as Susan let the man into the store. I heard him say, "Hey, honey bunch," and then the door closed.

Interesting. Susan had a significant other. Gordon was going to turn off the alimony spigot if she remarried, I suspected from Susan's comment, and unless the new man was richer than his worn jeans indicated, that would have meant a reduction in lifestyle. The man in the store with Susan was more than burly enough to have maneuvered Gordon's body over the roof wall. It might be useful to figure out who he was and where he'd been on Friday night. I didn't remember seeing him at the grand opening, but there was a crowd and I might have missed him.

Checking my phone, I read the text I'd received in the store: "Derek home. Family meeting tomorrow at seven so you can come before work." I knew it was from my mom without even checking the sender's phone number; she couldn't bring herself to abbreviate anything, even when texting, and she thought emoticons were a poor substitute for language. I thumbed back a quick "ok. cu@7."

My phone rang. I thought it might be my mom or Derek, but caller ID said "Lola." "Hey, Lo, what's going on?"

"Thank goodness," she said in a breathless voice unlike her usual slow, measured speech. "I'm in a bind. My delivery van won't start and I've still got a load of shrubs to deliver to that new housing development, Jubilee Acres. Is there any chance—?"

"Of course," I said immediately. My van had hauled much stranger things than shrubs in its day. "I'll run home and change and be there in twenty."

"You're a lifesaver, Amy-Faye," she said gratefully.

Chapter 16

When I pulled up at Bloomin' Wonderful, Lola's nursery, she was standing in front of two rows of potted shrubs, an anxious look on her espresso-colored face. Light winked off her glasses as I stopped. Two greenhouses rose behind her, condensation clouding the panes, and several acres of trees, shrubs, and daylilies surrounded us. The Bloomin' Wonderful van squatted under a tree, its hood up, like a yawning pink-and-yellow hippo. A small lavender farmhouse with a welcoming porch sat beyond the greenhouses. I looked for Lola's grandma, frequently to be found shelling peas, shucking corn, or knitting on the porch, but she wasn't there. Misty came running from under the porch when she heard the van and twined around my ankles when I got out. I bent to pat her and she mewed.

"Thank you so much," Lola said, hefting a five-gallon shrub before I'd even opened the van's back doors. "These have to be at the site by six. It's the first time this contractor has bought from me, and I need to keep him happy."

I helped her load the lavender, euonymus, barberry, and Russian sage (none of which I could have identified except for Lola's tutelage over the years), sliding the heavy pots into the van. Misty jumped in to inspect the job we were doing, nosing around.

"Where's Axie?" I asked. I knew her younger sister frequently helped out with Bloomin' Wonderful.

"At a friend's," Lola said, grunting as she lifted a mugho pine into the van. "Move, Misty. She was supposed to put in two hours with me after school, sorting the bulbs that came in yesterday, but she said she had a group project to do for history and that the kids were getting together this afternoon. She begged me to let her go, saying she'd make up her hours on Saturday, but she's been gone long enough to have written the Articles of Confederation or the Versailles Treaty now. I suspect pizza is involved," she added darkly.

I laughed. Lola's fifteen-year-old sister, Axie, short for "the accident," which she preferred to her given name, Violet, was a handful, much more outgoing, social, and reckless than Lola had ever been. With their parents dead in a car crash not long after Axie's birth, Lola and her grandmother had been responsible for raising the girl.

"She should owe you two hours of work, since you're the one giving up her evening to help me," Lola said. She wiped her brow.

"That's not a bad idea," I said, considering it. "I've been thinking about hiring another intern. Business is brisk enough that Al and I can't handle it all. If you think Axie might be interested, and if you can spare her, I could maybe use her a few hours a week. When does she get her driver's license?"

"Two months," Lola said. "God help us all. Out, Misty."

Laughing, I climbed into the van and we headed for the housing development, about two miles past Heaven's eastern border. The heat had bled out of the day by the time we arrived, and the setting sun silvered a pile of metal pipes and irrigation PVC at the entrance to the development. A tracked vehicle squatted, heavy and yellow, beside a shallow ditch. A series of holes were predug around the large stone sign with the bronze lettering announcing JUBILEE ACRES. Two workers, both Hispanic, came over when we stopped and immediately began to unload the plants from the back, gesturing us away when we tried to help. When the containers were off-loaded, one of the workers signed the form Lola handed him, and we took off.

"Thanks, Amy-Faye," Lola said as we made the turn onto the main road. "Let me buy you dinner?"

"Sure," I said.

Since we were grubby and casually dressed, we ended up at a fast-food burger joint. It teemed with rambunctious kids and tired parents, and the table was sticky, but I was hungry enough to overlook it all. I caved to the temptation of a burger and fries, liberally loaded with ketchup. Salad tomorrow, and the rest of the week, I told myself, thinking about the enchiladas I'd had with Doug earlier.

As if she'd read my mind, Lola said, "I hear Doug's back from his cruise."

"Sailing. He was crewing for a buddy with a yacht."

"Must be nice to have a buddy with a yacht," Lola said.

"Indeed."

She sipped tea through her straw and waited. A toddler in the booth behind her started wailing and thumping the bench seat so Lola jolted with every kick.

With a put-upon sigh, I said, "Yes, I saw him. He came by at lunchtime to show me the office he's rented." I told her about his plans.

Giving it some consideration, Lola said, "I think he'll be happier working for himself. I'm sure he was good at playing the corporate game, but Doug always was one to do things his way. Remember that game against Caprock Academy where the coach told him to pass to Donnelly and he ran the ball himself?"

"Won the game and we made it to states," I said, munching on a fry.

"Didn't stop Coach Evans from chewing him out."

We laughed at the memory. Lola, the most discreet and least pushy of my friends, didn't ask if Doug coming to see me so soon after he got back meant anything romantic. Good thing, because I didn't know. I didn't even know if I wanted it to mean anything romantic or not. Doug and I had been over for more than two years—which, admittedly, was only a fraction of the decade-plus we'd been together, off and on. Doug was recovering from being jilted and Hart and I were . . . something. I squeezed my burger so tightly that ketchup leaked out.

The family in the booth behind Lola got up to go—thank goodness—leaving the table looking like a troop of angry baboons had descended on it. Lola checked her cell phone for what must have been the fifth time since we sat down. She apologized and said, "I'm worried about that girl. She's always been such a good student, and pretty responsible, really, but since school started a couple of weeks ago, she's just been . . ." She shrugged, unable to describe her sister's behavior.

"She's what? A sophomore this year?"

Lola nodded. "Uh-huh. And the way her grades are looking, she may be a sophomore again next year, too."

I laughed at Lola's glum tone. "Stop! Axie's a good kid, a smart kid. She might be testing the limits a bit right now, but she'll straighten herself out. We did the same thing when we were fifteen."

"You did. I didn't," Lola said with a smile. "While you were sneaking out to meet Doug, I was putting diapers on Axie."

I could have slapped myself for being so insensitive. Lola's parents died that year and her grandmother needed Lola's help with baby Axie and the house. She'd lived the life of a single teenage mother without the fun of having sex first. "Sorry, Lo," I mumbled.

"Ancient history, A-Faye," she said calmly, slurping the last of her Coke through the straw.

Anxious to turn the subject, I told her about the other events of the day, starting with Derek's arrest and ending with my seeing a man go into Susan Marsh's shop after hours.

"That'd be Gideon Lohmeyer," Lola said, after asking if she could help Derek in any way. "They've been seeing each other for, oh, six or eight months. Gran says they're getting serious."

I stared at her. "Your gran knows the guy Susan Marsh is dating?"

Lola chuckled. "Of course she does. You know Gran! Gideon's mom is part of Gran's quilting circle and from what I can tell they don't talk about anything other than what their kids and grandkids are up to. Gran comes home and shares it all with us. Nancy Diaz and Martin Knipp, among others, would never show their faces in Heaven again if they knew what their moms have been sharing about them. I told Gran I'd leave home and stick her with Axie and the nursery to run if she ever said 'boo' about me to her friends."

Resisting the urge to ask for embarrassing details about Nancy Diaz, who, as Nancy Simpson, had tried to make my life miserable in high school, I asked instead about Gideon.

"He's the foreman on the Double A Ranch," she said, naming a spread about twenty-five miles northwest of Heaven, on the other side of I-70. "Nice guy, from what I hear. Lost his wife a while back. Breast cancer, I think Gran said."

"When you say 'nice guy,' do you mean too nice to help Susan kill Gordon?"

"Amy-Faye!" Lola looked at me, full lips pursed with faint disapproval. "You can't go around saying things like that about perfectly decent folks."

"I'm not *saying*, I'm *asking*," I said. "Big difference. Face it: Someone whacked Gordon over the head and threw him off the roof. Chances are it's someone we think of as a 'nice' guy or gal."

Lola looked troubled. "Since Ivy was poisoned, and now with Gordon's death, I find myself thinking about murder more than I'm comfortable with. And it strikes me that one of the worst things about it, beyond the taking of a life, is the way it rips at the fabric that binds folk together, making them look sideways at each other, question, worry. 'Where was my husband when so-and-so got killed?' 'My best friend had a fight with so-and-so the day before it happened. I wonder . . .' The wonderings are bad."

With Derek in jail, I wasn't in the mood to philosophize. "A murderer walking around loose is worse," I said, crumpling my trash together into a ball on my tray. Lola dropped the subject and looked at her silent phone again. "C'mon," I said. "I'll bet Axie is home by now and she just hasn't called."

When I pulled up outside the farmhouse ten minutes later, Axie came to the door and waved. I gave Lola a "told you so" grin and drove off with a toot of my horn. Getting home at a decent hour for the first time in days, I changed into my jammies, curled up in the den, and debated between the old Eighty-seventh Precinct novel I'd been reading and the Amelia Peabody book I'd read twice before. I went with the latter. I needed lighthearted, not a police procedural. There was too much police procedure in my life right now, as it was.

Chapter 17

Thinking I'd start the family meeting off on the right note, I arrived at the family home the next morning with a box of assorted bagels, and coffee for everyone. From the cars pulled into my parents' driveway, I knew Derek and my sister Peri had beaten me there. There were hugs all around and I hung on to Derek extra long, until he pushed me away and said, "I didn't pull a nickel in Supermax, sis."

He grinned at the look on my face. "A 'nickel' is five years in prison-speak," he explained, "and Supermax is—"

"I know what the Supermax Prison is," I said huffily. "It's where they put people like the Unabomber."

"Supermax—where prisoners check in, but they don't check out," Derek paraphrased the old roach motel commercial.

I guessed it was good he could make jokes about it. He didn't look too bad, considering. No worse than when I last saw him.

"Where's Zach?" I asked Peri. The oldest of us five siblings at thirty-nine (and holding), she lived here in Heaven with her husband, an engineer with the Colorado Department of Transportation, and my only nephew and niece, Blake and Blythe. The Johnson family red hair was more carrot on her, and her pale arms and face were freckly. She'd left college at nineteen to marry Zach and never regretted it. She managed an apartment complex and had an unending supply of funny (and sometimes gross) stories about tenants and their habits.

"Home with the munchkins," she said, smearing an onion bagel with strawberry cream cheese.

Ick.

"Blake took a foot in the face at tae kwon do last night and we had to take him to the urgent-care place. Thought a couple of teeth might be loose. I swear those places would go out of business if it weren't for adolescent boys. We've never had to take Blythe to an ER, but it feels like Blake is in there every other month. They should engrave our names on those nasty plastic chairs in the waiting room. Dr. Dreesen and Dr. Iwata know us by name, and the staff probably has our insurance number memorized."

"Is he okay?" I asked, suspecting I knew the answer from her breezy description of the visit.

"No permanent damage, but he'll be chewing on the left side of his mouth for a while. Zach'll drop them both at school before going to work. Hey, I saw Doug at the City Market. Did you know he's back? Please tell me that you aren't going to get hung up on him again, now that he's single and available, and looking pretty darn good with that tan. Rebound, A-Faye. Rebound. If he comes sniffing around, you keep in mind that that boy's on the rebound and steer clear. You've been doing great since you guys broke it off for real . . . Don't backslide now. I think—"

Luckily, Mom interrupted us before I could tell Peri that I didn't give a hoot what she thought on the topic of my romantic life, or lack thereof. Sisters! I settled for glaring at her as Mom herded us into the dining room. Why did everyone assume I was going to moon over Doug again, just because his marriage fell through? Okay, there might have been one or two—well, maybe four or five—occasions in the past where a similar thing had happened, but I was older and wiser. Plus, there was Hart.

Mom, still in a fluffy pink robe that made her look like one of the old Sno Ball snack cakes, brought our family meeting to order by making us sit around the dining room table, a slab of walnut she and Dad had found at a thrift store shortly after they married. Mom sat at the head of the table with Derek on her left and Dad on her right. I sat beside Derek with Peri beside me.

"Derek's in trouble," Mom announced.

"What's new?" Peri whispered to me. "He's been in trouble since he was two."

I swallowed a chuckle. Even when I was pissed at her, she could always make me laugh.

"His legal issues will be taking up a lot of his time—"

Peri leaned into my ear again. Her breath smelled like strawberries. "Getting sued is a 'legal issue.' Being

188 / Laura DiSilverio

tried for murder is a life-changing catastrophe. Or a great opportunity to write a book, go on the talk shows, and be set for life."

I swatted at her thigh to make her shut up. She straightened with a grin, and Derek sent us a suspicious look.

"—and he'll need to be helping his lawyer plan his defense in case the case goes to trial, which we devoutly hope it won't." She crossed herself. "So he won't be able to spend enough time at the pub to keep it running."

"You're going to close Elysium?" I gasped, getting cream cheese on my elbow when I leaned over my plate to stare at Derek.

"No—" he started.

"Your dad and I are taking over the day-to-day running of the pub," Mom announced, sounding like a general laying out a campaign plan. I tried to equate the rollers in her hair with a general's helmet, but couldn't make it work.

Peri and I looked at Dad, who confirmed it with a nod.

"Derek will still brew the beer, but I'm going to be responsible for food service, employee issues, and heaven knows what else," Mom said. She looked determined, but nervous, too. Forty years as a librarian and writing book reviews had not prepared her for the challenges of running a pub. "Your dad's going to take over the payroll and accounting. We're hoping that you girls can pull some shifts and help out where needed, as well." Her gaze went from Peri to me.

"Of course," we chorused.

"Zach will help, too." Peri recklessly committed her spouse. "Too bad the munchkins are too young to serve liquor. On second thought, the pub will have a better chance of staying in the black if it's not being drained by constant breakage."

"What about Nat and Rae?" I asked. My sister Natalie, the baby of the family, lived in Grand Junction and taught middle school social studies. Rae, the second oldest after Peri, lived in Denver with her partner and worked as an air traffic controller.

"We're going to talk to them about spelling us on weekends, if this drags on," Mom said. "They're too far away to do anything on a routine basis. Derek's going to call them tonight and let them know what the situation is."

Derek leaned forward with his forearms on the table, looking ill at ease. "I just want to say thanks," he said. "To Mom and Dad, especially, but also to you guys." He looked at me and Peri. "Courtney hopes this will never come to trial, but we've got to prepare as if it will, so my head's just not in the right place to be running the pub, you know? And I really need to make a go of it because Courtney's not working for free, for one thing. So, well, just thanks."

"Anytime, baby brother," Peri said, blowing him a kiss.

"I've made out a schedule," Mom said, passing a sheet of paper to each of us.

I looked at it. She had me down to work tonight, which I could manage because Al was handling the library fund-raiser we had organized.

"Let me know if any of the times don't work for you. I know you'll have to play it by ear, Amy-Faye, because of your events. That's okay. It's probably best that you concentrate on finding the real murderer. As long as you can do that without putting yourself in danger, of course. That goes without saying."

She said it so matter-of-factly that her mention of my investigating activities almost passed me by. "What?" I said, a beat late. "You think I can—?"

Dad nodded. "Of course. You've got my logical brain, even if it doesn't work with numbers. You figured out who killed your friend Ivy and we hear you've been making progress with this case. Clarence Uggams called me just last night to ask me to ask you to keep your 'pretty little nose'—that's a quote—out of police business, so you must be doing something right."

"I hope you told Chief Uggams that it's my Constitutional right to stick my nose anywhere I want to, especially when the police aren't following up on leads that might clear my brother's name." I crossed my arms over my chest.

"That's exactly what I told him," Dad said.

Peri and I got up to go. "Keep your chin up, Derek," Peri said, leaning down to give him a hug. "We'll run your pub so good you'll probably want us to stay on permanently. My terms are reasonable—Uncle Derek takes his favorite nephew and niece for a weekend so his favorite sister"—she stuck her tongue out at me— "and her hot husband can spend a weekend alone in Denver, doing what married couples do." She waggled her brows suggestively.

"Argue?" my father guessed.

Mom socked his arm and he rubbed it, saying, "Ow," with a mock-wounded look.

We all laughed, even Derek, and it felt good.

I worked all morning on the library fund-raiser we were in charge of tonight, finishing up the last-minute details that always leap up to bite you in the derriere. Al was going to be the on-site coordinator, the first time he'd been in charge of an event this big on his own. I'd decided a month ago that it was time to show him I trusted him to handle the tough stuff on his own. And I did trust him, mostly, but it still made me nervous to delegate such an important function. If I wanted him to sign on with me permanently, though, I needed to give him more responsibility.

"You up for this?" I asked as he headed out in his hatchback midafternoon, with a binder including the guest list, the evening's schedule, a diagram of the event area, bios for the presenters and special guests, phone numbers for the caterer, the party-supply company, and other vendors we'd hired for the evening, and more.

"I've got this, boss," he said, sounding confident, but tweaking at his polka-dot bow tie the way he did when he was nervous. "I just wish I didn't have a statistics test tomorrow."

"I can fill in—"

"Nope." He held up a hand to stop me. "This is mine. Time to pop my cherry." He blushed. "Er, I mean—"

"I know what you mean," I said, suppressing a grin. "Call me if you need *any*thing. I'll be at the pub, but I can always get away if you need—"

"Will do, boss."

"And stop calling me boss," I yelled after his car as he drove off.

Before he was out of sight, my phone rang. Hart. "Hey," I answered, a smile in my voice.

"Hey back. I saw your brother made bail. I'm glad."

"Yeah, me, too. Anything new?"

"Amy-Faye, you know I can't—"

"I know, I know," I said, walking into my office as I talked. "I thought you might blurt out something useful if I took you by surprise. I guess I'm not up to Hercule Poirot standards yet. Give me time."

He laughed. "Are you doing anything tonight? With the chief back, I'll get off a bit earlier, and I thought we might—"

"I'm bartending at Elysium for Derek," I said. "My parents have taken over running the pub while he's, well, you know. My sister and I are helping out. I'll buy you a beer if you want to drop by, though."

"It's a deal."

Clad in the orange shirt with "Sam" over the pocket, I took charge of the bar again Wednesday night. I felt more comfortable behind the bar tonight, maybe because I knew my way around, or maybe because we were all pulling together to help Derek. The orange upholstery was warmly welcoming inside, and the setting sun and cooling air made the outside patio equally hospitable. Mom was in the kitchen, talking to the cooks and figuring out what happened back there, and Dad was in Derek's office, familiarizing himself with the accounting system. There were more customers than there'd been last Wednesday when I filled in, and I took that as a positive sign, even though I knew some of them might only have been ghouls attracted by Friday's tragedy.

Bernie reported for her shift on time, and grinned at the sight of me slicing lemons and limes. "Just can't stay away from here, can you?" she said.

I started to explain what we were doing, but she said, "Yeah, I know. Your mom called earlier. I'm guessing she called all the employees. I think it's great that you all are sticking by Derek like this. When I got myself in trouble and Billy was on the way, my folks gave me the old heave-ho." She didn't sound bitter, but I eyed her as she pulled her round serving tray out from under the counter.

"How is Billy?" I asked.

"You know those Mayhem commercials for some insurance company? That's Billy. Things around him seem to erupt or explode or cave in, but he always walks away from it, even if on crutches or in a cast sometimes. Gawd. Take my advice: Girls are the way to go. What I wouldn't give for a daughter I could dress in those cute Gymboree dresses, who wanted to play quietly with Barbies or jacks."

I laughed, thinking of my niece, who was anything but quiet, and who was already a standout on the baseball team where she was the only girl. Before I could answer, a customer summoned Bernie and she took off, going into flirt-for-tips mode. The kitchen door opened and, to my astonishment, Kolby Marsh came out, clad in the orange Elysium Brewing Polo shirt and khakis. He slouched toward the bar and sent me a glance I couldn't read from the corners of his eyes.

"What are *you* doing here?" I blurted.

"I work here," he said, trying to sound nonchalant and failing.

I searched my brain. Had Derek told me Kolby had quit, or had I just assumed it? "Why?" I asked. "Your mom told me that you're going to inherit millions and that you've quit college."

"'Going to,'" Kolby said, snitching a lemon from the divided dish and sucking on it. He screwed up his face. "Turns out, I don't get the money right away. It's going to take, like, months even. Probate or something. I need something to live on in the meantime. And a place to live. Mom's moving in with that dude she's been dating, and I'm out on the street. That dude Mom's marrying, the cowpoke"—he gave the word a derogatory twist—"he's convinced Mom that working is good for me, told her I should stand on my own two feet for at least a few months before I never have to work again. He's worse than Dad. Said he could get me work on the ranch, mucking stalls or some such shit. Not the Kolbymeister, nosiree. I told him where he could stick his pitchfork. Mom was giving me grief about it, but I told her the job here was as much as I could handle and that I felt a responsibility to help out since the pub was important to Dad. She bought it." He tried to suppress the look that said his mother was a sap, and failed. "Of course, I'll need a salary now, but I figure Derek and me can come to terms, since he only has this place because of my dad."

Few things would have given me greater pleasure than to toss Mr. Entitlement out on his ear, but it wasn't my place. We were short-staffed as it was, and Mom was in charge in Derek's absence. I made a mental note to give her a heads-up about Kolby. "My mom's managing the pub for the moment," I told him, "so you'll have to negotiate salary with her."

Kolby's smile slipped slightly, but then he sauntered to a nearby booth and began taking orders. I made a pitcher of margaritas, a Bloody Mary, and a virgin daiquiri for one of Bernie's tables while he was gone, and when he returned to the server station, I said, "I never told you how sorry I am about your dad. Everything was so chaotic that night, with the police and everything, but I'm really sorry. It's got to be rough."

He looked at me through the fringe of dark blond hair. "That night was rough. Man! I've never been through anything like that. When I found him like that . . . I blew chunks. I'm not ashamed to admit it." He looked slightly paler.

"How did you manage to find him? I mean, why were you out at the Dumpster, in the rain?" A server's duties didn't take him or her out to the Dumpster, in the normal course of events.

His eyes slid away from mine, but then his mouth took on a sly twist. "Sometimes a man needs a break." He mimed holding a marijuana joint between his thumb and forefinger and sucked air noisily between pursed lips. "Know what I mean? I've got some good stuff and I'm willing to share." He leaned toward me and leered. "I'm going to be a very, very rich man, you know."

Humanity would go the way of the dodo before I would date Kolby Marsh. "You were out back getting high? Alone?"

"What can I say? The babes find the Kolby-meister irresistible. Just wait until they get a load of me in my new Ferrari California T. It's got a turbocharged V-8, a triple fence diffuser, and a T-top." He mimed one hand on the steering wheel with his arm resting along an open window. "I've already got one picked out. The color's called 'Rosso California.' That's red. The salesman is just waiting for me to give him the go-ahead. You can call shotgun now for the first time I take her for a spin." He winked, picked up his tray, and delivered it to his table.

I hadn't so much as touched his hand, but I felt the urge to wash mine. I did, lathering heavily, and wondering if Kolby was telling the truth. Had he really gone outside for a toke? Entirely possible. I found it harder to believe he'd convinced some girl to go with him in the pouring rain. I was mulling it over when a man's voice said, "Can a guy get some service around here?"

I jerked around, dropping the towel I was using to dry my hands. "Doug! I didn't know you were coming tonight." He sat on a stool, arms on the bar, grinning with pleasure at having surprised me. He had ditched his suit jacket and tie, but still wore a white Oxford shirt and slacks as though he'd come from the office.

"And I didn't know you were moonlighting as a bartender." He smiled. "I'll have an Angel Ale, please."

As I poured the brew and waited for the head to subside, I told him why I was there. "I can take a shift, too," he said immediately, "if you guys need me to. Who knows what kind of legal business I could pick up by sliding my card under each stein or pitcher?"

I was touched, and smiled at him gratefully. "That's really kind, Doug. Talk to my mom." I placed the glass mug in front of him, and declined his twenty. "On me."

Swiveling so his back was to me, he surveyed the pub and announced, "I like this place. It's got a nice feel. Homey, but funner." He spun back around.

"I don't think 'funner' is a word."

"'Livelier,' then."

Playing with synonyms made me think of Al and I wondered how the library event was going. I checked my phone, but there were no calls or texts from him. Maybe I should just cruise by the library to see—? I took a deep breath and made myself believe the event was going swimmingly. I couldn't leave. The crowd noise was increasing, people getting louder as happy hour wore on and they had more to drink. Over Doug's shoulder I saw the door open. Two women strolled in, followed by Lindell Hart. His eyes found mine across the crowd and he smiled. I smiled back. Doug turned to see whom I was smiling at.

"That's the new detective, right?"

"Right."

Hart had threaded his way through the crowd to us by then, and he shook hands with Doug. "Good to see you again, Elvaston." The two men presented a contrast. Doug, blond, handsome, shorter, and more compact. Hart, with his curly brown hair, taller and lankier, wearing jeans and a University of Georgia T-shirt. I felt a little awkward, seeing them together like this, but they didn't display any self-consciousness. Maybe Hart hadn't heard that Doug and I used to be a thing. Doug knew I was dating Hart because I'd told him so, even before it was true, not wanting to go to his wedding without a date.

Doug's brow crinkled and I knew he was trying to figure out where they'd met.

"The wedding," Hart supplied. "Sorry it didn't work out, man."

I liked that he tackled the tough subject casually, brought it out in the open as though it was nothing to be ashamed of. Which, of course, it wasn't. Not for anyone besides Madison.

Doug gave a rueful smile. "Better before the rings get put on than after, right? I hope you enjoyed the reception at least. My folks said it was a great party, even without a bride and groom. I heard the band's lead singer got drunk and fell off the stage—broke his thumb."

Hart took a swallow from the beer I'd poured him. "I didn't go. My date had to drive you to Denver, and I didn't think it'd be much fun on my own."

"That's right. You were there with Amy-Faye. Her plus one."

Was the look he was giving Hart an assessing one? I ducked away from the conversation to refill drinks along the bar and to take an order for the pub's signature burger from the middle-aged man at the far end. When I drifted back to Hart and Doug, they were deep into a discussion of the upcoming college football season, and they hardly acknowledged my return. A tad miffed, I wiped down the bar and collected dirty mugs, offering my thoughts on the Buffs' chances as I worked. Finally, some friends hailed Doug from a table and he excused himself to join them.

"Nice guy," Hart observed as Doug left.

"We've been friends a long time," I said.

"So I've heard." His eyes smiled at me. I must have looked a little flustered, because he added, "It's a small town."

"Yeah, I noticed."

He began to relate a story about a traffic stop earlier in the day that was complicated when the pet ferret in the car bit the officer giving its owner a ticket. I laughed and reciprocated by telling him about letting Al run the library fund-raiser on his own. "It's hard for me to let go," I confessed. "I guess I'm something of a control freak."

"Probably a good trait for an event organizer," Hart said. He hesitated, and then asked, "How's your brother holding up?"

"As well as can be expected, I guess," I said, appreciating that he was willing to skirt the edge of our "don't discuss the case" agreement by asking about Derek.

"I've heard good things about his lawyer. Word is she doesn't back down," he said.

"I got that feeling from her."

Before the conversation could veer to more neutral topics, my mom pushed through the kitchen's swinging door and headed toward us. Before the pub ever opened, Derek had gotten my folks orange shirts like the uniform shirt I wore. Mom's XXXL shirt made her look like a vast pumpkin, and had the phrase SHE WHO MUST BE OBEYED printed where her name should have gone. Little did Derek know when he did that as a joke that it would soon be true; as far as the pub went, Mom was the big boss now.

I introduced Hart to Mom and they chatted for a minute before Mom turned to me. "I've been told that this place hasn't been cleaned since you ran off that janitor three days ago. Not that I blame you after what he did to the grand opening. And he might have murdered Gordon, after all. Not a desirable employee at all."

I resisted the urge to look at Hart when she said that. I was half hoping he'd say whether or not he'd found Foster and what the janitor had said, but he remained silent.

Mom asked, "Do you have any recommendations for a service I could hire?"

I pulled out my phone and read her off the numbers of two companies I had used in the past. She didn't need to write them down; she'd always been able to memorize numbers.

"In the meantime, I'm afraid . . ." She trailed off and looked at me meaningfully. It took me a moment to catch on.

"Mo-om! You know I hate cleaning toilets."

"It's for your brother, dear," she said. "Just for tonight, until I can hire someone new."

"Fine," I grumbled, "but I'm not touching the men's room. Dad can do that."

Mom chuckled, the sound rich and cheering, and agreed that Derek or Dad could be responsible for the men's room. "The kitchen staff and I have got a handle on the kitchen," she said. "Once I explained to them that they wouldn't have jobs if the health inspector closed us down, they pulled out the Lysol and elbow grease." With a triumphant smile, she made her way back to the kitchen.

Hart hid a smile in his almost-empty beer glass and refused a second when I offered. "Feisty woman, your mom. I see where you get it."

"Hmph."

We chatted in between my bartending duties for another fifteen minutes and then he stood to go. He surprised me by leaning across the bar to kiss me lightly on the lips. "It feels weird to leave you a tip," he murmured, "so maybe this will do instead."

"Much better than twenty percent of nothing," I agreed, tingling with the effervescence that bubbled up in me every time he touched me.

I watched him go until the door closed behind him, and then I looked around. I realized with a start that Doug was gone and I hadn't even noticed when he'd left.

Chapter 18

My Thursday morning started with a breakfast meeting I'd organized for the Chamber of Commerce. Accordingly, it was after ten by the time I got to the office. Approaching the French doors from the garden, I noticed blobs of color seemingly floating around the office. I picked up my pace, puzzled and a little concerned. I opened the door on a forest of balloons trailing long ribbons. One drifted out and up before I could snag it.

"Close the door!" Al's voice came from behind a wall of latex globes.

I closed it. A strange hissing came from the direction of his desk. "What on earth—?"

I batted the balloons out of my path and saw Al, operating the lever on a helium tank. "Gilda at Balloons-r-Us had a family emergency," he said, tying off the inflated balloon and affixing a yellow ribbon tail. "She apologized in about eight languages and said we could have the helium tank for the day. No charge for any of this." He gestured widely and the balloons floated across the reception area like colorful ghosts. "I think Timothy will like them, don't you?"

"What seven-year-old doesn't like balloons?" I asked. "How'd it go last night?"

"Perfectly."

"Flawlessly?"

"Faultlessly."

I beamed at him. "Of course it did. I never had a moment's doubt."

"Ha! I know you checked your phone at least eight times, and probably got in the van twice to come over to the library." He smiled to show that he didn't mind that I had been the eensy-teensiest bit worried.

"I did not get in the van," I said with great dignity. "I served beers, blended margaritas, and cleaned toilets with nary a thought for you."

He snorted, but then asked, "Toilets?"

I explained.

"You're a good sister."

The sincerity in his voice touched me. "I try to be," I said, feeling awkward.

"I'm pretty sure my sister would rather visit me in jail than clean a toilet on my behalf," he said cheerfully, clearly bearing his sister no ill will. "In fact, I don't know if she knows how to clean a toilet. We shared a bathroom growing up, and the best thing about moving into the dorms was no more smelly, pink, powdery girlie stuff in my bathroom."

"Just good old man-stink and mildew, right?"

"Right." He grinned.

There was a knock on the door. I waded through the balloons to open it, surprised to find Courtney Spainhower, Derek's lawyer, standing on the patio.

"I was getting a cup of tea at the Divine Herb"—she held up the imprinted cup as proof—"and thought I'd stop by to see if you had time to talk about your brother's case."

"Sure. Come in."

She cast a curious look at the balloons and I explained about the birthday party we were responsible for this evening.

"I guess you've got to be able to tackle anything, if you're an event organizer," she said, considering.

"Pretty much. Livestock, feuding relatives, nudity, food fights, incontinence, fires, floods . . . I've dealt with it all."

"I can see what Derek means when he says you're the most amazingly competent person he's ever known."

"He said that? Derek? My brother?"

Courtney laughed. "Cross my heart."

My second warm fuzzy of the day.

I introduced her to Al, who looked smitten with her dark beauty, and led her into my office. "Nice," she said, gazing at my table desk, whiteboard, window, lemon walls, and green chairs. "Refreshing. I have an office smaller than my pantry at home, with file folders piled to head height against one wall and my desk against the other with about eight inches to push my chair back. If I gain five pounds, I won't be able to squeeze into my chair."

I laughed and invited her to sit in one of the grass green club chairs. I joined her, rather than sitting at my desk. Pulling a bulky accordion folder from her briefcase, she opened it and spread some papers on the table between us. "You know, Amy-Faye—may I call you Amy-Faye?"

"Of course."

She smiled. "The police actually did your brother a favor by arresting him, I think."

My brows soared. "Really? How so?"

"The lead detective, Detective Hart, has been very forthcoming with discovery, turning over documents and reports to the defense. That's me and Derek."

I knew what discovery was from reading so many legal thrillers. What I gathered from those books was that the police and prosecution usually tried to delay turning over documents the law required them to provide to the defense, or inundate the defense with so much extraneous paper that the defense team had to waste thousands of billable hours sorting through coal to get at the diamond.

"If he hadn't arrested Derek, I wouldn't have access yet to all this"—she waved a hand over the piles of paper—"that lets me know who the police have talked to, who had what alibis, what investigatory paths they wandered down, et cetera. If you have time, I thought we could go over some of it together, since you've also done a fair amount of investigating on Derek's behalf."

"Sure." I felt warmly toward Hart for playing fair with my brother's case and turning over the documents. I was eager to dive into his reports and find out the sorts of things it took a badge to discover. Telling Al to handle anything that came up, and refilling my coffee cup, I kicked off my shoes and plunged in, sitting on the floor to have easier access to all the documents. Without hesitation, Courtney joined me, sitting cross-legged.

I left the autopsy report to Courtney (since I'd already had access, via Maud, to a purloined copy) and started in on the witness statements. There were at least a couple of hundred, I figured, riffling through them—most of the grand opening attendees. I yanked the ones I was most interested in: all of Gordon's relatives (Susan and Kolby Marsh, and Angie and Gene Dreesen), the WOSC contingent, and Foster. They were the ones I knew had a serious grudge against Gordon, or who benefited financially from his death. After a second's thought, I pulled Derek's statement, too.

Courtney produced a couple of legal pads and I took one to draw a timeline on. I read through the witness reports with an eye for who had been where when. Motive is all well and good, but opportunity is equally if not more important. I must have picked that piece of wisdom up from a police procedural. I decided to tune into my inner J. P. Beaumont, Jance's Seattle cop, as I read.

No one admitted to being on the roof at any point in the evening. Surprise. Angie Dreesen and Kolby and Foster were at the pub by six o'clock for the preparty. The WOSCers arrived right at seven—I'd seen them myself. The two whose names I didn't know turned out to be Sally Braverman from Fruita and Veronica

Kuykendal from a Denver suburb. I put them all on my timeline. So far, so good. From there, everything got hazy. From what I could tell, no one could produce any witnesses who could account for every minute of their time during the party. People mingled, went to the bathroom or the bar, and generally behaved the way people do at a party that's not a sit-down dinner. Shoot.

Courtney finished with the autopsy report and helped herself to a couple of the witness interviews as I tackled Foster's statement. It was unilluminating. His last name was Quinlan and he'd been at the pub since midday, prepping for the opening. His definition of "prepping" had been different from mine, I knew now. After the party started, people reported seeing glimpses of "a janitor" but mostly couldn't nail down the times. A kitchen worker mentioned seeing him by the Dumpster shortly before seven o'clock. In and of itself, that didn't mean much because he was probably hauling trash out to the Dumpsters on and off all day and evening, when he wasn't blowing up microwaves. On the other hand, maybe he was checking on Gordon, assuring himself that he hadn't survived the fall. Stapled to his statement was my statement about our encounter, the log of a call from his wife reporting him missing when he didn't come home Sunday night after our talk in Elysium's kitchen, and an officer's write-up of finding him intoxicated in the Lost Alice Lake gazebo at noon on Monday. I made a note to talk to Foster's wife.

One or another of the WOSCers claimed to have been with Susan Marsh all evening. Except for a five-minute bathroom visit, she hadn't left the corner table until the fire alarm sounded. No one had seen her during the evacuation, but that was after the ME's time of death, so it probably didn't matter.

Courtney interrupted me. "I kind of liked Gene Dreesen for it; he and his wife, Gordon's stepsister, Angie, went off the rails when their daughter died, saying Gordon was culpable, accusing him of driving the car when it crashed, and basically making out like he was responsible for everything from ISIS to Ebola. Additionally, Gene's accounting firm used to have a lock on all of GTM's business—thousands of billable hours a year—but Gordon yanked it all away after Gene and Angie filed a civil suit against him related to Kinleigh's death. Left Gene with a bunch of egg on his face in front of his partners. But he's got an alibi." She waved the page. "He got to the pub around seven thirty, after the window the ME established for Gordon's death. There's a note here that says his alibi checked out: He left his office late and stopped to help a motorist with a flat tire. The police talked to the driver, who corroborates the times." She set the page down with a disappointed look.

"Angie's time isn't so closely accounted for," I said, riffling through the pile until I found the right statement. "She was gone for twenty or thirty minutes soon after the party started; she said she was having 'digestive system difficulties'—you suppose that means diarrhea?— and had been in the second-floor bathroom."

"Maybe she's anorexic." Courtney mimed putting a finger down her throat.

"She's tiny," I agreed. "There's no way she could

have thrown Gordon from the roof by herself. How about if she had an accomplice who wasn't her hubby?"

Courtney scrunched her face doubtfully. "Like who?"

I shrugged, not having a suspect in mind. I read farther down the form. "Anyway, she rejoined the party before her husband arrived—several witnesses, including my folks, corroborate that—and they left together. I saw them get into the car myself."

Courtney had been only half listening to my last remarks and now read from another document, rectangular reading glasses perched on the end of her elegant nose. "The police haven't found the weapon, but they describe it as metal, approximately one half inch to one inch in diameter."

I circled my thumb and forefinger to what I thought was an inch and then shrank the circle to half an inch. "So, a golf club shaft," I said, thinking of the clubs in Gordon's office. Surely the police would have tested them.

"Or a tire iron, or a cane."

"An umbrella? There were lots of them around Friday night."

Courtney considered, but then shook her head. "I wouldn't think so. Too light, right? You could poke someone's eye out, but I wouldn't think you could knock someone unconscious with one."

"How about a mop handle!" I said.

Courtney caught on immediately. "The janitor. Do you have his statement?"

I passed it to her with a comment about how much

Foster had hated Gordon. She read it with a speed I envied; *Moby-Dick* wouldn't have been such a slog if I could have read that quickly. The skill had probably served her well in law school.

"Hmm, he certainly bears further scrutiny. I'll have my investigator look at him more closely—background, work history, financials."

We worked side by side for another hour, and my timeline still had more bare spots than a monk's head when Al rapped on the door and brought in two bags from the Divine Herb. The room filled with the mouthwatering smells of pastrami and chicken. "Thought you might be hungry," he said, his adoring eyes on Courtney.

"You are so kind." She took a bag with a smile and I thought he was going to melt into a puddle.

"Ahem." I cleared my throat and he all but tossed me the other bag without taking his eyes off Courtney. "Don't you have class this afternoon?" I reminded him.

He started. "Accounting. Oh, right. I'm going to be late. Nice to meet you, Miss Spainhower." He bolted.

"Any messages from this morning?" I called after him.

"Nothing important." The door slammed.

Courtney was already back into the documents. She sat cross-legged on the floor, munching her sandwich while she read. Tucking a comma of dark hair behind her ear, she said, "I like the son for it." She looked up. "He's inheriting millions and Doretta, my investigator, says there was no love lost between them. Kolby's classmates and friends all say he hated his dad for leaving him and his mom, talked about what he'd do with the money when it was his, and was generally a weaselly person, not above stealing from friends or cheating on tests. People at the college don't seem to like him much."

I told Courtney about Kolby maybe accidentally-on-purpose running Gordon down when he was sixteen. While she mulled that over, I pulled his statement from my pile and scanned it quickly. He hadn't mentioned marijuana to the police as his reason for being outside, or the girl he'd tried to tell me he'd been smoking dope with. I summarized what he'd said for Courtney. "He told me he went out to smoke a joint with some girl, but he told the police he was taking a trash bag out. Ha! Not likely. He barely did his own job and I can't see him volunteering to help the kitchen staff."

Courtney got an alert expression, as though something I'd said had struck a chord. "Marijuana, marijuana," she muttered, flipping through some papers still in her briefcase. "Here it is."

The page she showed me was a line drawing of the Elysium Brewing rooftop with dimensions annotated and little squares drawn to represent the shed, the planters, and the AC unit. Neat numbers freckled the page and corresponded with a list attached on the second page. Studying it, I realized it listed all the items found and marked at the scene by the crime scene technicians. Cigarette butts made up at least half the list.

"Number twenty-two," Courtney said, pointing.

"'Marijuana joint, half inch,'" I read. "Kolby! He was toking up on the roof. He could've gotten into it with his father, lost his temper, and pushed him off."

"We don't know when he was up there," Courtney pointed out. "He could have dropped that joint days or even weeks earlier. Judging by the number of cigarette butts, no one ever swept the roof. And even if he was in the habit of sneaking a joint on the roof now and then, it doesn't rule out the possibility that he also liked to smoke behind the Dumpster on occasion."

I reluctantly conceded her point, but added, "I still think he was lying about why he was out there."

"Most people lie," Courtney said cynically. "The trick is sorting out what they're lying about and why. People might lie about their whereabouts at the time of the crime because they were having an affair, or doing a line of coke, or something else embarrassing or criminal, not because they were involved in the crime being investigated. It didn't take me more than one case as an associate to realize that. I'll bet you there's a lie in every one of those statements. Except yours, of course," she added politely.

"And Derek's!"

She remained silent and studied the page in her hand.

I studied her, hovering between anger and curiosity. "You think Derek lied to the police about something? What?"

"I don't know, but he was drunk and facing a tough situation when they interviewed him that night. It would be miraculous if there weren't any . . . discrepancies."

"Discrepancies" sounded so much better than the *L* word. "Will you be able to get him off?" I asked.

She gave me a straight look. "Probably. The scene was chaotic, lots of people had motive and opportunity, there are no witnesses—juries love witnesses, even though they're notoriously unreliable—and the only physical evidence is Gordon's blood on Derek's shirt, and I've got a plan for handling that. On the downside, several people, including you, know he and Gordon were fighting about money and how to run the pub, and he gets that million-dollar insurance payout."

Big downsides. I eyed the striking lawyer curiously. It was none of my business, but I asked anyway. "Are you and Derek . . . ?"

"Derek and I are lawyer and client," Courtney said with an enigmatic smile. "Look, I've got a meeting in half an hour, so I've got to go." She rose to her feet in one graceful movement and began to gather the documents together.

After showing her out, I threaded my way through the balloons and worked hard on upcoming events until five o'clock.

Chapter 19

This being Thursday, I headed for movie night with the Readaholics. When the book we were reading had been made into a movie, we usually watched it together after we discussed the book. Movie nights were usually at Maud's or Brooke's, because they had the nicest TV-viewing setups. Brooke, of course, had a full-up home theater with stadium seating and a projection screen. Maud had a big-screen TV in her living room, which had ample seating. You had to take a sweater, though, because her house was always chilly. Lola didn't even own a TV and Roman and his buddies usually took over Kerry's television for their Xbox games.

Driving to Maud's, I thought through the case, wishing I'd had time to read more of the documents Hart had turned over to Courtney. The thought made me think of him, and as I pulled into Maud's driveway, I dialed his number.

"Thank you," I said when he answered.

"For what?"

"Arresting Derek."

He choked on a laugh. "I never thought I'd hear you say that."

"I never thought I'd say it," I admitted, "but Courtney Spainhower explained about discovery and mentioned that the HPD was really cooperative about turning over documents and reports, and whether you thought that through before you arrested Derek, or you're just being decent, I appreciate it."

"If it comes to trial, I'll have to testify," Hart warned me.

"It won't come to trial," I said with more confidence than I felt. "And if it does, Courtney will tear you apart on the stand, shred your testimony, and make you wish you'd decided to open a bakery instead of become a cop." I let a little humor creep into my voice to show that I was kidding . . . sort of.

"She can try." Hart's tone said he didn't think she'd succeed. "It's not exactly my first go-round as the lead investigator in a homicide, you know, and I rather suspect it is Ms. Spainhower's first appearance as lead counsel on a murder-one case. Let's hope it doesn't come to trial."

"Amen." I realized that a trial would almost certainly end my just-beginning relationship with Hart. Whether or not Derek got convicted, I was sure I wouldn't be able to get the images of Hart testifying against him out of my mind. I could tell myself until the cows came home that he was only doing his job, but Derek was my brother. The thought crushed me and I struggled for something to say. Kerry's Outback pulled up to the curb and she got out. "I've got to go," I said.

"Thanks for calling," Hart said, his rising inflection asking if we were okay.

"Sure," I said, not feeling sure about anything.

"Any chance of seeing you Friday night?"

"I've got a bachelorette party."

"Wow, that was sudden. Who's the lucky guy?"

I laughed, feeling lighter again. "No one you know—he's from Oklahoma. The bride is a sorority sister of Brooke's. It's a hen party, of course, but I could maybe sneak you in if you want to wear a cop uniform and take it off while singing 'I'm Too Sexy for My Shirt.'"

Hart made a gagging sound, and I rang off, still laughing, and got out of the van to greet Kerry.

Inside, the happy aroma of popcorn pulled us into Maud's living room, where she, Lola, and Brooke had already staked out positions on the charcoal gray sectional sofa. I sat on the floor with my back against the sofa, between Lola and Brooke, because I didn't like the couch's too-squashy cushions. The opening credits for the movie were frozen on the huge television screen.

"We're having sidecars tonight, in honor of the Orient Express," Maud said, waving to a tray with martini glasses filled with a golden yellow drink. "They're a classic 'thirties cocktail with cognac, Cointreau, and lemon juice. I never thought I'd find a way to use the Cointreau someone gave Joe for his birthday two or three years ago, but this fits the bill nicely." She held a glass up to the light. "I remember my mom drinking them, with a precious little spiral of lemon rind. I'm not the garnish type, so you'll have to make do." She urged us toward the tray. "It would be more authentic if we had a steward to bring them to us, but I'm afraid we'll have to settle for self-service."

We laughed. When everyone had a drink, Maud dimmed the lights and clicked the remote. The rumble of the train, the elegance of the 1930s costumes and hairstyles, and the edgy tension of the dialogue held us spellbound for the first half of the movie, although there were some complaints about the casting.

"They did a good job casting the men," Kerry said, crunching on popcorn, "but the women—good grief! Lauren Bacall as an 'elderly' American lady, who I pictured as overweight, and Ingrid Bergman as a woman the book described as having a 'sheeplike' face. Come on! There is nothing in the world less sheeplike than Ingrid Bergman."

"Jacqueline Bisset is lovely as the young countess," Lola said.

"Albert Finney makes a good Poirot," Maud put in. "Arrogant and obnoxious."

"Shush," I commanded, trying to catch the dialogue.

"It would be easier to find Gordon Marsh's real murderer if you had a finite set of suspects," Kerry observed later during a quiet moment. "Poirot had it easy—no one could come and go."

"True," I said. "I drew up a timetable today, like Poirot did. Here." I had made copies of it and I passed them out, explaining about Courtney and the discovery materials she had shared with me. "I'm afraid it doesn't help much. This other page"—I passed it out—"is the crime scene sketch that was in the file."

"You know," Lola said slowly, studying the latter, "I don't know if I could have dragged a man Gordon's size fifteen or twenty feet and then gotten him up and over the wall, and I'm stronger than most women."

Biting my lip, I nodded in agreement. Lola wasn't tall, but she had muscular arms and legs, a product of hauling heavy plants and sacks of fertilizer and soil around all day at Bloomin' Wonderful.

"She's got a point," Maud said. "Gordon must have weighed—what?—two twenty, at least? And a dead body is just plain awkward. I've only got experience with deer and elk, of course, but moving a body is not like lifting a nice, stable weight bar at the gym."

"We should try it," Brooke announced, startling me. "We need to know if we can rule out the women suspects."

I turned to look at her. "We should try throwing someone off the pub roof?"

"No." She laughed, but didn't look any less determined. "We try an experiment here. How high was the wall?"

I held my hand just below my rib cage. "About here."

"Okay. Maud, do you have anything around here that's about that height?"

Maud thought for a moment, upper lip pushing out over the lower. "I think the deck rail's just a bit lower."

Kerry, getting into the spirit of the experiment,

asked, "Who's going to be Gordon? None of us weigh anything like two twenty."

Mischief sparkled in Maud's pale blue eyes. "Joe's home." She disappeared down the hallway and reappeared a moment later with Joe Wrobleski, a rumpled-looking guy of her height and age, sporting a closely trimmed, mostly gray beard.

"I hear you need a guinea pig," he said good humoredly, his voice a bass rumble.

"Do you mind?" Brooke asked.

Like most males, he was not proof against her hopeful green eyes. "Heck no. I was only watching a *Big Bang* rerun."

"To the deck," Brooke said, twirling her hand over her head and pointing.

We trooped through the kitchen and out the back door onto the deck. Only a thin line of yellow showed on the western horizon, so Maud turned on a light so we could see what we were doing. It startled a great horned owl that took off from a lodge pole pine near Maud's boat shed. Moving the picnic table and grill, which took up most of the room on the deck, we cleared a space for Joe to lie down.

"He needs a towel," I said, "so he won't get splinters when we drag him."

"Good thinking." Maud whisked away and came back with a ratty army blanket, which she folded into a pad and spread on the deck.

"Okay," Brooke said, apparently appointing herself director, "who wants to be the murderer?"

"Should I be faceup or facedown?" Joe interrupted, lowering himself to the blanket with an audible creak from his knees.

We looked at one another. "I don't think it matters," I finally said. "Faceup will probably be more comfortable, since we're going to drag you."

"Absolutely," Kerry said. When no one moved forward to be the murderer, she said, "Oh, heavens, I'll do it." She positioned herself behind Joe's head, reached down, and hooked her hands under his armpits. Her bangs flopped into her eyes and she tossed her head impatiently so she could see. In a crouch, she began to drag him across the deck. Joe stiffened initially, but when Brooke ordered him to go limp, he let his head loll and asked, "How's this?"

"Corpses don't talk," Maud reminded him.

Corpses don't have muscle control, either, but I noticed he gripped handfuls of the blanket in either fist so it slid along with him and he didn't get pulled off it.

Kerry was breathing hard after five steps and grunting before she was halfway to the rail. She paused, lowering Joe to the deck. "You're sure you only weigh two twenty?" she asked the corpse.

Without opening his eyes, he mumbled, "Two fourteen this morning," from the side of his mouth.

Trying a new approach, she hooked her elbows under his calves and began to drag him. She managed to get to the deck rail with only a couple of complaints from the corpse about splinters, but we could all tell there was no way she was going to be able to maneuver him to waist height and dump him over. Wiping sweat from her brow with the back of her hand, Kerry said, "There have got to be easier ways to kill someone."

Maud handed her her drink. "Let me see if I can get him up in a fireman's rescue carry."

With a great deal of effort, Maud finally managed to get Joe slumped over her shoulder, head down her back, her arm clamped around the back of his thighs at chest level. To his credit, Joe didn't object once, not even when he started to slip and we all jumped forward to wedge him against her shoulder. She staggered to the deck rail with him and tried to heft him up and forward enough to get him over the rail.

"Ow," Joe complained as she banged his spine against the wood.

After two more tries, Maud told him to stand up. He brushed himself off and rubbed his back. "This has given me a new perspective on hazardous occupations," he said. "Next time I'm inching down a canyon wall to get a shot of cliff swallows, I'll remember this and not complain."

"You were a good sport," Brooke said.

"A strong man might just have been able to get him over the railing," said Lola, who'd stood a bit away observing the whole process like the scientist she was, "but I have trouble seeing any woman managing it on her own."

"She'd have blood on her, too," Brooke pointed out, "if she'd done that rescue carry. And her clothes and hair would be a mess. Surely someone would have noticed if a woman disappeared for twenty minutes or so and then came back looking like she'd been wrestling a bear?"

"Hey," Joe objected.

"I meant a very handsome, gentle bear." Brooke smiled at him.

"That's okay, then," he said. He drew his hands down his beard to smooth it. "The corpse needs a drink. What's that you're having?"

Once Joe had a sidecar, we reassembled in the living room. "I still think it was more than one person," Maud said stubbornly. "It's too awkward for one person alone, even a man."

"You might be right," Kerry said reluctantly (because she hated to agree with Maud on anything conspiracy-related). "If so, who are the obvious coconspirators?"

"Kolby and Susan," I said.

"I nominate the WOSCers," Maud said. "Hell hath no fury like a woman scorned, never mind dozens of women scorned."

"I'll keep that in mind," Joe teased. He sat beside her, their thighs touching, and their obvious respect and affection for each other made me happy.

"His sister and her husband had the most visceral motive," Lola said. "They think he's responsible for their daughter's death. I'm a Christian woman, and Axie's my sister, not daughter, but I'd sure want to hurt anyone who hurt her." Her eyes behind her glasses were quite fierce.

"Angie's too small and he's got an alibi," I pointed out.

Lola's shrug said she wasn't convinced.

"Anyone know Gene Dreesen, Angie's husband?" I asked.

"He's an accountant," Brooke said. "He does the books for the dealership, but I've never met him."

How would Hercule Poirot finagle a meeting with a suspect? He'd march in and introduce himself as the world's greatest detective. That wasn't going to work for me. What would Lydia Chin do? Or V. I. Warshawski? Before I could figure that out, Kerry interrupted my thoughts.

"Money makes the world go round," Kerry said, pulling off a clip earring and massaging her earlobe. "I'm with Amy-Faye. I think it was the ex and the son. They're the ones who benefit most."

"Except she sat at the WOSC table all night—wasn't gone for more than five minutes at a crack, according to the other women," I said. I pointed to my timeline.

"But you don't have anything down here for Kolby," Brooke said.

"He was moving around too much, serving drinks, going to the kitchen to pick up food orders, and who knows what else? We could maybe track his movements more closely with the receipts from that night," I said, the thought striking me so quickly that I sat up and spilled a couple of drops of my second sidecar on my thigh. "Every server has a code that they enter into the computer when logging an order. I could pull up the data from that night and see what it tells us."

"Good thinking," Maud said with an approving nod.

Brooke, who had been looking thoughtful, said, "I think you—we—need to look at the *un*likely allies. I mean, look at *Orient Express*." She nodded toward the TV screen, which was frozen on a still of Albert Finney as Hercule Poirot. "You'd never think half those people would even know each other, much less conspire to kill someone together. Maybe some of the suspects have connections we don't know about."

Kerry threw up her hands and sucked in a deep breath through flared nostrils. "This is hopeless," she said. She immediately added, "I'm sorry, Amy-Faye; I didn't mean that. Even if we don't discover who killed Gordon, I'm sure Derek won't get convicted. If the moving parts and timelines and possible suspects are confusing us, just think how the poor jurors will feel. There's enough reasonable doubt in all this to fill an Olympic-size swimming pool."

"It's okay," I said, knowing she hadn't meant anything by her outburst. I was frustrated, too. I rose to go. "Thanks for having us over, Maud. And thanks for playing corpse, Joe. You've got a real future in the acting biz if you ever decide to give up on photography."

"Be on the other side of the lens? No, thanks," he said, unexpectedly rising and folding me into a comforting bear hug. "Don't let it get to you, Amy-Faye. It'll all come out right."

I sniffed. "Thanks, Joe." I was grateful for the kindness of this man I didn't even know very well. "I'm sure you're right." I looked around at the Readaholics. "Thanks to all of you for helping, and for caring about Derek. Keep drinking Elysium beer—it's paying his legal bills."

They laughed, and some of the others also got ready to leave. As we walked out in a clump, I reflected on how blessed I was to have such wonderful friends. The thought warmed me all the way home. For my bedtime reading, I picked up the latest Royal Spyness book from my to-be-read pile. The 1930s setting reminded me of the movie we'd just watched, and I was in the mood for Lady Georgie's antics. Snuggling into the crisp white sheets, I drifted off to sleeping, thinking hazily that if only America were a monarchy, I could have been a minor royal, too.

Chapter 20

I woke Friday morning with an idea for getting in touch with Gene Dreesen. It had come to me in a jumbled dream that included both the Albert Finney and Peter Ustinov Hercule Poirots, Lady Georgie, a train that went round and round on a circular track, and, for some unknown reason, a ballerina dancing to the Sugar Plum Fairy song. She broke her arm halfway through her solo and had to finish dancing in a cast. Somewhere out of that strange collage had come the idea: Gene Dreesen was an accountant and I was a business owner who employed an accountant. Suppose I met with him, pretending I was looking for a new CPA to do my books and taxes? I said a silent apology to Perdita Coss, my real accountant, and hoped word wouldn't get back to her that I was looking to replace her.

Accordingly, after stopping for a large coffee at the Divine Herb, and eyeing the women coming downstairs from yoga enviously—I needed to put yoga back in my schedule—I called Dreesen's firm as soon as I walked into the office. When I explained that it was urgent, they were happy to give me an appointment at one o'clock.

I put thoughts of Derek and the investigation out of my mind, working feverishly all morning on the events we had on the books for this weekend. Chasing down murder suspects had cut into my work time and I was not as prepared as I liked to be for what was shaping up to be a busy weekend with a bachelorette party tonight, a community yard sale Saturday morning, an anniversary do Saturday night, and a brunch Sunday morning. Al drifted into my office midmorning, wanting to talk about Courtney, but I wasn't able to tell him anything about her relationship status.

"All I can say is, she's not dating my brother." I remained focused on the toast I was editing for the husband of the anniversary couple tomorrow night. When I'd started out in event organizing, I'd had no idea my English degree would actually come in useful, but it did on occasion. I was constantly amazed by the number of best men; maids of honors; corporate honchos making remarks at promotions, retirements, or other events; and others who asked me to either write their remarks or edit them.

"Eliminating one possible boyfriend still leaves her a lot of scope," he pointed out dolefully.

"Look her up on Facebook."

"Already did. She's not on there."

I finally looked up from the notes I was making. "Call her and ask her out."

"Like on a date?" He looked comically surprised at the notion.

"Exactly like that. An assignation, a rendezvous, dinner and a movie . . . a *date*."

Al wandered out so gobsmacked by the idea that he couldn't even respond.

I grinned and returned to my editing.

At twelve forty-five, I climbed into the van and headed for the east end of town and the office building where Madrid, Dreesen, and Jones had their CPA firm. I climbed the stairs to their third-floor office, wanting the time to collect myself and go over the new approach I planned to take. Instead of impugning Perdita by hinting that there was something amiss with Eventful!'s books, I was going to say that we—my family—needed Elysium's books audited by an independent firm because we thought there was something amiss in the wake of Gordon's death. I'd called to discuss the idea with my mother and Derek, and they were on board with it, as long as I didn't actually turn over the books to Gene Dreesen.

"He's got a conflict of interest, doesn't he?" Derek asked. "Being Gordon's brother-in-law?"

"Probably." I didn't know what the CPA code of ethics looked like. "I'm just using it as an excuse to get in and see him, so it won't matter if he ends up saying he can't do the audit. In fact, it makes it easier if he recuses himself, because then I won't have to come up with an excuse for not giving him the job."

Smoothing my pale blue skirt over my thighs, and lifting my hair off my neck for a moment, I pushed through the door and into the CPA firm's reception area. I barely had time to note glass end tables flanking a black leather sofa, and a flourishing ficus tree before the male receptionist whisked me back to Gene Dreesen's office.

"Your one o'clock," the receptionist said, reducing me to an appointment time. He hurried back to the reception desk to answer the ringing phone.

The office was minimalist, the desk a slice of black acrylic or some kind of space-age material, the desk lamp made of industrial pipe with a wire basket over the bulb, and no desk clutter except a slim laptop and a framed photo of a girl who had to be Kinleigh. A gray cellular shade cut the glare from the large window but allowed plenty of natural light. There wasn't a piece of paper in sight—Maud would approve.

"Amy-Faye Johnson," I said, smiling and extending my hand.

"Eugene Dreesen. Call me Gene."

He was about ten years older than Dr. Angie Dreesen, I thought, which put him in his mid-fifties. His hair was prematurely white, but full, framing a long face and mostly covering thick-lobed ears. When he stood to shake my hand, I saw that he was tall and slightly stooped. His charcoal pin-striped jacket fit loosely, as if he'd recently lost weight, and I suspected the groove between his brows and the lines bracketing his mouth were deeper now than they had been six months ago, before his daughter's death.

"How can I help you, Ms. Johnson? You own an event-organizing business, I understand."

He must have looked up my Web site after I called.

"Amy-Faye," I said, "and yes, I do, but that's not why I'm here."

"Oh?"

"I don't know if you've heard," I lied, "but a new brewpub opened in Heaven last weekend and one of the investment partners was killed. My brother owns the pub and my parents are currently managing it, and we want to have an independent audit of the books conducted."

Dreesen gave me an assessing stare from deep-set eyes. "Gordon Marsh was my brother-in-law. I was at the party last Friday."

"No!" I hoped I didn't overdo the astonished bit. "I don't remember seeing you." Actually, I remembered seeing him leave with Angie, head bowed against the torrential downpour.

"I got there late . . . got tied up here and then stopped to help a distressed motorist." He linked his fingers together and rested his hands on the desk. "I got there right in time to evacuate for the fire alarm. I never even got to congratulate Gordon that night, never laid eyes on him. It's strange . . . You rarely think that the last time you see someone is going to be the last time. It must have been a week earlier that I last saw Gordon, and that was a chance encounter at the Pancake Pig, where I was meeting a client for breakfast. He was there with Kolby, reading him the riot act, it looked like, and we didn't say more than 'Good morning' to each other." He looked pensive.

"Yeah, Gordon didn't hang around long after the preparty with the VIPs. He disappeared when he saw the Women Outing Serial Cheaters marching across the parking lot," I said. "Did you know about them?"

He waved a dismissive hand. "Susan was mixed up with them, right? I think she told Angie about them. Sounded like an utter waste of time and money to me. And possibly actionable if their slander harmed some man's reputation.

"Do you have reason to suspect there are irregularities in the pub's books? Are you saying you think Gordon was embezzling?" He scratched the side of his nose.

"Not necessarily," I said, wanting to keep all options open. "We recently found out that one of the pub employees was a man with a grudge against Gordon—"

"No shortage of those." He caught himself up short and pressed his lips together. "I apologize. You were saying?"

"—who sabotaged the pub opening in various ways. We want to make sure he wasn't also stealing or monkeying with the books."

"I'm sure the executor will order an audit as part of the probate process, and maybe GTM as well," Dreesen said, "so you should probably wait for that. Regardless, I'm sure you can understand why I'm not the man to do the job." His tone said *wrap it up* and his gaze flicked to his computer screen.

"No, of course not. I feel so silly for calling you. I must have subconsciously recognized your name from the grand opening attendees' list when I was searching for accountants last night. You know"—I wrinkled my brow in pretend puzzlement—"I thought Gordon said he didn't expect to see you and his sister at the party even though he put you on the guest list?"

"Gordon was family," Dreesen said, putting his palms flat on the desk and pushing himself up. "We wouldn't have missed it. I'm only sorry the evening ended so tragically. And now, Ms. Johnson, if you'll excuse me . . . ?"

I had no choice but to stand, thank him for his time, and go. He sat again as I passed through the door. When I reached the reception area, the receptionist was finishing a call. Feeling as sly as Kinsey Millhone, I said, "I guess you work some long hours here, huh? Mr. Dreesen was telling me how late he was here last Friday."

"Tax season is our busy time of year," the young man said. He wore suspenders with whales on them over a crisp yellow shirt. "We're pretty slow right now. And, honey, I'm just the receptionist. That five o'clock whistle blows and I'm outta here." The phone rang and he turned away to answer it.

I left slowly, pondering what I'd learned. Not much. Dreesen hadn't come across as a man bent on vengeance, and he might or might not have been here late on Friday as he said. Just because the receptionist hadn't confirmed his alibi didn't mean he wasn't here. As I well knew, partners in a firm frequently worked longer and harder than employees. All in all, I'd say my visit to Gene Dreesen was a waste of time.

Since I'd be working late tonight, I decided to take a small break on my way to the office and detour by the pub to see Derek and my folks. I hadn't eaten, and I was starving. At two o'clock, it was past the standard lunch hour, but a handful of people still lingered over burgers and fish and chips. Derek was behind the bar, looking better than he had seemed in days.

"I'm working on a new IPA," he greeted me when I plunked myself onto a stool, "and I think it's an award winner."

That was why he looked better. Nothing revived Derek like creating a new brew. "When can I taste it?"

"A couple weeks, maybe. I'm still tinkering with it."

"Could I get a bowl of the beer-and-cheddar soup?" I asked. The rich, creamy soup was my favorite thing on the menu, even though I'd guess it had four thousand calories per spoonful.

"Sure thing." He put a glass of water in front of me and went to get the soup from the kitchen.

He returned moments later, bearing a tray with the soup, utensils, and crackers. Savory steam rising from the bowl made me salivate and I took the first ambrosial spoonful as soon as the bowl hit the counter.

"Doing your starving-wolf impression, sis?" Derek asked, drawing his hand away quickly, in mock fear that I would tear into it next.

"Hungry," I muttered. After a few more bites, I felt human enough to ask, "Mom and Dad around?"

"In the office. Dad's paying bills. I think Mom's making up next week's schedule, or else she's redecorating." He rolled his eyes. "She got rid of my poker-playing dogs and brought in a bunch of flowers and plants."

234 / Laura DiSilverio

The way he said "flowers" made it sound like she'd brought in a cockroach farm.

I laughed. "They'll brighten the place up for her. You can dump them when you're back at this full-time." Crumbling crackers into the soup, I finished it off and resisted the urge to lick the bowl. Not couth.

He shrugged one shoulder. "Aw, I don't know—maybe I'll keep 'em. If they're not too stinky."

I took a swallow of water, stood, and left a ten by my bowl. "I'll say hi to the folks, and then I've got to put my nose back to the grindstone. I've got a bachelorette party tonight, and then that big community garage sale and the anniversary party tomorrow. Busy weekend."

Derek slid the ten back toward me. "On me. I owe you a lot more than a bowl of soup."

"You don't—" I stopped as if I'd suddenly had a thought. "I do need some help tonight. Raven, the male stripper I usually hire for these types of things, has come down with the flu. Do you still have that George of the Jungle costume you wore to the Aikens' Halloween party a few years back? If you could dress in that and come dance for the ladies, we'd be square. Nine o'clock? I'm sure Mom and Dad can hold down the fort here for an hour. I've got a sound track, and, oh, you'll need to wax your chest and maybe oil it. Or use some spray tan—you're looking pretty pale."

He was staring at me in horror. The glass he was filling from the tap began to overflow. I reached over the bar and turned off the tap for him while he gobbled, "You can't—I can't—Amy-Faye, I can't even keep a beat. My only dance move is the moonwalk. I can't dance naked in front of—"

"Oh, not totally naked," I said reassuringly. "Just down to one of those glittery jockstraps. Or lamé. Your choice."

"I don't have—" His hand raked his auburn hair, making it stand out.

I couldn't hold back my giggles any longer. He glared at me, caught between relief and pissed off. "You were joking. Thank God. I thought—"

"We're fam. You don't owe me squat. Besides, I've got my reputation to think of and you doing a Chippendales routine for fifty women would not enhance it. Sorry, bro, but there it is." I levered myself up on the bar so I was balanced at my waist and leaned over to kiss his cheek.

"Ick, girl cooties," he said, scrubbing at his cheek in pretend horror.

I could tell he was pleased. I waggled my fingers at him in farewell and trotted up the stairs to the third-floor offices. I found my dad in Gordon's office, writing checks. His head was bent so I could see the bald spot on top, and he wore a chunky gray cardigan Natalie, or maybe Peri, had given him for Christmas a couple of years back. A vase of coral-colored gladioli brightened the desk, floral throw pillows had been placed on each of the visitor chairs, and the window was open to let in a soft breeze, sure signs that Mom had been here. I hugged Dad and asked how it was going.

"Pretty well," he said. "The pub's not as deep in the

hole as I thought it might be—no more than is reasonable for a restaurant in its first months—and the books are in fairly decent shape. He flipped a hand at the open checkbook. "Just catching up with some tax payments and payroll stuff that's in arrears. I don't suppose you know how to get hold of that janitor, Foster Quinlan, do you? He hasn't been in for his last check, and Derek doesn't have an address on file for him."

"Tear it up," I suggested. Foster didn't deserve a penny after what he'd pulled during the grand opening.

Dad frowned. "You know we can't do that, honey. It's not much, not after we subtracted the damages, but he's entitled to it."

"Give it to me. I'll get it to him."

Dad pulled an envelope from a drawer, slid the check inside, sealed it, and printed Foster's name on it neatly. His meticulous way of doing professional things used to drive me crazy, but now I merely grinned, finding it endearing. I'd never understand how a man who was so precise about his research and classes and professional obligations could let the house and yard go the way he did. Maybe it had something to do with chaos theory, whatever that was.

Taking the envelope from him and promising to deliver it safely, I asked for Mom. "At the library," he said. "The new librarian, that Chianti—"

"Chardonnay," I corrected him.

"—is having trouble with the computer system again. You know your mom's the only one who can fix it."

My mom's forty years as Heaven's librarian had left her the expert on anything related to the library's collection, history, computing systems, and technical services, and her replacement, a twentysomething with good intentions but little practical experience, frequently called on her for help. I suspected she was happy to still be needed.

I wished him and Mom luck with their first weekend night at the pub, and returned to my office briefly to get Foster's address. I recognized it as being out near the Cresta Community College, in an apartment complex largely inhabited by students, and hoped that showing up with a check might gain me entrance to Foster's lair.

Chapter 21

The Crestview Apartments parking lot, when I pulled in, had numerous potholes that I had to steer around, and was more than half-empty on a Friday afternoon. The vehicles that remained tended more toward beaters, cheap compacts, and well-used pickups than anything Matthew McConaughey would be an advertising spokesman for. Two buildings on either side of a rectangular pool bounded by a sagging chain-link fence made up the complex. The exterior was pitted tan stucco with rusty drips washing down from window air-conditioning units. The landscaping consisted of various cacti, rocks liberally dotted with cigarette butts, and tired annuals in pots on either side of the leasing office door. The pool should have been a cheerful oasis, but its harsh turquoise color and strong chlorine odor were somehow off-putting, although three college-aged kids were baking themselves on loungers. The contentious voices of a courtroom "reality" show drifted from an open window. Merely standing in the parking lot was depressing me; I was grateful for my cozy house.

Clutching the envelope, I looped around the pool enclosure to hunt for Foster's apartment. I couldn't find the building numbers, so I wandered through the nearest building without any luck before deciding the apartment must be in the other building. I passed the pool again and finally found Foster's apartment, an end unit on the second floor. Two towels hung over the wrought-iron rail fencing off the landing, flapping in the growing breeze. I knocked.

The apartment was so silent I was convinced no one was home. Then the door opened, startling me, and I stepped back. A woman stood there, middle-aged but fierce, with dark hair showing gray roots drawn into a low bun, deep-set eyes, and a red-lipsticked mouth. She balanced a plastic laundry basket on one hip. Despite the pile of soiled laundry, she made me think of an aging flamenco dancer I'd seen in a painting somewhere, mouth drawn down with weariness or disillusion, but still holding herself with a dancer's erect posture. She wore a linen sheath and low-heeled pumps more suited to after-work cocktails at an upscale bar than schlepping dirty clothes to the complex's laundry room. The dress showed off truly stunning legs. She did not remotely fit the picture of the long-suffering but loyal wife Foster had drawn for me during his kitchen confession. I knew immediately that Mrs. Quinlan had not adjusted well to the change in her economic circumstances.

"I don't need magazines, or candy bars, or whatever you're selling," she said.

I led with my trump card. "I've got a check for Foster," I said, holding up the envelope.

She gave me a "try it on someone else" look. "If you'd said you were a bill collector, I might have believed you."

"No, really. It's from Elysium Brewing. He said he'd be back to get it, but he never came in, so I brought it over. I'm Amy-Faye Johnson. My brother, Derek, owns the pub."

Mrs. Quinlan let out a long, whistley sigh, like a leaky balloon. "Damn him."

Damn who? Derek? Foster? Gordon?

"I don't imagine it was worth the gas you burned coming over here, but thank you." Her tone was grudging. She held out her hand and I had no choice but to place the envelope in it.

Sensing that she was about to herd me down the stairs with the laundry basket, I fought for a way to continue the conversation. "Look, I really need to use the bathroom. Do you mind?" Not up to Kinsey Millhone's standards, but it would have to do.

For a moment I thought she was going to tell me to hold it until I got home, but she finally stepped inside and set the laundry basket on an ottoman. She gestured me in and shut the door. "Through the bedroom."

Averting my eyes from the unmade bed, I entered the small master bathroom, locked the door, and ran the tap. I didn't really have to pee, so I peeked into the medicine cabinet while waiting for a believable length of time to elapse. Enough prescription bottles crammed the shelves to stock a pharmacy. I recognized some of the drug names as antianxiety meds and antidepressants. Her name was apparently Anita and it appeared on roughly half the bottles. Foster's was on the other half. I eased the cabinet shut quietly, flushed, swished my hands under the faucet, and rejoined her.

The furniture in the living room was too big for the space, and I imagined it was a small fraction of the furnishings from their prelayoff house. There was a tiny parqueted square meant to be an eating area, but an ornate desk, a grandfather clock, and what looked like antique fire tools with enameled handles—a poker, brush, and tongs in a stand—family heirlooms they couldn't bear to part with, perhaps, took up all the space. They must eat standing at the kitchen counter or sitting on the oversize leather sofa.

While I was in the bathroom, Anita had pulled a two-liter bottle of diet lemon-lime soda from the refrigerator and now offered me some. I was wary of her sudden friendliness, but accepted. Getting ice from the freezer, she filled two heavy tumblers and added the clear soda. The carbonation tickled my nose when I drank.

"I was hoping to see Foster," I said, sitting on the oversize ottoman when she sat on the sofa, which was angled across the living room because it was too big to fit against either of the walls. "He told me some things . . . Well, I have a few questions."

"He's at an interview," Anita lied smoothly, running one hand up and down the glass's smooth sides. "He, er, told me a little bit about your conversation, and, well, I'm hoping you—your brother—that there won't be any legal ramifications? Foster's really not himself. He's not responsible for his actions, not since . . ."

Ah, here was the reason for her more welcoming manner. She was afraid we were going to have Foster arrested for the vandalism. I was surprised to realize the idea had never crossed my mind. I was about to deny any such intention, when I decided to let her stew and see what she had to say. "I can't speak for my brother," I said, setting my glass on the Oriental carpet, a murky mix of reds, blues, and peach, since the only end table was unreachable.

"It's all Gordon Marsh's fault," Anita burst out, her red mouth tightening to an angry slash. "He had no right to fire Foster. No right! Foster was a good worker, a hard worker. He had a history with the company. He was months from retirement eligibility and his pension. You can't just throw that away." Anger deepened the lines at the corners of her eyes. "People are not paper plates, not disposable. After all we—after all Foster did for the company—he had no right."

"You knew what Foster was planning to do?"

"Knew? It was my idea. He balked at the idea of becoming a janitor, said if I was so set on the idea I should apply for the job, but no one would believe that I was janitor material," she said, clearly thinking her designer dress and manicured nails proclaimed her lack of fitness for honest labor. "Besides, I already had a job."

"Teaching, right?"

Her eyes slid away. "I was. Preschool. But I couldn't stand the dirty little . . . I had to hand in my notice when the principal objected to my discipline methods. No one today wants to hold kids accountable, or teach them manners or the correct way to behave. They're positively encouraged to run around like wild animals and 'express themselves.'" She sneered the last words.

I resisted the urge to ask what her methods were, and banished images of medieval torture chambers from my mind. "So you hatched the plan . . ."

"To ruin Gordon like he ruined us." She curled her fingers into her palms. "It was only what he deserved."

"Getting thrown off the roof?"

"Yes." The word ended with a drawn-out hiss.

I had a sudden vision of her standing on the pub's roof, arms upraised in triumph, hair whipped by the wind, as Gordon's body tumbled into the Dumpster. I added a couple of bolts of lightning and a rumble of thunder to the scene for atmosphere. "Where were you Friday night?"

"Where am I always?" she asked bitterly. "Here. We don't have enough money to even go to the movies, and it's not like any of my old friends are going to drop by here to have a cocktail." Ice clinked as she jiggled her glass.

I took a stab in the dark, hoping to scare her into revealing something. "I saw you at the pub. In the parking lot. You're very striking, easy to remember." I hadn't really seen her, but she might have been there.

Confusion and what I thought was a flash of fear flitted across her face. "You're mistaken. I wasn't— well, of course I had to drop him off. We can only afford the one car now. I didn't go in. I've never been in the

244 / Laura DiSilverio

pub. Frankly, I was afraid of what I would do to Gordon Marsh if I came face-to-face with him." She crossed one lovely leg over the other.

Her pseudo-openness left me unconvinced. "So how did Foster get home?"

"He didn't come home." She lengthened her neck so she could peer down her nose at me. "I called the police and tried to report him missing, but they wouldn't do anything. Said he was a grown man and would come home in his own time. It's not the first time. Since he was let go, Foster stops by a bar now and again and . . . well, you know."

I remembered the police report that said Foster had turned up, dead drunk, in the gazebo at Lost Alice Lake. "That must have worried you."

My sympathy made her eyes shimmer. "Of course it did! This . . . this"—she gestured at the apartment in a way that said she was encompassing their entire life—"is almost unbearable, even with Foster. Without him, I don't think I could stand it." She set her glass down with a trembling hand and the ropy blue-green veins twining across the back made me think how hard it must be to start over from scratch at almost sixty. I tried to envision my parents near penniless, having to give up our family home and most of their belongings, cooped up in a small apartment. Somehow I knew there'd still be flowers and open windows.

I believed Anita and felt sorry for her, sort of, but also suspected that she and Foster together were more than strong enough, and motivated enough, to have clonked Gordon over the head and flung him off the roof.

"Look, Miss Johnson, nothing Foster did was intended to hurt your brother—it was all aimed at Gordon Marsh—so I hope he, your brother, will take that into consideration. Foster didn't do any real damage, after all." She stood and looked down at me, a supplicant, yet unable to totally shed her lady-of-the-manor air.

Anger burned away my pity. "He's collateral damage, not your target, and so he should be okay with that?" I asked, standing so quickly I knocked over my half-full glass.

"My Bokhara!" Anita Quinlan ran for the kitchen and began unspooling the paper towel roll.

Without even apologizing (my mother would lecture me if she knew), I let myself out, closed the door, and trotted down the stairs and back to my car, ignoring a wolf whistle from the pool area. I drove halfway back to my office in an angry blur, but then my brain started working again. Anita Quinlan had been at the pub Friday night, even though she'd initially denied it. She'd also said something about people not being disposable, something about "after all *we*—" and cut herself off. I couldn't help thinking that she was a darn attractive woman, only a few years older than Gordon, and wondering if all her anger at Gordon was on her husband's behalf. Maybe she'd been one of Gordon's all-too-disposable women, wanting the kind of revenge that joining up with WOSC wouldn't supply.

I imagined a little scenario. She could have snuck onto the roof without anyone noticing, maybe even before the party got going, and waited for Gordon to come up for a smoke. Foster could have told her that was his habit, or if she really had had an affair with Gordon, she could have known. She could have texted Foster, busily plugging up toilets, when Gordon appeared. Foster could have crept upstairs and beaned Gordon with—what?—his mop or some other weapon, taking him by surprise if he was already arguing with Anita. Together, they could have heaved him up and over the wall. Foster could have returned to the first floor, pretending he was mopping up a mess or something if anyone caught him in the elevator or on the stairs, and Anita could have waited on the roof until after the party—

I wrinkled my brow. No, she couldn't know how long it would be until Gordon's body was discovered, so she'd have had to escape quickly. The fire! Foster blew up the microwave to set off the fire alarms so she'd have the opportunity to blend in with the exiting crowd and escape. I caught my breath. Then he confessed to the sabotage, hoping it would distract from their real crime. I didn't have any proof, but Foster and Anita had motive and opportunity. It all fit. I banged the steering wheel with excitement. I needed to tell Hart.

Chapter 22

"That's a whole boatload of 'could haves' you've got there, and not much proof," Hart observed twenty minutes later.

We were seated in his office and I had blurted my theory out, barely stopping for breath, when he invited me back and offered me a chair. His office in the Heaven Police Department was a small room with windows on two sides. Paint, flooring, and furniture were all institutional blah and utilitarian, but a full set of Sherlock Holmes novels and short stories were bookended by a plaster deerstalker cap and pipe, a bag with bat handles peeking out slouched in one corner, and Ugga, the University of Georgia's bulldog mascot, perched atop the printer, wearing a red jersey. A vinegary odor confused me until I noticed the remains of a take-out salad in his trash can.

"But it all fits," I said, leaning forward to convince him. "They had motive, means, and opportunity. You should have heard her—she hated Gordon. And Foster does, too. I was nervous of him in the kitchen, how gleeful he was telling me about his sabotage."

"That doesn't make either of them killers," Hart said, eyeing me, not without sympathy. "Look, we can reinterview her, focusing on her whereabouts rather than her husband's, but even if she wasn't home, that doesn't prove anything."

"What do you want?" I flashed. "Another blood-spattered shirt?" Even as I said it, I knew I wasn't being fair. He was a police officer, trying to build a case that would earn a conviction.

"That would be a strong piece of physical evidence, yes," he said, remaining calm in the face of my attack. "The murder weapon with their fingerprints on it would also suffice. I could even pressure them if a witness saw her inside the pub. I'll ask some questions."

I must have made a doubtful face, because he reiterated, "I will. You know Derek's still the strongest suspect, but that doesn't mean I'm not open to evidence that suggests otherwise." His expression was sympathetic but firm; I was only going to piss him off if I pushed more.

"Thanks," I muttered, standing. Hearing how ungracious I sounded, I smiled ruefully. "No, really. Thank you. I know you don't have to look into it, or even listen to my theories—"

"Like you'd let me ignore you," he murmured.

"—but I really think I'm right about this. The Reada-holics were all talking about how there was probably more than one person involved—"

"There's no proof of that, either."

He was sure fond of the *P* word. "—and we were looking at trying to pair up people who don't have an obvious connection, but this makes so much more sense. Anita and Foster hate Gordon with a passion, whatever their individual reasons, and I could see how they would spur each other on, how every time Anita had to forgo a manicure she probably said something nasty about Gordon, and how whenever he heard about his old buddies playing eighteen holes without him, Foster would add it to his tally against Gordon, until it felt *right* to them to go after him."

"I saw that dynamic at work once in Atlanta," he admitted. "I'm not saying you're wrong, just that we need to get—"

"Proof. I know." I grinned at him. "That's why I channel Annie Laurance Darling or Stephanie Plum when I'm investigating, rather than Jane Rizzoli or some other cop who has to be all hung up on proving things in court."

He rolled his eyes and made shooing motions. "Go. I have to give a talk to a middle school class about the joys of serving the community as a police officer. Maybe I'll channel T. J. Hooker."

I stuck my tongue out, blew him a kiss, and left in a better mood than I'd been in for a week. I knew that if Hart looked into Anita and Foster's story, it would unravel and he'd find the proof that they had killed Gordon. Derek would be freed, I would no longer have to bartend, and life would go back to normal.

*   *   *

I needed a distraction that night, and the bachelorette party I was in charge of was just the ticket. It was for a sorority sister of Brooke's and was being held at another friend's house. I'd ordered the custom invitations for fifty of the bride's closest friends, coordinated with the caterer and the party-supplies rental company, ordered party favors for the attendees, planned games, and, yes, booked a male stripper. The hostess, a thin blonde who still looked like she could be living in the Kappa Delta house at CSU, had insisted that she wanted a "tasteful" stripper. "Good-looking and built, of course," she'd said, "and a good dancer, but nothing *dirty*. Tasteful."

"Of course," I'd said, nodding as if that made sense. It made as much sense as painting the town's gazebo pink. I'd immediately called Tom Smith, whose stage name was Raven, and booked him. He was my go-to guy for parties of this nature; he was reliable, had a wide repertoire of numbers ranging from cop to doctor to cowboy to Tarzan, and was smokin' hot. He wasn't shy, like Derek, about strutting his stuff in front of strange women. Also, he had a sense of humor, which I appreciated even if my clients were more appreciative of his other—*ahem*—assets.

Brooke waved to me when she came in, but I didn't have a chance to talk to her until after the women had giggled while playing the silly bridal games, tossed out bawdy remarks worthy of a *Hangover* movie while opening the presents (all lingerie somewhere on the scale from tasteful to hooker), eaten, and consumed an entire case of champagne. When the doorbell rang and Raven entered to hoots and catcalls in his fireman's outfit, Brooke managed to draw me aside.

Beside the horse sculpture in the entryway, she whispered, "There's a girl who wants to meet us. Tuesday!"

It took me a moment to switch my brain from strippers to adoptions, but when I caught on I hugged her hard. "Oh, Brooke, I'm so happy for you."

"It's not a done deal," she said, twirling a strand of hair. "She could decide she doesn't like us, or find a couple she likes better, or decide to keep the baby." I knew she was managing her own expectations more than mine. Raucous hoots and a loud rendition of "I'm Your Fireman" blasting from the living room made it hard to hear her.

"Still, it's a start. A good sign."

Her green eyes sparkled with hope. "Keep your fingers crossed, okay?"

"My toes, too," I promised.

"And don't tell anyone. I don't want to be answering lots of questions about it, especially if it falls through."

I mimed zipping my lips. She hugged me again with a little squeal. "This is it, A-Faye. I can just feel it."

Someone called to her and she slipped back into the party. I gave Raven his check when he finished, standing on the front stoop while the partiers finished drinking themselves into a coma. Frat boys had nothing on thirty-year-old women freed from their toddlers and husbands for a night. The night air was pleasantly cool and three moths bumped the glass porch light. Raven was sweating from his exertions, and his long black hair was damp at the temples. He had the fireman's jacket draped over his shoulders, so I could still admire his tanned and oiled six-pack and pecs. We talked about his day job as a piano tuner and how my business was going. I watched as he counted the ones and fives that had been tucked into his G-string. I'd supplied them, of course (after suggesting it to the maid of honor hosting the party and getting her approval to bill for it), in a Ziploc baggie, and passed them out before he arrived, so I knew he'd made something in the three-hundred-dollar ballpark. Not bad for half an hour's work.

He kissed my cheek before he left. "When am I going to be dancing at your bachelorette party, Amy-Faye?" he asked, teasing.

"Not in this lifetime," I said. Not because I was never getting married, but because I didn't plan to be ogling other men on the eve of my wedding, or ever again, hopefully. My husband would be my one and only oglee.

"With all the business you've thrown my way, I'd do it for free. In fact"—he took a step closer until I could feel the heat coming off of him—"I'd dance for you privately, anytime."

I flattened my palm on his rock-solid chest and pushed him back. "Sheena break up with you again?" I asked.

He shrugged and gave a "you caught me" smile. "Yeah. She says she's done with me forever this time."

I was unimpressed. "She said that the last three times, too. To everyone at the salon. I heard some of her clients were running a pool to guess when she'd take you back."

Nodding, he said, "Yeah, that's why I thought I'd put the moves on you quick, while I'm still unattached."

Laughing, I pushed him off the stoop and said good night.

Chapter 23

I groaned and rolled over, burying my face in my pillow when my alarm went off at six o'clock the next morning. Saturdays were for sleeping in. Why, oh why, had I agreed to organize the Cherubim Glen community garage sale? Because the HOA president had asked me to and I foresaw a fair amount of business from future HOA functions and Cherubim Glen homeowners, I reminded myself. After dragging myself to the shower, I felt almost human when I emerged fifteen minutes later. I snagged a boiled egg from the fridge and a bowl of Cap'n Crunch and snarfed them down standing at the counter. Then I gathered my supplies and hit the road.

I'd actually enjoyed the garage sale challenge, right up until I had to roll out of bed before the early birds were patrolling for worms. This was the first one I'd been hired for, and I'd had fun contacting homeowners to see who wanted to participate, drawing up a map and having it printed, arranging advertising, suggesting parking and a shuttle from a nearby middle school so heavy traffic wouldn't disturb shoppers walking from sale to sale, contacting local high schools to see if they had any clubs who wanted to make some money selling concessions on various street corners, hiring an off-duty cop to direct traffic, and more.

Cherubim Glen was a community of about a hundred homes and fifty patio homes located on the southwest corner of Heaven, not too far from the country club. It had its own landing strip, and some of the homeowners kept small planes parked out in back of their homes, as casually as I parked my van at the curb. Usually, a rolling gate barred entrance, but today it was wide-open, inviting shoppers and the merely curious into the exclusive enclave. I waved at the gate guard as I drove through and was relieved to see that many of the participants were already lugging stuff from their houses to their driveways, as I'd recommended. The sale was set to start at seven. I recognized Axie Paget with three friends, busy setting up a baked goods concession on one side of the most traveled intersection. I gave her a thumbs-up and she grinned. I made a mental note to stop by later, buy some cookies, and ask if she was interested in working for me a few hours a week.

The HOA president, a retired admiral, lived in a four-thousand-square-foot home he called a "cottage." It was built to resemble an Adirondacks lodge and was decorated in what I thought of as "early-modern Hemingway," with animal or fish trophies on every wall. Notwithstanding his penchant for killing any critter that swam, snarled, or had antlers or horns, Admiral

Beaubridge was a nice guy who volunteered at the library and the hospital, and turned his powerful leadership abilities to many town projects. He had hired me with the approval of his HOA board, given me an idea of the kind of event he wanted, and left me to it. My kind of client. He awaited me on his porch, hands on hips, looking like a fireplug in a crisp white shirt and khaki slacks that managed to suggest the uniform he had given up twenty years earlier. Iron gray hair was slicked back from a high forehead, making his Roman nose even more prominent. I always got the urge to hum "I Am the Very Model of a Modern Major General" when I spent time with him.

"Top o' the morning to you, Miss Johnson," he called. "Lovely day for a tag sale."

"Good morning, Admiral," I answered, smiling. "I think we're all set."

"Come aboard, come aboard," he invited, gesturing me inside. "Coffee's on. You can brief me once we've been properly fortified."

Gratefully sipping his superb coffee in a kitchen that was, of course, shipshape, I briefed him on all the arrangements.

"Excellent work, excellent work," he said, beaming. "You'd have made an outstanding executive officer."

I had no idea what an executive officer did, but he made it sound like high praise, so I said, "Thank you, Admiral." I drained my cup. "I'm happy to work under your command anytime. Now, if you'll excuse me, I'm going to make sure the shuttle driver knows the route and that the signs are all posted."

I carried out those tasks and then drove slowly around the community, watching as perhaps half of the homeowners buzzed their garage doors up and dragged outgrown, unneeded, unwanted, or otherwise excess stuff onto their driveways and lawns. I could have furnished my whole house with the lamps, chairs, headboards, dressers, tables, linens, knickknacks, and small appliances for sale. Of course, the lamp needed a new cord, the headboard's brass needed lots of elbow grease and polish, the dresser needed leveling, the table refinishing, and the linens a good bleaching, but still. And the books! There were books at every other house, it seemed, ranging from pristine hardcovers to ratty paperbacks. I'd found a hardback Elizabeth George novel I didn't own a copy of, and a paperback Travis McGee mystery I didn't think I'd ever read, and asked the seller to put them aside for me. I knew I would be going home with ten or fifteen books for my to-be-read stack. One home had a pile of throw pillows I would check out later, and I called Lola to let her know there were twenty or so ceramic planters at another house. She could pick them up for a song and resell them at Bloomin' Wonderful.

I made my way around the neighborhood, stopping to chat with people I knew and lots I didn't. A boy on a Big Wheel zoomed down a sidewalk, and a large black cat with a white bib lurked under a garaged SUV, tail twitching back and forth. Grackles settled into the trees surrounding a lawn with a bird feeder and began their crackly gossiping. With sunlight slanting down and a cloudless sky, it was a beautiful day. Let the hordes descend, I thought, as my watch showed seven o'clock and the first shuttle arrived.

I'd been to the bank to get rolls of quarters and packets of ones and I was busy for the first hour distributing change to sellers who hadn't planned ahead. I settled a dispute between two rival groups of high schoolers who both wanted the same corner for their soda and water sales, and helped an old woman roll a rack of what looked like 1950s–era clothes from her house to the sidewalk.

"This would look lovely on you, dear," she said, "with your tiny waist." She held up a nip-waisted jacket on a hanger. Moss green, it had padded shoulders and two big buttons crusted with sparkly rhinestones in shades of green, brown, and amber.

Beguiled by her comment about my tiny waist, I bought it for five dollars. She was telling another customer how becomingly a hat framed her lovely face when I walked away. I had to admire her sales technique.

I spotted Brooke and Troy looking at a crib and waved to them. Brooke's smile looked forced and I suspected her dark sunglasses hid a hangover from last night's bridal shower. Lola pulled over in the Bloomin' Wonderful van to thank me for the tip about the planters she had just loaded into the van. Two houses farther down, I came across Maud, stripping line from a reel she was obviously considering buying. She looked ready for a day on the river in her waffle-weave red Henley, cargo shorts, and Tevas. Of course, Maud always looked ready for a hunting, fishing, snowshoeing, hiking, or skiing adventure.

"I love garage sales," she said. "Did I ever tell you I once went for two years without buying anything—besides food and undergarments—other than at a thrift shop or yard sale? I still own some of those clothes—could probably make money off them at a vintage consignment store." Her blue eyes, framed by crow's-feet, had a reminiscent look. She handed the reel to the waiting store owner and said, "I'll give you ten."

"Why'd you do that?" I asked.

"Wanted to prove to my folks that their materialistic approach to life was shallow and crass. Of course, it didn't stop me from letting them pay my tuition at Berkeley," she added. "I was a hypocrite." She said it matter-of-factly, obviously having come to terms with her younger self's inadequacies long ago.

"Twelve-fifty," the seller said.

"Done." Maud handed over her money, accepted her change and the reel, and moved along with me.

Bargain hunters crowded the sidewalks and we stepped into the street. As we walked, I told Maud about my encounter with Anita Quinlan and my theory that she and Foster had conspired to kill Gordon.

Maud's eyes lit up. "Excellent work, Amy-Faye. Now, how do we get them to confess? It's too bad we're not trapped on a train with them. Wouldn't it be grand to get all the suspects in one place and present our theory?"

Maud sounded wistful, and I could see she really wanted to play Hercule Poirot and wow the suspects with our unraveling of the conspiracy, even the small two-person conspiracy that wasn't nearly as exciting as the fictional one that resulted in Ratchett's stabbing death. She turned to face me with a grimace. "I have a feeling the police won't want to move without more evidence."

"They don't. I already talked to Hart." I kicked an acorn and watched it skitter down the street before disappearing into a storm drain.

"We should bug their phone. I have a couple of devices left over from—"

"That's against the law!"

She shrugged. "You've got to fight fire with fire. If the government has the means and the will to spy on its citizens, then the people have to—"

I stopped her before she could get too far on her hobby horse. "We're not talking about the government," I objected.

She looked as though she was going to continue arguing in favor of wiretapping the Quinlans, but Kerry hailed us from a yard across the street. Roman, arm still in a cast wrapped in bright orange tape, stood a few feet away, sorting through a box of video games. Maud and I crossed over.

"Great event," Kerry said to me. She rattled a box of kitchen gadgets. "Maybe I can get my neighborhood to do something similar. I wouldn't mind making a few bucks off some of the junk in my attic." She considered a garlic press but set it back down with a muttered "Clutter."

"I'd be happy to help you set it up," I said.

"Have you told Kerry?" Maud asked me.

"Told me what?"

I shook my head and Maud summed up my suspicions of the Quinlans.

"That hangs together very well," she said with a brisk nod. "I think you've cracked it."

"Yeah, well, it won't do Derek any good unless I can prove it," I said. "The police—"

"Your hot detective?" Kerry asked.

"—are hung up on proof," I finished, ignoring her.

"Then we should get them some." Kerry put her hands on her hips. "How hard can it be? You've got two pissed-off people, both of whom seem eager to run down Gordon Marsh to anyone who will sit still long enough to listen. Didn't you say the janitor had a drinking problem?"

"Well, the police found him drunk at the lake," I said, "and I got the feeling he wasn't really at an interview, like Anita said, but that doesn't mean he was at a bar."

"He was at a bar," Kerry and Maud said together. "My father—" Kerry started. "My first husband—" Maud began.

Kerry and I stared at her. "You were married?" Kerry asked.

"Twice," Maud said, looking amused at our astonishment. "A story for another time."

I held up my hands, surrendering to their superior knowledge of drunks. "So, what's the plan? Drag him to a bar, get him drunk, and pump him for details? Seems . . . unethical, to say the least."

"We won't have to get him drunk," Maud said. "He'll be drunk any time past ten a.m. if my ex is anything to go by."

262 / Laura DiSilverio

"One of us will have to make nice, get him talking about Gordon."

"He knows me," I said.

"And he might know my face," Kerry put in. "My Realtor signs are on all those benches, and he might have seen me at a city function or something. Not to say I'm a celebrity, but I'm pretty well known in Heaven."

She tried to hide it, but I could see her satisfaction in that. Coming from one of the poorest families in the county, Kerry had worked and scraped and saved to go to community college and then get her four-year degree. Her Realtor's license was the cherry on top, and she quickly became the most successful Realtor in a three-county area before marrying the former police chief, having two kids, and getting elected mayor when she decided town politics were too corrupt to allow the incumbent to continue in office. She had a lot to be proud of.

"Too well known to take a chance," Maud agreed. "I'll do it." Her eyes sparkled with anticipation. "I'll put on one of my old suits—I knew I had a reason for not letting Joe haul them to Goodwill—and feed the target a story about being laid off when my company got bought up. I don't think I can say Gordon was involved—that might be suspicious, don't you think?"

"Too much of a coincidence," I agreed.

"I'll let him buy me a drink, cry a little—"

I couldn't imagine Maud crying.

"And he'll spill his guts," Kerry finished for her. "Men always do," she added. "Women get a bad rap for spilling secrets, but in my experience it's men who can't resist yapping, especially if it's something they're proud of, or want credit for."

"How do we find his bar?" I asked.

"Start with any watering hole within walking distance of his apartment," Kerry suggested. "He won't be driving—he doesn't need a DUI on top of his other troubles."

"When?" I looked from Kerry to Maud.

"Tonight," Maud said. "Joe's photographing geese in Canada, as if there aren't enough of those pooping pests here. He won't be back for a week. I was going to do my estimated taxes, but this will be more fun. It's against my principles to fund a government that wastes my money the way this one does, but Joe insists. He says another stint in jail would send me round the bend."

Another? I definitely needed to prime Maud's pump with a bottle of good wine and hear the story of her pre-Heaven life.

"I promised Roman I'd watch that new zombie movie with him tonight," Kerry said, with a sideways look at her son, now chatting (if one could call monosyllabic responses "chatting") with a pretty redhead who was signing his cast.

"I've got a function," I said.

"It doesn't matter," Maud said. "I can fly solo."

"You should have backup," I said, chewing on my lip. "Maybe I can let Al—"

"Pish. I'm having a drink in a bar. Nothing safer," Maud said.

"You can't do this by yourself," I said firmly. I'd feel

guilty if anything went wrong when I was the one who got her all revved up with my suspicions about Foster and Anita. "Wait until after I get the anniversary party going. I'll turn it over to Al and meet you somewhere. Say, eight o'clock?"

"Fine. Foster should be good and plowed by then," Maud said cheerfully. "I'll go home and figure out which bars are closest to his place." She strode off, a woman on a mission, gray-white hair swishing across her collar.

"You going to buy that?" A hopeful woman stood beside Kerry, pointing to the mushroom brush Kerry had been holding for several minutes.

"All yours," Kerry said, handing it over. "I wish I could go with you tonight, but a mom's gotta seize the moment to spend time with a teenager, especially a boy. Amanda wasn't so bad, at least not until she got hot and heavy with Cormac. She used to talk to me about her classes, her friends. Not Roman, though. You'd think words cost ten dollars each, the way he doles them out, at least to me. One day, you, too, will be happy to watch a zombie movie if it means you might get three sentences out of your teenager." She raised her voice. "C'mon, Roman."

I laughed and called, "Enjoy the movie," as she and Roman walked away.

Chapter 24

As it turned out, the anniversary wife came down with a migraine midway through the party and it broke up early. Al and I finished supervising departures and cleanup a little before eight. On impulse, I invited him to join me and Maud on the Great Foster Stakeout, thinking that Foster would be less likely to notice me if I was with someone.

Al agreed to accompany me with a degree of enthusiasm that gave me pause, but I couldn't uninvite him. "We're just having a drink together, making sure Maud's okay," I said. "No Rambo stuff."

"Rambo?"

I tried to think of a more contemporary action hero. "No Iron Man heroics. Maud can handle herself."

"I believe that," Al said, clearly remembering some of his run-ins with Maud. "Are you wearing a disguise?"

"Sort of." I had a floppy sunhat in the car that Mom had left there. I planned to stuff my hair under it, keep my sunglasses on, and hope the bar was dim enough Foster wouldn't notice me.

"That apartment complex is by the university," Al said. "I'll bet he's at the Long Shot. The only other bar that's walkable is Steve-O's, and no one over thirty goes there."

I called Maud to give her that news and we agreed to meet at the Long Shot. Al was fairly bouncing in the passenger seat with excitement as we drove to the bar. "Chill," I said when we arrived and got out in the parking lot. Neon lights advertising beer brands sputtered from the bar's windows, and lamps in the parking lot gave plenty of illumination. The sedans and SUVs in the lot said it wasn't a student hangout, and I began to hope we wouldn't have to troll through several bars to find Foster. Maud arrived a minute after we did, and dismounted from her Jeep. I almost didn't recognize her.

She wore a sharp gray suit with a skirt that skimmed her bare knees, and high-heeled pumps. She had smoothed her hair so it fell in an elegant swath against her jaw, and wore discreet but expertly applied makeup. I wouldn't have guessed that Maud even owned mascara. She moved with assurance, like a woman who wore heels every day and ground subordinates under them, and grinned when she saw my expression.

"Didn't know I cleaned up so well, did you?" she greeted me. "Hi, Frink."

"You look like that actress in *The Devil Wears Prada*," Al said, eyes round. "The old one."

"Thanks," Maud said drily.

"No one's going to believe anyone fired you when you look like that," I said, trying to soften Al's "old" remark. "You reek of competence."

"Don't you worry—I'll 'loser' myself up a bit." Maud grinned. "I'll go in and scout the place. If I'm not out in five minutes, assume I've acquired the target and come on in to enjoy the show." Without waiting for us to agree, she strode across the parking lot, every line of her singing with power and confidence. I couldn't wait to hear more about Maud's pre-Heaven life.

Al started the timer on his watch, and I was relieved no one had said, "Synchronize your watches." This whole thing was feeling too "James Bond meets the Three Stooges" for me already. A lone man and a pair of women in their fifties entered the bar while we waited, and then Al's alarm went *pip-pip-pip* and he said, "She must have found him. Let's move in."

"Stop with the spy lingo, okay? I feel silly enough as it is." Twisting my hair up and cramming the hat onto my head, I put on my sunglasses, even though it was almost dark, and we headed into the Long Shot. Al held the door for me, and I entered a dreary space where the order of the day seemed to be serious drinking. Utilitarian tables and chairs occupied most of the space, and a bar with five stools ran along one wall. The guy manning it wore a white T-shirt, none too clean, and an apron, ditto. A two-day growth of beard speckled his jowls. The odor of cigarettes hung heavy in the air, even though smoking indoors was illegal and I didn't see anyone with a cigarette. I realized after a moment that it was leftover smoke, from decades back, soaked into the wooden floors, vinyl chairs, and wall-board. Major *eew*.

On a Saturday night, the place was not exactly hop-ping, but it was decently busy. Four of the seats at the bar were taken, and several of the tables held men and women in various stages of inebriation. A small televi-sion high in one corner broadcast a college football game that a couple of people were watching, and a country lament thrummed from a jukebox. This place was no threat to Elysium Brewing, I decided.

I spotted Maud immediately, seated at the bar, shoulders slumped forward as she pounded back what looked like whiskey. One of her pumps was on the floor beneath the stool and the other dangled from her toes. Her hair was more disheveled than in the parking lot, her jacket hung off the back of the stool, and her posture made her the very picture of dejection.

"There's Ms. Bell," Al whispered. "Is that the target next to her?"

"Shh." I studied the back of the man seated beside Maud and decided it probably was Foster. Black hair, a little longer than I remembered, a checked shirt, khakis, and high-end trainers. As I watched, he turned his head a fraction and said something to Maud. I recog-nized his profile.

"Yes," I said. "Let's snag that table over there." I pointed to one that might be within hearing distance.

Al sprinted for it like he was trying to outrun Usain Bolt, and slid into one of the straight-backed chairs with black vinyl padding a second ahead of a man holding a beer in one hand and a bowl of popcorn in the other. I gave the man an apologetic smile and he glared before wandering to a booth closer to the television. "Way to be inconspicuous," I muttered to Al.

"Sorry." He looked abashed. "It's my first stakeout."

I rolled my eyes but didn't say anything. Pulling out a ten, I gave it to Al and said, "Get us a couple of beers and some popcorn."

He popped up eagerly and wedged himself between Foster and the man on his right to signal the bartender. He carefully avoided looking at Foster, but the way his head was cocked toward him, any moron could tell he was eavesdropping. Fortunately, Foster was snockered and more interested in Maud than in the skinny kid in the bow tie trying to get the bartender's attention. I strained to hear what Foster and Maud were saying.

"—with that effing company for twenty-eight years. Wouldn't you think that deserved some consideration, some loyalty on their part? Oh no. I'm out on my ear. Two weeks' severance. Have a nice life. One minute I'm an HR executive and vice president, looking forward to a comfortable retirement, maybe a condo in Florida, and two seconds later I'm on the unemployment line, hoping I don't lose my house. They had security escort me out, like I was embezzling or stealing company secrets. It was humiliating."

Maud's voice blended bitterness and pathos very effectively. She swallowed the last of her drink in one extravagant gesture, and snapped the glass onto the bar. "I'm sorry. I shouldn't be bothering you with my troubles. You can't understand unless you've been there." She signaled for another drink. If she'd looked like

Meryl Streep earlier, now she reminded me of Charlotte Rampling in that Paul Newman lawyer movie: sexy, disillusioned, angry.

"I've been there," Foster said eagerly, almost slipping off the stool as he swiveled to face Maud. His eyes were bleary and his lips slack, but his diction was hyperprecise, not slurry. I'd bet he'd been here drinking since noon. "Laid off by a man not fit to shine my shoes. Fact. Not that they need shining." He waggled one foot and the untied laces danced. "'Laid off.' What does that even mean? Let's call it what it is, right? Fired. The other *F* word." He laughed at his wit and insisted on adding Maud's drink to his tab.

"She should be an actress," Al said, setting down two foaming mugs and a plastic bowl of popcorn. "I was right there by them, heard every word, and she should absolutely be in Hollywood."

Having learned so many new things about Maud recently, I wouldn't have been surprised to learn that she *had* been a Hollywood actress.

Putting a finger to my lips to shush him, I leaned toward the bar as far as I dared, pretending to stretch and scooting my chair back several inches. My hat slipped over my eyes and I pushed it back a hair so I could see. Al had his eyes fixed on the pair like he was watching a movie, totally unsubtle. He shoveled a handful of popcorn into his mouth, reinforcing the movie idea.

"—out on my ass—just like that." Foster tried to snap his fingers. "But that bastard got his." He nodded slyly.

"How so?" Maud asked, keeping her voice casual.

"Got what he deserved," Foster said, nodding like a bobblehead. "Arrogant bastard."

Maud tried again. "What did he get?"

"Dead."

Maud leaned her upper body toward Foster, ready to receive his confidence. "You killed him?" she whispered, her look suggesting he deserved a prize, if so. I didn't hear the words so much as read her lips.

Al started, his knee bumping the rickety table, and his mug toppled. Pale golden beer spilled across the table, dribbling to the floor and into my lap. The cold liquid immediately saturated my slacks. Al flushed beet red, stuttered, "I'm so sorry," and tried to sop up the mess with his four-inch-square bar napkin, which dissolved on contact with the beer.

Maud and Foster, along with half the other patrons, looked at us. I kept my head bowed, dabbing ineffectually at my slacks with my napkin, hoping Foster wouldn't recognize me.

"Use this," the bartender said, slinging a damp cloth toward Al. He caught it and stood to make a better job of blotting up the beer.

"Hey, I know you," Foster said.

I peeped through my lashes to see him staring at me.

"You're her." He seemed to struggle for my name or a descriptor that didn't cover half the population. He failed. "That one. Her."

"I'm going to clean up in the restroom," I announced. Trying to keep my back to Foster, I rose and started to squelch toward a dark hall where I hoped to find the facilities.

272 / Laura DiSilverio

"You were telling me what you did to get back at the jerk who laid you off," Maud said.

Her attempt at distraction didn't work. "You're her. From that other bar where Marsh got killed."

That stopped conversation bar-wide. Only the announcer's voice from the football game, lamenting a fumble, and Carrie Underwood singing about a wife and mistress killing the man who done them wrong kept the room from total silence.

Why did Hercule Poirot not have moments like this? No one ever soaked his pants so it looked as if he'd peed himself. No one ever caught on to his game when he was staking them out or leading them into a clever interview trap. Should I hide in the restroom or confront Foster? "I don't think we've met," I mumbled, continuing toward the ladies' room. I tried the door. It was locked.

"Just a minute," a voice called from inside.

I heard the thud as Foster slid off the stool and his feet hit the floor. "Are you following me?" he asked. "Spying on me?"

I half turned. "No, of course not! I—"

" 'Cause you're not the kinda woman hangs out in a dive like this. You must be—"

"Hey," the bartender (and owner?) said in a wounded voice. "If the Long Shot ain't good enough for you, Foster, you can haul your heinie out of here. In fact, I'm gonna call your wife." He pulled a cell phone out of his apron pocket and dialed from memory. It obviously wasn't the first time he'd had to call Anita Quinlan to haul her husband home.

That got a few titters from onlookers, who went back to their drinking, game watching, and conversations. The woman in the restroom came out and I ducked inside. It was small but surprisingly clean. I used paper towels to try to rinse some of the beer out of my slacks and then splashed water on my flushed cheeks. When I emerged, Al was sitting beside Maud at the bar, and Foster was nowhere in sight.

"Where's Foster?" I asked when I reached them.

"Waiting for his ride outside," Maud said. "He tried to follow you into the restroom, so Mel here"—she nodded toward the bartender—"suggested he get some fresh air."

"I'm so incredibly sorry," Al said, looking downcast. "I ruined our operation, alerted our target to our presence, and just totally tubed it."

Maud said, "I guess we need to pull your double-oh rating." She grinned. "Really, Frink, it's no big deal."

"But he was right on the verge of saying he killed Gordon," Al said.

"Maybe yes, maybe no," I said. "Did you hear how he said 'that bar where Marsh got killed,' or something like that? He didn't say 'that bar where I killed Marsh,' or 'that pub where I tossed Marsh off the roof.' He's three sheets to the wind, so he probably isn't thinking too quickly, and yet he didn't say anything incriminating in the heat of the moment." I shrugged. "I'm just not sure he did it anymore."

"Let's go out there and ask him," Maud said, sliding off the stool in one graceful move. She searched for her pumps with her toes and slid them on. "I'd forgotten how these suckers pinch. Stilettos are proof of the fashion industry's conspiracy to keep women subordinate to men. I need to write a blog post about that." She marched toward the door.

Al and I exchanged a look and hurried after her. We opened the door onto a parking lot devoid of people. Brake lights flared at the turn-in, and a car slid into the street and purred away.

"You win some, you lose some," Maud said.

Chapter 25

Sunday morning was busy with the brunch I'd organized for a group from our sister city in Bulgaria that the community college had brought to town, but the afternoon was low-key. I lazed around my folks' house, helping make dinner and discussing books with my mom, who'd managed to read and review six this week, despite her new pub responsibilities. The pub was closed on Sundays, and I think we were all relieved to have a day off. I filled Derek in on my investigative efforts when he returned from playing basketball with some friends. He listened intently while I related Maud's efforts to trick Foster into a confession, and laughed about the beer spill.

"Yeah, you can laugh," I said. "I'll send you the dry-cleaning bill."

"And I'll pay it, right after I pay my lawyer," he responded. "So, 2022?" He slung an arm around my shoulders and squeezed. "Seriously, thanks for trying. You're the only one who is. I sure don't get the feeling the cops are out there busting their butts to find another suspect."

There was nothing to say to that, so I changed the subject. "How are Peri and Zach doing at the pub?" I asked. My shifts hadn't overlapped with theirs. Peri was the family klutz from way back, so I was curious.

"Zach's not much for chatting up the customers, so I've got him supervising in the kitchen," Mom said. "Peri—my little chatterbox—is very popular, and she's doing a good job behind the bar, although our breakage rate is up slightly. I've got you down to work tomorrow evening," Mom told me, "with Bernie and Kolby." She forestalled my objections. "Now, I know that boy's not the hardest worker, but his daddy just died and he deserves our consideration. I told him we'd keep him on for two weeks and reevaluate then."

"Great," I said unenthusiastically.

Work on Monday was interrupted by Derek's lawyer, Doug Elvaston, and Hart, in that order.

Courtney called first, wanting to know if I'd had any further thoughts about Derek's case. I told her about Foster and Anita and our attempt to get a confession or something incriminating out of Foster.

She took our failure in good part. "They're still viable suspects," she said. "Reasonable doubt. That's my mantra, baby, reasonable doubt."

She rang off and Doug swung by. He brought me a coffee, doctored just the way I liked it, and stayed to chat for fifteen minutes. He'd added a couple of clients to his caseload, he was enjoying his new life off the corporate hamster wheel, and Madison had called to apologize for ditching him at the altar.

"Big of her," I observed, blowing on my coffee and observing him through my lashes. His tan had faded a bit already, but he still looked more relaxed than I'd seen him in years.

He grinned at my tone. "Yeah, well. She wants to stay friends, says to give her a call next time I'm in New York."

"And will you?" If he said yes, I was done with him. I wasn't going to watch him let Madison stomp all over his heart with her stiletto heels.

"Hell no. I've learned my lesson. Even though I am pretty good about staying friends with my exes." He waggled his brows at me.

"Plural?"

"Well, no. Just you."

The look in his eyes warmed me. *Uh-oh.* "I've got to work," I said, bending over the file on my desk. "So, shoo."

"Maybe we could hang out this weekend?" He lingered in the doorway.

I looked up. Those green eyes could still melt me. "Uh, I think Hart and I have plans," I heard myself say, even though we didn't.

He shrugged it off and flashed a smile. "Another time."

After he left, I continued to stare at the empty doorway. Decision time had come and gone. I hadn't been ready for it, hadn't thought about it, but when it came to it, I went with Hart. Spontaneously. Satisfied with myself, I hummed as I worked my way down the list for Troy Widefield's state senate announcement event.

"'Da Doo Ron Ron'?" Hart asked, appearing in the doorway. The way he slouched against the jamb was eerily reminiscent of Doug's presence there not half an hour ago. "Who even remembers the Crystals?"

I quit humming. His question was lighthearted, but his expression was more serious. "To what do I owe the pleasure?" I asked, standing. He remained in the doorway, hands shoved into the pocket of his charcoal slacks. I could hear Al talking on the phone in the reception area.

"Foster Quinlan came in this morning to complain about you 'stalking' him," he said.

"He did not!" It had never crossed my mind that Foster would go to the police about me. If it had, I would have dismissed the idea, figuring he wouldn't want to draw any attention to himself.

"He did." A lift of Hart's brows questioned me.

"Al and I happened to have a drink at the Long Shot last night after an event broke up early," I said, fiddling with my pen. "Foster was there and recognized me."

"Despite your hat and sunglasses," Hart said drily. "Oh yes." He correctly interpreted my expression. "He told me you were in disguise."

"I didn't do anything to him," I said. "Didn't accost him or follow him home or accuse him of anything." I paced two steps in each direction, relieved that I hadn't let Maud talk me into tapping Foster's phone.

Hart held up his hands against my heated words.

"Calm down. I explained to him that your presence in the bar did not constitute stalking. You need to back off, though. What with interviewing his wife the other day, and the bar last night . . . you need to steer clear of Foster Quinlan. I told you I'll talk to him, and I will. I got in a few questions while he was complaining about you, and it certainly doesn't feel as if either he or his wife has rock-solid alibis for last Friday. I'll follow up."

I paused in my pacing and gave him a rueful look. "It was stupid, right?"

"You love your brother and you're trying to help him," he said, with the hint of a smile. "We all do stupid things for love."

"Have you?" I asked, sure from the expression on his face that he was remembering something specific.

"Most definitely," he said.

"You're not going to tell me, are you?"

He shook his head. "Not a chance."

"It can't be that bad," I coaxed.

"Not bad, just embarrassing on an Olympic scale."

"You have to tell me now!"

He shook his head, smiling, and pointed his finger at me. "No more sniffing around Foster Quinlan or his wife, okay? I don't want to have to arrest you."

"And I don't want to be arrested," I concurred, letting that serve as my agreement to stop pestering Foster.

"Any chance you're free one night this week?" he asked, lowering his voice so Al wouldn't overhear.

"I'm bartending again tonight," I said morosely.

"Between working at the pub and last night, I'm beginning to feel like I spend more time in bars than at home. Not good, right?"

"It's for a good cause," he said.

"I know." I glanced at the schedule on the whiteboard, even though I knew it by heart. "I can do tomorrow or Thursday, and there are no events next Sunday, either."

"Dinner on Tuesday." He smiled in a way that made heat curl in my belly.

As soon as Hart left, Al scooted into the office. "Are we in trouble for last night?" he asked. "I couldn't help overhearing part of what the detective said."

"Not you, just me," I said. "And not in very much trouble. That weasel Foster Quinlan told the police I was stalking him."

"What a douche. So we're not going to try again?" He sounded disappointed that his spy career was over before he got to sample his first martini shaken, not stirred.

Shaking my head loosed a strand of hair and I tucked it back into my French braid. "Nuh-uh. Hart says he'll follow up, and I believe him."

"Just as well," Al said philosophically. He straightened his bow tie. "I'm falling behind in my accounting class. Would you mind if I left a couple of hours early today? I've got a big test tomorrow. The only thing outstanding for tomorrow's barbecue is to make sure the propane tanks get delivered, and I can take care of that in the morning."

"No problem." I made a note to call Axie, which I

hadn't gotten around to yet. It would be perfect if she could do a few hours in the office each week, spelling me and Al. She wasn't old enough to do events, but she could answer the phone, schedule meetings, and the like. I could give her more responsibility if she liked the work and proved reliable. The last thought made me grin: No way would Lola let her *not* be reliable.

Chapter 26

In my usual reliable way, I showed up at Elysium a few minutes before my shift started at five. If this went on for much longer, I was going to get myself an orange shirt with my own name on it; I was tired of being "Sam." Mom had called to say she and my dad were held up in Grand Junction, where they'd gone to visit the pub's main food vendor, and they asked me to take charge until they could arrive. Derek, Mom said, was at Courtney's office, meeting with her and her investigator. I poked my nose into the kitchen, to let the staff know I was there, and returned to the bar, which was devoid of customers on a Monday evening. I was grateful that Derek was short a bartender and not a kitchen worker; I could handle mixing a few drinks and pouring pitchers of beer, but flipping burgers and dunking fries in oil was not a skill I had ever acquired.

To my great surprise, Kolby was already behind the bar when I emerged from the kitchen, albeit texting rather than working. His blondish hair hung lankly over his collar, but his thumbs flew with more energy than I'd seen him commit to any paying task. I told him to put the device away and bring in a new keg of the Demons IPA. He gave me a disgruntled look, but complied. I disconnected the empty one while waiting for him to return. He reappeared with the keg on a dolly as Bernie came through the door. An adolescent boy trailed her, moving stiffly in a walking cast.

"Sorry I'm late," Bernie apologized, shoving her sunglasses into her corkscrewing hair. "And sorry about Billy here. He's supposed to be with his father, but Jackson got called out on an emergency, so he can't get him until later. My sitter wasn't available, so I had to bring him with. My little guy's at a sleepover with a buddy, but I didn't have anywhere to leave Billy. I hope it's okay if he waits here somewhere?" She gave me an anxious look. "He promises to behave, don't you, Billy?" She nudged the boy.

"You don't need to say that all the time, Mom, not in front of other people." He shuffled his feet and managed to look both embarrassed and defiant. He had crew cut hair and freckled jug ears, and looked a lot like the way I'd always pictured Tom Sawyer. He peeped at me from under sandy lashes. "There's pool tables, right? I could play pool until Dad gets here." His pleading gaze went from his mother to me.

"I don't see why not," I said.

A grin lit his face. He was an engaging kid and I smiled. "How are you going to play pool with your leg in a cast like that?" My eyes went to his foot. The plaster extended from just above his grubby toes to mid-shin. Orange tape covered most of it. It looked just like Roman's . . .

My eyes widened as I made a connection that up-ended all my previous theories about Gordon's murder. The truth plowed into me with the force of a boulder hurtling down a hill. I swallowed and looked from Billy to Bernie, who didn't seem to sense my new discomfort. "I'm sure it'll be okay if you hang out in the pool lounge," I said. "There's no one up there yet. Take the elevator." I pointed to it.

"I'll show him," Kolby volunteered, having off-loaded the new keg and moved it into position. He brushed hair off his face. I had a feeling he was also volunteering to waste an hour playing pool with an eleven-year-old.

"Thanks," Bernie said, giving me a grateful look as Billy thumped his way to the elevator, already chattering to Kolby as if he'd known him for years. "I don't like playing the single-mom card, but sometimes it's the only one I'm holding."

I didn't know how to say what I needed to say, so I started obliquely. "They do a good job with broken bones at Alliance Urgent Care, don't they? I had to take a friend's son there a few nights ago and I was impressed with their efficiency."

"Yeah, they do a good job," Bernie agreed, putting her purse behind the bar. She grabbed a wet rag and began to scrub at a spot on the gleaming surface. "The docs are real good with Billy."

"You told me you didn't know Angie Dreesen, but if Billy gets hurt as often as you say, you must know her."

Silence followed my statement. Bernie's hand slowed until she was merely holding the rag pressed against the bar. Finally, she looked up at me. Her eyes were brown pools of worry and guilt, but she didn't say anything.

"You were late last Friday, too. You said you'd had car trouble. Gene Dreesen didn't get to the party until late, too." I suddenly realized I'd seen Gene get into a car with Angie when they left the party—if he'd arrived late, why wasn't his car still in the lot when I left much later? "He told the police he helped someone with a flat tire. I'm betting that someone was you, only you didn't really have a flat, did you? You told the police you did, though—you gave Gene Dreesen an alibi for the time Gordon was killed. Why, Bernie? Why?"

Every muscle in her body seemed to quiver and for a moment I thought she was going to bolt. The futility of it must have struck her—Billy was upstairs, after all—because the tension melted away and she went as limp as a rag doll. I knew then she was going to tell me everything.

"You're right. I've known Dr. Dreesen for a few years now. She's treated Billy for everything from ear infections to broken bones. Kids always seem to get hurt or sick in the middle of the night or on a weekend when the family doc is playing golf or asleep in bed, right?" She tried to smile, but it was a poor effort. "This last time, with Billy's ankle, we got to talking. Gordon . . . Gordon and I . . . I'd thought Dr. Dreesen and I were going to be sisters-in-law, you know? Gawd, was I a fool!" She put her elbows on the bar and dropped her face into her hands. "He cheated on me with Sam, just like he'd cheated on some other woman with me. I don't know why I thought he'd be different with me. Any woman who was ever the 'other woman' and thinks her man will behave differently once he's hers is a fool. Tattoo it on my forehead." She slapped a hand to her forehead. "F.O.O.L.

"He dumped me the same day Billy broke his ankle. I broke down at the clinic, burst into tears, told Dr. Dreesen everything. I told her how I loved Gordon and had believed him when he said he was going to take care of me and the kids. You don't know how that felt, Amy-Faye, looking forward to not having to scrimp and scrape and save and do without all the time. I wanted to get Billy a pair of jeans that didn't come from Goodwill, to sign Chester up for Little League. I don't mind working, but I thought I could drop back to one job when Gordon and I were married, and have more time to spend with the boys. They need me."

She turned her head to look at me, her eyes begging me to understand. Tears streamed down her face.

"I'm sorry," I said, aching with the inadequacy of it.

"Gordon dangled that new life in front of me, and then he jerked it away." Her mouth tightened into a thin line. "I was hurt, but I was also angry. So angry. Gawd."

She used her palms to rub her tears away so hard I thought she'd tear skin from her face. I passed her a handful of bar napkins to use as tissues.

"So when Dr. Dreesen suggested . . . suggested *it*, and offered to pay me to give Gene an alibi, I said yes.

They gave me ten thousand dollars," Bernie said, straightening and looking me in the eye. "Ten thousand dollars to be late for work, to wait for them to call before I showed up, and then to tell the police if they asked that Gene had stopped to help me change a flat tire. Ten thousand dollars for one little lie."

My expression must have accused her of more because she said, "I didn't kill Gordon! I didn't even know for sure they were going to—" She couldn't go on. She shook like she was freezing.

"Would you have let Derek go to prison?" I asked, anger getting the better of me for a moment.

"No! No, I . . . of course not. I'd have—it wouldn't have come to that. They had no proof. He wouldn't have been convicted." Her teeth chattered.

Most of my sympathy for her evaporated. Not that I was sympathetic toward murder, but I could see how she'd gotten to the point where she could convince herself that telling a lie for enough money to make her boys' lives better was an acceptable moral trade-off. Letting an innocent man go to prison for the crime, though . . . there was no way she could justify that.

I pulled out my phone and dialed Hart without taking my eyes off Bernie. "I'm at Elysium," I said when he answered. "You need to come here. It's important."

Something in my voice must have convinced him, because he didn't ask any questions. "On my way," he said.

"Want a drink?" I asked Bernie when I hung up. "On the house."

"A Coke."

She waited while I put ice in a glass and filled it from the soda hose. Taking long, thirsty gulps as the glass clinked against her teeth, she said, "Don't tell Billy, okay? I mean . . ." Realization dawned. "Oh my Gawd, what will happen to Billy and Chet? I won't go to jail, will I? Not for telling a lie? Do I need a lawyer?"

I couldn't tell her what was likely to happen, but I advised her to get a lawyer and to call someone who could look after Billy and his little brother for a couple of days, at least.

"I can't call my ex. He'll use this to take the boys away from me." Panic filled her eyes as the full range of consequences opened like a bottomless pit in front of her. "My sister, maybe she can come." She made a couple of frantic phone calls while we waited for Hart.

I served the first three customers through the door, filling a pitcher with beer, chatting, and swiping the credit card on autopilot. They moved toward a table, laughing and joking, when Hart came through the door. His eyes asked a question. I cut my eyes toward Bernie, sobbing into her cell phone. His brows rose and I nodded in confirmation. When he reached the bar, I gave him the thirty-second version of what Bernie had told me, and then introduced him to her. He led her to a booth, where they talked. I kept an eye on them as I served a trickle of customers, but they were too far away for me to hear anything and their profiles didn't tell me much. After ten minutes, Hart approached me again, leaving Bernie slumped in the booth.

"I've got to take her in," he said in a low voice. "She

says her sister is coming from Rifle to pick up her son. I can send a social worker if you don't want to be responsible for him until then. It could be an hour." He quirked a questioning eyebrow.

"No, it's okay. He can stay here. What do I tell him?" The thought panicked me. How do you tell an eleven-year-old his mom has been arrested for—what?—conspiracy to commit murder?

"I'm going to give her five minutes with him," he said. "She can tell him what she wants to. How did you get onto her?" he asked.

"It was the cast." I told him how I'd figured it out. I thought about how Maud or one of the others had said to look for connections people didn't know about, like the ones between Poirot's suspects, when trying to ID the murderer. Since our body-dragging experiment on Maud's deck, I'd been thinking in terms of two people killing Gordon. I'd focused on Foster and Anita because they were so noisy about hating Gordon, but Angie and Gene Dreesen had much more powerful motives for wanting him dead: their daughter's death at his hands (as they thought), the blow to Gene's business, the lawsuits back and forth, even pent-up hatred and envy from Angie's childhood.

He shook his head, smiling in admiration and disbelief when I finished. "First time I've heard of a criminal being tripped up by orange tape," he said. "I hope Derek appreciates you."

Thinking of Derek filled me with joy. "Can I tell him?"

Hart hesitated but then said, "I don't see why not. It

290 / Laura DiSilverio

might take a couple of days for the DA to formally drop the charges, but you can let him and his lawyer know that I'm arresting Ms. Kloster and will shortly be picking up Angie and Gene Dreesen for questioning. Even if they don't confess, I'm sure we'll be able to follow the money trail. That ten thousand and the clinic's records will tie them to Ms. Kloster."

"And Gene's car wasn't in the parking lot," I said.

"What?"

"The Friday it happened. I waited in the parking lot until you were done with Derek. By the time he came out, there were no cars there except police cars. I saw Gene go home with Angie in her Lexus, so where was his car if he came late after helping Bernie?"

"A very good question," Hart said. "I'll be sure to ask him. We're still on for tomorrow night, right?"

"Most definitely." Derek would be cleared by then, with any luck, and we'd really have something to celebrate. A smile took over my face.

Hart patted the bar twice and returned to Bernie, leading her upstairs to talk to Billy. They returned less than ten minutes later, Bernie staring blindly ahead as he guided her down the stairs and out the door. He'd been discreet enough that I didn't think any of the customers knew an arrest had taken place under their noses. I appreciated his consideration for Bernie and for the pub's bottom line. Although—who knows?—an arrest might be a plus for business.

I thought about calling Derek, but wanted to break the news in person. I was on tenterhooks until Bernie's sister, easily identified by the spirals of sandy hair crowning her head, burst through the door, asking, "Where's Billy?"

I abandoned the bar for a few minutes to lead her upstairs to the pool area. When she had collected Billy and hustled the subdued boy downstairs, Kolby trailed me back to the bar, a suspicious frown tweaking his brows together.

"What's going on?" he asked. "First that cop drags Bernie out of here, and then that other woman—her sister?—hauls Billy away. What gives?"

I bit my lip, wondering what I should tell him. I finally decided on the truth. Gordon was his father and he deserved to know. "Bernie might have had something to do with your dad's death," I said. "The police need to talk to her."

"Bernie killed my dad?" His mouth hung open.

"No. She just knows something about it. She was . . . involved."

"Why didn't she say something sooner? What—? Will she go to prison?"

"I don't know."

He looked dazed. He flipped his hair off his face, but it fell into his eyes again when he shook his head and said, "That poor kid."

I gave him a puzzled look.

"Billy. He seems like a decent kid."

Kolby's moment of humanity surprised me and made me feel more kindly to him. "It'll be hard on all of them."

"Does Bernie know who killed him? Is that it? Who—? Aunt Angie!"

It was my turn to be astonished. How had he guessed? Then I noticed he was staring over my shoulder, toward the door. I turned to see Angie Dreesen crossing the floor toward us.

Chapter 27

Gordon's sister looked thinner and older than she had a mere week ago, a couple of breakouts marring her complexion, and muddy circles under her eyes. Her blond hair was the only bright note. She wore maroon scrubs and I guessed she'd come from the clinic. I knew immediately that Bernie must have called her. For a fleeting second, I thought she might be here to shut me up, keeping me from telling the police what I knew, and adrenaline zinged through me, but a second later the thought was gone.

She didn't look like a murderer prepared to kill again to cover her tracks. She looked utterly defeated. Broken. A woman who has done herself irreparable harm by abandoning her moral compass and doing something so heinous she'd never forgive herself. She stopped in front of us and no one said anything for a long moment.

Finally, Angie licked dry lips and said, "I'm looking for Derek Johnson. Is he here?"

"No," I said.

Her eyes met mine with what might have been her last ounce of resolve. "I've come to apologize to him. Bernie called me. I might not have the opportunity later to tell him how sorry I am."

"What do you have to be sorry for, Aunt Angie?" Kolby asked.

She hesitated, clearly not wanting to tell her nephew she'd killed his father. I wondered when she'd realize she owed Kolby the biggest apology.

"Kolby," I said, "I need you to hold down the fort for half an hour or so. Your aunt and I need to find Derek." I ducked under the bar. "My folks should be here soon."

"You mean I'm in charge?" he asked, clearly taken with the idea. "My dad never let me be in charge."

"You're in charge," I affirmed. I'd only be gone half an hour—he couldn't do any damage in thirty minutes, could he?

I escorted Angie from the bar and walked her to my van. It was probably stupid, to hop into a vehicle with a murderer, but I didn't feel threatened at all. "Derek's with his lawyer," I told Angie. "We can find him there. I'll call and let them know we're coming." While Angie got in on the passenger side, I dialed not Derek's number, but Hart's. He didn't answer, but I left a message telling him Angie and I were headed to Courtney's office. Disconnecting, I hopped into the driver's seat and we rolled out of the parking lot.

"The police are probably looking for me already," Angie said. "And Gene. I should have called him. After

Bernadette told me. But he might have made a run for it, and I couldn't let him do that. We need to pay for what we did. I thought killing Gordon would make me feel better about Kinleigh, and it did, in the moment, but then . . ." She angled the vents to focus the air-conditioning on her face.

We idled at a stoplight and I asked, "How did you—?"

"It wasn't so hard," she said, understanding my question. "Not once we had Bernadette on board. We knew Gordon spent a lot of time on the roof, smoking, so we decided to do it there. We picked the night of the opening because there would be so many people there it would be hard to keep track of any one person's movements, and because there would be lots of suspects. I dropped Gene off a few blocks away early in the afternoon. He waited for his chance and snuck up to the roof and hid. He had the tire iron from his car with him, and an umbrella, because we could see it was going to rain."

The light turned green and I depressed the accelerator a bit too hard. We rocked back in our seats.

"I got to the party as early as I could and kept an eye on Gordon. When I saw him heading for a smoke, I waited a few seconds and followed him. I told people I was going to the bathroom. He was at the wall, smoking, when I came onto the roof. I wasn't trying to be quiet—I wanted him to know what was happening and why, that it was for Kinleigh." Her voice shook. "It was for Kinleigh. When he saw me, he started saying things, things that didn't even make sense, calling me names.

He lurched toward me like he was going to hit me. That made it easier.

"Gene hit him. The tire iron hitting his head made the ugliest sound. A wet cracking sound, like dropping a cantaloupe. You know, I've treated people with horrible injuries—from knives and guns, tractors, falls, car accidents—and I never thought of the sound a body makes when it's assaulted."

I swallowed hard. I didn't want to think of it now.

"Gordon went down. Gene took his shoulders and I took his feet, and we got him up onto the wall and rolled him off. We didn't know how professional the HPD was; we were hoping his death might be called an accident, or maybe suicide. When it wasn't, when the police arrested your brother, that's when it all began to unravel for me. I couldn't live with the idea of putting an innocent man in prison. I'm not proud to say I killed Gordon, but he deserved it for what he did to Kinleigh. But your brother . . . he didn't deserve what was happening to him."

I could feel her gaze on my profile as I drove. She said, "I like to think that even if Bernie hadn't given us up, I'd have come forward if it looked like your brother was going to get convicted. I told Gene we had to tell if he went to trial."

I didn't point out that Derek was going through hell and might lose his business because of the arrest, never mind the trial. "How did you get off the roof without being spotted?" I asked instead. "And what did you do with the tire iron?"

A hint of pride showed on her face. "The plan was for me to rejoin the party and say I was in the bathroom, if anyone asked. Gene was supposed to come down on the elevator and mingle with the crowd. There was some risk that he'd be seen, but if he summoned the elevator, the chances that someone would be in it were slim, since the roof was off-limits, and if someone saw him get off on the first floor, he could say he'd come down from the pool room on the second floor. But then the fire alarm went off and that was so much easier with everyone rushing outside. We tucked the tire iron inside the umbrella."

I remembered wondering why they didn't put up the umbrella when they ran across the parking lot to her car.

We pulled up in front of the office building where Courtney's firm had its offices. Angie unbuckled her seat belt and said, "It was all easy. Too easy."

She made a move to get out, but I stopped her. "You know Gordon had a brain tumor, right? It was growing. It was terminal. That's probably why he spouted gobbledygook at you on the roof. And it's probably why he was dizzy the night Kinleigh drove him home. He wasn't drunk—he was ill."

"You're lying," she breathed. "Why is everyone lying to us about that night? He was driving the night of the accident, and the police covered it up. He was drunk—the PI we hired found witnesses that said he was staggering around, but the cops told us the blood test came back negative. Liars! He probably bribed them; that was the way he did business. Kinleigh's friend, the one who said Kinleigh was driving, she was lying, and now you are, too!" Her voice had gotten shrill.

"No, I'm not. It's in the autopsy report." It sounded as though she hadn't seen it—and why would she?—and hadn't known about Gordon's tumor. When the truth sank in and she realized that he truly hadn't been drunk or driving the night of her daughter's death, I didn't know what it would do to her. I'd never lost someone I loved like that, but I suspected it had broken something inside her. Something in her needed to blame someone other than her daughter or capricious fate for what had happened. I wondered if Lola had experienced similar feelings when the drunk killed her parents.

She looked stricken. "But then—"

Hart's Chevy Tahoe and an HPD patrol car with its light bar flashing pulled in beside us and behind us. I sat still, with my hands on the steering wheel, while an officer helped Angie out of the van. Hart came to my window, his face stormy.

"What in the world were you thinking, Amy-Faye, to be alone with a murder suspect—?" He pulled open my door and I got out. He didn't back away, so we were standing chest to chest, the open door partially shielding us from others' view.

"Look at her," I said, pointing to Angie, who stood docilely as the officer cuffed her. She looked blank and frail, as brittle as an autumn leaf.

"That's not the point," Hart said, more quietly. "You put yourself in harm's way."

"She wants to apologize to Derek," I said. "Can't she—"

"Derek can hear her say 'I'm sorry' at the jail, if he

wants to," Hart said. "She's not going anywhere except to the station. We've already picked up her husband. He hasn't told us anything, though. Asked for a lawyer first thing. Did she—?"

I nodded. "Full confession. Every detail. She's eaten up with guilt."

"Good." His hand reached for mine, down at my side, and squeezed it. "I'm glad you're okay. I'll need a full statement from you, but you can run up and tell Derek everything while I get her processed at the station. Don't take too long, okay?"

"Okay."

His smile was almost as good as a kiss, and I jogged into the building to tell Derek he was off the hook, feeling like someone had replaced my blood with helium.

Chapter 28

After I told Derek and he slumped across the table with relief, and Courtney high-fived me so hard my hand stung for half an hour, we decided to hold an impromptu victory party at the pub Tuesday night, a private gathering. Derek insisted that I tell everyone how I worked out who the killers were and got him released. I demurred, but he insisted, so the next night, clad in jeans and a kelly green scoop-neck shirt, I sat on the bar at Elysium, legs swinging, and regaled my friends and family with the details of the investigation. All the Readaholics were there: Troy was with Brooke, and Lola had brought her grandmother and Axie. Kerry had brought Roman and I used his cast as "Exhibit A" when I explained how I came to suspect Bernie. He blushed red and tried to slump down in the booth. My family was there, of course, as were Hart, Doug, Courtney, Al Frink (who had promised me his response to my offer next week), and a handful of Derek's friends. A sign on the front door said CLOSED FOR PRIVATE PARTY.

Several times during my narrative, would-be customers rattled the door and then left. One or two thumped on it, but we ignored them. I felt a little like Hercule Poirot revealing his insights and strategies in the restaurant car of the Orient Express, only I was talking to friends and family instead of suspects.

Derek was serving his Purgatory Porter, to celebrate his release from purgatory, he said. I was not playing bartender; in fact, I'd turned Sam's orange uniform shirt over to Derek and told him I was retiring. He told me I hadn't worked long enough to get a pension. I socked his shoulder and looked around. Bernie not being here was weird. Even though what she'd done was truly awful, I missed her humor and her quirky take on things. I'd heard that her sister was keeping the boys for now. I felt my eyes misting, a combination of sadness for Bernie and her boys, and relief for Derek. It had been an emotional week.

"What about the blood on Derek's shirt?" Peri asked when I'd given them the bare bones of events, including my conversations with Bernie and Angie Marsh. "The blood that got him arrested?"

Hart spoke up. "I can answer that." Everyone swiveled to look at him where he stood near the entrance door, beer mug dwarfed by his large, strong hand. "The lab has stated that it's possibly a case of transfer, especially given that there was so little blood on the shirt Derek wore the night of Marsh's murder." Noting some puzzled looks, he elaborated. "The blood from Gordon's nosebleed after he and Derek fought was transferred to the trash can when Derek threw out the shirt he was wearing that day. Then, when he dumped the other shirt in the can, the night of the murder, the dried blood transferred from the metal trash can to the new shirt."

"I was going to argue that as part of my defense strategy," Courtney said.

"Because you're brilliant," Derek said.

Courtney gave a bow with a small flourish. "That's why you hired me."

"Damn right. That, and because you've got a wicked free throw percentage."

We laughed. Everything Derek said was a little too loud, his relief at being out from under suspicion exploding out of him. He was grinning like a maniacal jack-o'-lantern, and he kept foisting beer and munchies on everyone. I hoped it would wear off soon; watching him was tiring me out.

"I knew it was a conspiracy all along," Maud said. She sat with Lola and her family at a table right in front of me, her long jeans-clad legs stretched out and crossed at the ankle. "Although I'll admit I didn't ever suspect Bernie was involved. I thought it would turn out to be the son and the ex-wife, or the ex-wife and one of the WOSCers."

A few people didn't know who she meant by "the WOSCers," so she had a great time telling them. When she finished, one of Derek's basketball buddies in the back squirmed and said, "Harassment like that shouldn't be allowed."

If I were his girlfriend or wife, I'd be suspicious.

"I went to see Angie Dreesen at the jail," Mom said

unexpectedly. Unlike me, she was still wearing her orange uniform shirt and her chestnut hair was freshly dyed and curled, poofing out in a way that made her round face seem even rounder.

"You did?" That wiped the smile off Derek's face.

She nodded, chins jiggling. "I wanted to see what kind of woman could do what she did to my son. Her husband is still denying everything, but she told me she's made a full confession—"

I looked at Hart to see him nodding.

"—and she's ready to pay for what she did. She's still insisting that Gordon is responsible for her daughter's death and she's refusing to believe he had brain cancer. She won't even look at the autopsy report or X-rays. Her daughter dying clearly knocked her off the rails. She needs help, medical help."

"Do you feel sorry for her, June?" Lola asked.

I expected Mom, a famous bleeding heart who gave everyone the benefit of the doubt, to say yes.

"No." Mom's lips compressed to a thin tangerine line. "Well, I feel sorry that she lost her daughter the way she did—I'd feel sorry for anyone that happened to—but I can't be sorry she's going to prison. Not after what she did to her brother and Derek."

Derek crossed to Mom and slung his arm over her shoulders, squeezing her against him. "Amen, Mom." He kissed her cheek with a loud smack.

The serious moment had drained some of the fun out of the gathering, and Derek released Mom and turned back to the group, saying, "More beer for everyone!"

With my turn in the spotlight done, I swung myself off the bar, landing with a plop. Hart appeared at my side, smiling down at me. "Ready to go?"

I was more than ready for dinner, more than ready to be alone with him, but I held up a finger. "Give me a moment."

I wove my way to the table where Lola, Maud, Axie, and Mrs. Paget sat. Exchanging a few words with Lola's grandmother, I turned to Axie and asked if she'd like to work for me a few hours a week. Her pretty face lit up.

She looked at Lola. "Can I? If I stay on top of my homework?"

"And still put in your hours in the greenhouse," Lola said. "You'll have less time to spend with Cassie and Lorenzo," she warned, "and you might have to cut back on your extracurriculars."

"How much are you paying me?" Axie asked, brown eyes meeting mine directly.

I liked that she was assertive enough to ask. That boded well for her interactions with clients and potential clients. "Minimum wage at first," I said. "Then, if you like it and show some promise, I can give you more responsibility and more money."

Axie stuck out her hand with an air of resolution. "It's a deal," she said. A huge grin chased her adult air away. "My first real job! I don't count babysitting and working for Lo. When can I start?"

"How about next week?" We hashed out the details, and I moved on after a few minutes, catching up with Brooke and Troy, who were headed for the door.

"Wait, wait, wait," I said, latching onto Brooke's arm. She and Troy stopped. Troy Widefield Jr. was an attractive man with a slightly droopy posture who seemed younger than thirty-two. Tall and slender, he had a pleasant, open face and light brown hair that waved around his ears. I'd always thought he had a weak chin, but he and Brooke made an attractive couple. "How'd it go today?" I asked.

Today was the day she and Troy had met with the teenage mother who was looking to give up her baby for adoption. I'd called Brooke last night to wish her luck, and told her I was praying for her. She'd been hovering between hopeful, anxious, and pessimistic.

A tremulous smile wavered across Brooke's face. "She was really nice. Anastasia. Pretty, and smart, too, didn't you think, Troy?"

"Yeah," he said, "although you gotta wonder how smart any of these girls are, when they get themselves pregnant by accident."

"Troy!" She slapped his arm lightly. "She didn't get pregnant by herself, you know. I thought you liked her?"

"I did. No one's going to believe that the baby is really ours, though. Not with that white-blond hair she has, and the father being a redhead."

A troubled look clouded Brooke's eyes as she studied her husband. "Of course the baby will be 'really' ours," she said. "We're not going to try to convince people he's our biological child."

"Anyway . . . ?" I prompted.

Twirling a lock of hair, Brooke said, "Anastasia said

she's talking to two other couples, but she'll let us know by the end of the week. We had a good talk. She's a senior this year, and is applying to CSU. She wants to be a vet. I told her about CSU and Fort Collins. I think she liked me—us."

"She liked you," Troy affirmed. "What's not to like?" He smiled and dropped a kiss on Brooke's hair, but I could see it cost him something.

I got the feeling he wasn't as gung ho about adopting a baby as Brooke was. Maybe, I thought, as I wished them luck, hugged Brooke, and they left, he was just uncomfortable with an open adoption, worried that the baby's birth mother might want to insinuate herself into their lives. The Widefields were one of the richest families in town and I was sure that Troy had experience with people wanting to be his friend only because he had money, and with people trying to take advantage of him. More likely, I decided as Hart joined me by the door, his parents, especially his mother, were dripping poison in his ear about polluting the Widefield gene pool.

"Trouble?" Hart asked, reading my expression.

"No, I'm just worried Brooke will get her heart broken if this girl they met with doesn't choose them to adopt her baby."

"You can't fix everything for everyone, Amy-Faye," he said. "If this girl doesn't pick them, the next one will. Or the one after that."

"You're right," I said, looking up at him and smiling.

He put on a face of mock amazement. "That may be the first time you've told me I'm right."

"I like to give credit where credit is due, but don't get used to it," I said, nudging him to the door.

The celebration noise faded when the door swung shut behind us. "Shall I tell you what I'd like to get used to?" Hart asked.

The huskiness in his voice made my breath hitch and I looked at him instead of watching where I was going when I stepped onto the graveled parking lot. I half tripped and he caught me around the waist to keep me from falling. Arched back over his encircling arms, I fixated on the way the sun, low on the horizon behind him, lit his hair, seeming to make individual strands glow from within, turning the light brown to amber.

"Or maybe I should show you," he said. His hand tipped my chin up while his other arm drew me in close for a long kiss. His lips had drifted to my neck when Brooke and Troy drove past us in his BMW. Troy tooted the horn and both of them grinned. Hart released me with a sigh.

"Later?" he asked, lacing his fingers with mine and drawing me toward his Tahoe and our delayed dinner.

"Absolutely," I promised, thinking later couldn't get here soon enough.

Read on for a sneak peek
at Laura DiSilverio's next
Book Club Mystery,

The Readaholics and the Gothic Gala

Coming from Obsidian in August 2016.

Normally, when I was surrounded by books, I was in a state of bliss. Today, I could feel a headache coming on. That wasn't the books' fault; no, it was a by-product of dealing with the people who wrote them. I'd never had much contact with authors. Barring the one signing I'd gone to some years ago in Boulder, where the author had entertained the small audience with humorous stories about writing his police procedurals and life in Wyoming, I didn't think I'd ever met an author. I'd blithely assumed they'd all be something like the Boulder author—affable, entertaining, happy to interact with fans. First wrong assumption . . .

I'd discovered the hard way that attending an author signing bore no resemblance to organizing a multiple-author event. When Gemma Frant, owner of Heaven's only bookstore, Book Bliss, had hired me to put together a "Celebration of Gothic Novels" to coincide with the September birthdays of her favorite twentieth-century gothic authors, I jumped at the chance. What could be more fun than organizing an event focused on books? After all, I'd grown up in a house with more books than dust mites, with a mother who was a librarian. I had read voraciously since sounding out my first Dr. Seuss book, and would just as soon have gotten on a plane or gone to a doctor's waiting room naked as without a book. Five years ago, I'd started the Readaholics, the book club that was currently reading du Maurier's *Rebecca* in honor of this event. It's one of the most widely read gothic novels of all time, after all. So, I'd figured any event that revolved around books had to be fun, right? Second off-base assumption . . .

I'd had fun decorating Book Bliss for today's activities and I smiled with satisfaction as I scanned the effect I'd created. Thinking "gothic," I'd borrowed the Heaven High School theater department's backdrops from last year's production of *Dracula*. They depicted a spooky stone castle, complete with painted bats and sickle moon. Arranged in a semicircle behind the signing table, the flats gave the bookstore an appropriately eerie air, I thought. I'd added to it by having my friend Lola Paget, who owns Bloomin' Wonderful, the best nursery in a five-county area, rent me some potted trees, which I'd clumped together near the door to make it feel as if customers were entering a forest. Once the signing was over, Lola and her crew would relocate the trees to the Rocky Peaks Golf and Country Club, which was hosting tonight's gothic-themed costume party. My assistant, Al Frink, had put together a sound track for the event, downloading music from the sound tracks of *Dracula*, *Phantom of the Opera*, some Hitchcock flicks, and *Sweeney Todd*. It was all gothicky and atmospheric and I was hugely pleased with myself and Al. Gemma was oohing and aahing while the photographer I'd hired was taking dozens of photos that would go on the store's and my Web site and Facebook page.

Gemma wanted a full day of activities, starting with a birthday party and author panel this morning and culminating in the costume party with all the guests dressing as their favorite gothic characters from books, TV, or movies. She thought it was wonderfully appropriate because there was that disastrous costume party sequence in *Rebecca*, and costumes play a large role in many gothic works. Think of the masquerade scene in *Phantom of the Opera*, and the protagonist's mask, for that matter. Since Heaven, Colorado (population 10,096, according to the sign as you drive into town), was, sadly, devoid of gothic castles, we were holding it at the Club tonight.

The birthday party was because all of Gemma's favorite gothic authors were born in September. They included Victoria Holt (September 1), Joan Aiken (September 4), Phyllis Whitney (September 9), Mary Stewart (September 17) and Barbara Michaels (September 29). I had to admit it was almost eerie how many of them were born in the same month. To top it off, this September would have been Mary Stewart's hundredth birthday, so my go-to baker had constructed a cake decorated with icing replicas of some of the birthday authors' covers, and crowned it with a hundred candles.

Following the birthday party and panel, we had media interviews for the visiting authors, a high school writing contest for the authors to judge, and an auction of donated merchandise, including a collection of first-edition books by the birthday novelists. The auction was to fund a scholarship for a Heaven High School student to attend the Pikes Peak Writers Conference in Colorado Springs. Gemma had proposed naming the scholarship after du Maurier, but when the high school administrators found out that she was apparently bisexual and had had an affair with the novelist Gertrude Lawrence, they put the kibosh on naming it after her. They'd christened it simply the Book Bliss Scholarship for Creative Writing Students.

Even though gothic novels weren't my reading material of choice, I'd heard of all of the event's headliners: Constance Aldringham, perennial bestseller of gothic romance; Francesca Bugle, the midlister rumored to have a hit and a major studio movie deal on her hands with her forthcoming novel; and Mary Stewart, the much-ballyhooed debut novelist. Apparently, the latter's birth certificate name was actually Mary Stewart, although she was no relation to the gothic romance author of the same name who had been big in the genre in the 1950s and '60s. It made me wonder if names were destiny. Were all Mary Stewarts fated to become gothic novelists? If so, what did being named Amy-Faye Johnson portend?

Aggravation.

"I simply must be seated in the middle," Constance Aldringham was telling my assistant, Al Frink. She rearranged the nameplates he had set on the table for the

author panel that would start in half an hour. "And
don't forget to have a bottle of Perrier and fresh sliced
limes at my place. Talking to fans parches me, simply
parches me, and I must rehydrate. I count on you to
attend to these details for me. I cannot, simply cannot,
waste my creative energies on such mundane matters."
This last was apparently directed at her mousy-looking
assistant, who quailed at the sharp note in her boss's
voice. Or it might have been meant for her husband, a
bearded man with stooped shoulders who had made
his way to the bookshelf with World War II histories
immediately upon entering the shop, and was now
hiding behind a study of tank warfare tactics.

The acknowledged grand dame of modern gothic
romances, Constance Aldringham was a well-preserved
sixtysomething who had wisely let her hair go white.
Smoothed back from a wide forehead and caught up in
a low chignon, it emphasized her pale skin, which was
minimally lined for a woman her age. Her eyebrows
were darker, peaked instead of arched, framing skill-
fully made-up light blue eyes. She affected clothes in
dark hues that set off her hair. Today's dress was navy
blue, sweeping almost to her ankles, and accented with
a paisley silk scarf chosen, I suspected, to obscure the
slightest hint of jowls and a crepey neck.

Al gave me a "what do I do?" look, and I signed for
him to let it be. We had intended to have the authors sit
in alphabetical order, but if no one else complained it
didn't make much difference if Constance sat in the
middle. On the short side, wearing a sweater vest and
a bow tie, and with his sandy hair recently buzz-cut, Al

looked like a refugee from the 1950s, the "good kid" Mrs. Cleaver and her ilk would have trusted without hesitation. In truth, he'd been a bit of a troublemaker in high school and it had taken him a couple of years to straighten up and enroll in college. The university had matched him with me as an intern for my event organizing business, Eventful!, a couple of years ago and it had worked out great. I'd recently asked him to come on board full-time when he graduated, and he was still thinking about the offer.

Now he straightened Constance's name tent, gave the table skirt a twitch, and disappeared into Gemma's stockroom, where we had parked the refreshments for the signing. I was about to follow him to set out the three cakes iced to look like the covers of the guest authors' most recent releases, when there was a knock on the still-locked front door. Gemma hurried to let in a stocky woman I recognized from book jackets as Francesca Bugle. She wore a red jacket with wide lapels that did not flatter her top-heavy figure, and a felt hat decked with red poppies.

A man followed her, his attire making it plain he wasn't from around here. I'd bet tonight's paycheck he was from L.A. He wore a black linen blazer over a black silk T-shirt, slacks, and loafers without socks. Facial hair that was several days past "forgot to shave" but not quite up to "mustache and goatee" framed his mouth. I figured he worked hard to keep it at that exact in-between stage. Maybe ten years older than me—in his early forties—he had a round bald spot on the crown of his head and kept the rest of his hair cut short.

A pair of trendy glasses was shoved up on his head and I wondered if they were meant to hide the bald spot.

"Gemma! Hon!" Francesca threw her arms around slim Gemma and squeezed so hard she knocked Gemma's glasses askew. "Nice to meet you finally."

"Thank you for joining us for our Celebration of Gothic Novels," Gemma said in her fluttery way. She smoothed the ruffle at her neckline. "I enjoy your books so much."

"Especially the naughty bits, hey?" Francesca winked, then drew the man forward. "This is Cosmo Zeller, president of Zeller Productions. That's the company that's turning *Barbary Close* into a blockbuster. Right, Cos?"

Cosmo slouched forward and pulled one hand out of his pocket to shake hands with Gemma. "Spot-on, Frannie. It's going to be big. Bigger than big. Huge. I think the opening weekend gross will beat the numbers *Fifty Shades* put up." His gaze went to the smartphone in his other hand.

"He's scouting locations since a large part of the book takes place in a small town in the mountains. It's really in Oregon, but Cosmo says Colorado's been offering filmmakers a lot of incentives. We're staying the whole week—I'm fascinated by everything that goes into making a movie."

The photographer approached and took a photo of the duo. Francesca smiled for the camera, stood beside Gemma for another photo, and then looked around the store. Spotting Constance and her entourage, she called, "Hey, Connie, Merle, Allyson. Good to see you."

Constance dipped her head like a queen recognizing

a peasant. "Francesca." Her husband and assistant copied her, their nods tentative, as if Constance might divorce or fire them for acknowledging Francesca.

"A little bird told me sales of your latest are way down," Francesca said, mobile mouth puckering into a moue of seeming concern. "Is it true Oubliette Press isn't picking up the option on your next book?"

Constance sent her an icy look from narrowed eyes. Before she could reply, Francesca laughed heartily and sailed toward me, hand out. "I'm Francesca Bugle. And you are?"

"Amy-Faye Johnson. I'm the event organizer."

We shook and my fingers tingled when she released her grip.

"Bang-up job you've done," she said with a decisive nod that set the poppies on her hat bobbing. "Love the castle." She gestured toward the painted flats. "I've never been to Heaven before, but it's a nice-looking little town you've got here. Love that B and B, the Columbine."

I'd managed to get all the writers and their various relatives and hangers-on into Heaven's most exclusive B and B, the Columbine. In fact, they'd taken over the whole house for the week. Francesca and Cosmo were staying to scout for movie locations, Constance Aldringham and her family were taking advantage of the free accommodations and lovely surroundings to have their first vacation in eight years (or so Constance had told Gemma), and Mary Stewart was using the charming inn as a writing retreat.

"I'm ready for a change of pace," Francesca said.

"Just turned in a manuscript, so I'm in no hurry to get back to Winnetka. It was twenty-two degrees there when I left yesterday. Felt more like December than September. *Brrr*." She gave an exaggerated shiver. "Scouting for movie locations will be fun."

"I hope you enjoy—" But before I could finish, she was turning away, introducing herself to Al as he came out of the stockroom bearing the birthday cake decorated with frosting replicas of some of the birthday authors' books.

"That is the most beautiful thing I've ever seen," Francesca exclaimed. "Who is the genius that did that? I've got to get a cake like that for my next book launch. I can just see the cover of *Never Again, My Lovely* done up in buttercream and fondant. The mist, the seascape— it'll be gorgeous."

I gave her one of the baker's cards. She was tucking it into the structured purse hanging from her elbow when there was another knock, Gemma unlocked the door, and a light voice said, "I'm not late, am I?"

We all turned to look at the willowy young woman glowing on the threshold. The sun shone through her white dress—my mother would have insisted on a slip—and set her red hair on fire. Pleased that we had been struck dumb by her entrance, Mary Stewart the Living (which was how I differentiated between her and the author of *Madam, Will You Talk?*, the Merlin trilogy, and other books I'd enjoyed when I stumbled on them as a college freshman) glided into the room and shook hands with Gemma. Behind her, one of the most handsome men I'd ever seen carried in a box and set it on a table. I couldn't help thinking that he was a gothic hero come to life, tall, dark, and brooding, with full lips that would have landed him a men's cologne commercial if he was an actor, and springy black hair that I knew would feel crisp if I ran my fingers through it.

What was I thinking? I was happily involved with Lindell Hart, Heaven's chief of detectives. I didn't need to be fantasizing about a man who hadn't yet hit thirty and who looked as if he might be the model for the vampire on the cover of Mary's book *Blood Will Out*. He politely backed out of the frame when the photographer came forward to take a photo of Mary Stewart.

Mary hugged Francesca and told Constance, "*Simply* lovely to see you again."

While I was wondering if her emphasis on "simply" was a sly dig at Constance or if that was how all authors talked, she took the gorgeous man's hand and said, "Everybody, this is my brother, Lucas."

We all chorused, "Hi, Lucas," as if we were at an AA meeting.

He flashed a brilliant smile that dispelled the broodiness. "Nice to meet you all."

"There's quite a crowd out there already," Mary said, apparently delighted. She had a way of talking that made every sentence sound as if it ended with an exclamation point. "Scads of people waiting to meet us and hear about our books. This is going to be such *fun*!"

Strike three . . .

ALSO AVAILABLE FROM

Laura DiSilverio

The Mall Cop Mystery Series

Emma-Joy Ferris likes mall cop work, even though it's a bit more humdrum than the military policing she did in the army. But there's no time to be bored when there are conniving killers on the loose...

Die Buying
All Sales Fatal
Malled To Death

"Put this series at the top of your shopping list."
—National bestselling author Elaine Viets

Available wherever books are sold or at
penguin.com

facebook.com/TheCrimeSceneBooks